the problem with perfect

JILLIAN LIOTA

Love Is A Verb Books

Book Cover Design and Layout by Blue Moon Creative Studio

Cover Photo by Madison Maltby

Editing by C. Marie

ISBN 978-1-952549-38-0 (paperback)
ISBN 978-1-952549-36-6 (eBook)
ISBN 978-1-952549-37-3 (kindle)

for Adeline
welcome to the world

chapter one
bellamy

I stroll through the small group surrounding the fire, my hands tucked into the pockets of my jacket to ward off the light chill that clings to the air. It's the first bonfire night of the summer, the weather still a little crisp in the evenings and the crowd thin since not everyone has finished up the semester and traveled home from college yet. At the height of the summer season, there will be over a hundred people here, cars lined all down the dirt path leading into the closed-down campsite. But tonight, there are only about 20 or so folks scattered about, drinking and listening to music and reveling in the feeling of summer just on the horizon.

To be honest, I'm not really sure why I decided to come. I guess I feel bored…maybe a little impatient. It's this unfamiliar feeling that's been skittering beneath my skin recently, a sense of not knowing exactly what to do with myself. It's as if I'm just sitting around, waiting for life to happen.

Normally, I'm fairly relaxed, so this sensation is very unlike me. That's why I'm here, trying to find something to do, someone to talk to, something to take my mind off this feeling of stagnation.

My eyes scan the attendees littered around the gravel and dirt circle, taking stock of everyone and trying to decide who to approach. Unsurprisingly, most of the people here tonight are locals who graduated a few years before or after me. Familiar faces from around town, people I know of but don't really know.

Until my eyes halt on a familiar old Chevy Blazer in red with a white cover.

"What are *you* doing here?" I ask, my voice light and teasing as I approach the broad-shouldered back of a man I've known almost my entire life. "Aren't you too old to be at one of these things?"

Rusty pins me with an unimpressed look then returns to whatever he's doing at the tail end of his car. "I'm not here to party, Bellamy. Those days are in my past."

I snort and shake my head, watching as he tugs out a box of beer. "I didn't think you were here to party, Rusty. Besides, how long has it been since you graduated high school? Twenty years?"

He pauses and looks back at me over his shoulder with narrowed eyes. "Fourteen." Then he gives me his back again.

"Same thing." I lean against the Blazer and kick one foot over the other, tilting my head up to look at the sky, the stars slightly obscured by the smoke rising in the clearing between the trees.

I hear Rusty snort. "It is most certainly *not* the same thing." He passes by me and thunks a box onto the hood. "I thought you were supposed to be good at math."

I ignore his comment.

"So, what exactly *are* you doing here tonight?" I ask. "Because it looks like you're planning to dole out booze to Cedar Point's youth. Does Boyd know you're selling your product at the bonfire?"

He lets out an irritated sigh. "I'm not selling beer to Cedar Point's *youth*, Bellamy. Everyone is of legal age. A sale is a sale, and someday, when you've moved out of that plush house your parents own and you actually *need* the money you work for, you'll see what I mean."

I roll my eyes, not surprised by his bristly attitude. Rusty's always been that way—angry at the world. I don't make that statement with judgment; it makes sense considering the shitty hand life has dealt him. Still, it's rare for me to see him talk to anyone without a scowl on his face, besides his younger sister, Abby, and my brother, Boyd. The two of them have been friends since they were really young, which is why I'm not intimidated by his irritable bear act the way everyone else in town is.

That doesn't stop me from noticing what a dick he can be sometimes.

"You know, you have a way of being incredibly condescending."

Rusty heaves one of the boxes up on his shoulder then grabs the other and slides it forward until it's tucked against his hip.

"I *do* know. I figure it's the best way to keep you from annoying me with your jabs about how old I am." He starts walking away, heading over to where Corinne Paulson is standing with a group surrounding her dad's Saab.

I glare at his retreating form, cross my arms, and watch the slowly growing crowd. I've been here all of five minutes and it's easy to see that coming tonight was a mistake. Instead of chitchatting and laughing with friends to distract myself, I'm stuck volleying insults with a guy who barely tolerates me.

Sighing, I push off of Rusty's car and round to the back, nosily eyeing the contents in the trunk: a few more beer boxes, what looks to be a box of tile samples, a flannel blanket, and—I huff a laugh.

A box of condoms. Classy.

I snag the box and glance inside, unsurprised when I see there's only one left. If I know anything about Rusty Fuller, it's that he is a man about town, and if I put stock in town gossip, it seems like he mostly gets his kicks with tourists passing through and looking for a good time with a guy who looks like a lumberjack.

Gross.

I could never sleep with someone like that—without emotion, without connection. Sex is special, something to be shared with people who mean something.

I glance back over to where Rusty is still talking with Corinne and roll my eyes at myself. Clearly it's time to leave. Standing around, snooping through the back of Rusty's Blazer is *not* what I had in mind for the evening. I should have just stayed home and done absolutely anything else until it was time to leave for my late shift at The Mitch.

Part of me thinks I should wait to say bye to Rusty, though I doubt he even cares. When I walk around to the front of the car, giving one final glance to the crowd before heading out, I hear my name in a familiar voice that has my heart swooping down into my stomach before launching itself into my throat.

Connor.

My eyes scan to the right until I spot him a few feet away, walking toward me, and I can't help the way a smile explodes on my face. God, I wish I could be more subtle, but that's just not how I was made.

"Hey, Connor!" I say, cringing only slightly at the overly enthusiastic way my voice has hit such a high note.

"Hey, Bells," he says, the sound of my nickname rolling off his tongue sending something warm through my chest. "You taking off?"

I shake my head, my plans changing on a dime now that Connor is here.

"No, I was just…"

But my voice trails off when I spot the body that emerges from behind him as he comes to a stop a few feet away.

As *they* come to a stop.

And I know instantly that they are a *they*.

She's beautiful. Short, thick, brunette hair that flips in a little bob around her jawline and wide beautiful eyes.

"Hey, Rusty," Connor says, and I glance briefly to the side, spotting Rusty's approaching form.

"Pruitt." Rusty's response is just as gruff as always.

I can't do anything except stare wide-eyed at Connor and the girl next to him…the one holding his hand.

"Hi, I'm Stace," she says, smiling at all of us. "Like Stacy, but without the *e* sound. Except my name ends with an *e* so…" She shrugs. "It can be *really* confusing."

I blink a few times then look at Connor.

"Stace, this is Rusty and Bellamy. Bellamy and I knew each other in high school."

Knew each other in high school. I almost want to laugh. That's how he wants to describe us? As people who knew each other in high school?

As if we don't know each other anymore?

As if we mean nothing to each other now?

"And Rusty owns Cedar Cider," he continues, "which is the

best beer in town."

Rusty steps forward, and when I glance up at him, I see the tight smile on his face, his hands on his hips.

"Thanks for the compliment, Pruitt, and nice to meet you, Stace, but I need to take off."

"No worries, no worries," Connor says. "We can't stay long anyway. Just wanted to bring my fiancée by and introduce her to anyone who's back in town, though it looks like not too many people are out tonight."

I think that's what he says, but I can't be sure, because the ringing in my ears began when I heard him refer to Stace as his fiancée. I must stand there staring with my mouth agape for too long, because it isn't until I receive a physical nudge from behind me that I snap out of it.

"Huh?"

I glance at Rusty, who is looking at me with a quirked eyebrow.

"You alright?"

I look back at Connor, who is still watching me with an easy smile on his face like he hasn't just obliterated the very foundation of my heart.

"Yeah, sorry." I shake my head and try not to look like I'm dying inside. "What did you just say?"

"I said," Connor says slowly, "are you gonna be here a while? I was gonna walk Stace around…"

I clear my throat then shake my head. "I actually have to leave soon. I have… I'm closing at The Mitch tonight."

He bobs his head. "Yeah, okay. Well, we'll see you around. Maybe we can swing through later and grab a drink."

"Nice to meet you," Stace says, giving a friendly wave before she and Connor are turning and heading off toward a group of people a little ways away from us.

I watch them go, not even caring how awkward and weird I'm surely being by staring after them. Everything inside me feels dead.

What the hell is happening? He's *engaged*? I didn't even know he was dating anyone.

My stomach rolls.

How long have they been together?

I spin around and put my back to the light of the fire, shielding my face from anyone who might be watching as a tear streaks down my cheek. I bat it away with the sleeve of my jacket, but just as quickly as the first popped up, another follows, and I know I need to get out of here immediately.

Without thinking, I walk to the passenger side of Rusty's car and tug the door open, climbing in next to him.

"What are you doing?" His question is tinged with that same irritation from earlier.

"I need a ride."

"Tough shit, Bellamy. I have somewhere to be."

I yank the seatbelt forward and click it into place.

"Please?" I ask, scrunching up my eyes trying to hold back the tears.

Rusty says something else—something equally as dismissive—and it's clear he doesn't want me here with him right now. But I don't hear him, because I bend forward and put my face in my hands as I burst into tears, my emotions slamming through me.

"I'm so sorry," I say, choking the words out between sobs.

I hear Rusty sigh and then feel the car begin to roll forward, hopefully carrying us far, far away from what is surely the worst moment of my life.

When I glance out the window 15 minutes later and see that he's pulled up outside The Mitch, my stomach turns over. I feel like I can barely breathe right now, let alone go in for a closing shift where I might have to face Connor and Stace later on top of dealing with every drunk in town.

Though downing a bottle of tequila sounds like it might be a good idea.

"Can you just take me home?" I ask, my voice small.

"I literally just drove you in the *opposite* direction of your house. You couldn't have said that earlier?"

"I'm sorry, I was…" But I don't get the sentence out before my eyes scrunch up and I break into tears again.

I hear him grumble something about my brother, then the car moves forward, through the gravel of the dirt lot and back out onto the main road. He doesn't turn in the direction of my house on the other side of the lake, though. Instead, he drives the few minutes back into town and then out onto the road that exits Cedar Point and leads down the mountain. It only briefly occurs to me to ask where he's going, but I resolve to just sit in silence and wait until he eventually takes me home.

I've never missed a shift before, so when I text my co-worker Emily to let her know I'm not feeling well and won't be able to head in, it only takes a split second before I get her reply saying she can cover for me, which I appreciate since I've covered for Emily on many, many occasions.

The tiny distraction her text provides is gone in a blink, leaving me with a stark reminder of what I learned tonight.

Connor has a fiancée.

Thinking about it again sends another wave of tears to my eyes, but this time I manage to sit and cry silently as Rusty drives us along the winding road out of town.

Connor was just here, in Cedar Point, not even three months ago for his mother's birthday. He came into The Mitch, sat at the bar, and talked with me all night like nothing had changed between us since last summer. He did that thing, the tucking my hair behind my ear thing that he's always done. Maybe I'm just incredibly naïve, but I feel like that's way too intimate of a thing to do to someone who is not your fiancée when you're engaged.

My train of thought is cut off as we come to a stop. I sit up straighter, wondering where we are. I've driven up and down this mountain for my entire life and have never stopped here before, at what looks to be a random turnout about ten minutes from town.

When I glance at Rusty, he's staring out the windshield, his jaw tight and his hands squeezing the wheel like he's hoping to rip it out.

A few minutes go by, and we just sit in silence.

Five minutes.

Six.

Seven.

Then, without a word, Rusty shifts the car out of park and turns us around to head back into town. I glance back, wondering what the hell that was abou...

And then it hits me.

I look at Rusty where he sits, taking in the emotion that's rolling off of him in waves. Today is the anniversary of when his parents died, when they were run off the road by a drunk driver just a few minutes outside of town.

It was the most horrible kind of tragedy. Cedar Point was devastated. Rusty and his sister Abby barely held it together. I was pretty young at the time—junior high, I think—but I remember the service like it was for someone in *my* family. It was the very first time I'd been to a funeral, and it left a mark I've never been able to wipe clean.

I want to say something to him.

Anything. Anything at all that might soothe him or ease some of the pain I'm sure he must be feeling, but I've never been good with words. I never know what to say or how to make anything better. Instead, somehow, I always seem to say something that makes it worse.

It's why I like numbers. There's no emotion in numbers, always a right answer.

With people, with situations like this, there's always the probability to get it wrong, and I hate to be wrong. I stay silent, eyeing him frequently as he drives us back into town and up the east side of the lake toward my parents' house.

"You gonna be okay?" he asks once he pulls into our driveway and comes to a stop.

I nod and try to give him some kind of smile. "Yeah. I'll be..." But a wave hits me, and I break into tears again. "I'm so sorry," I say, dropping my face into my hands again. "I feel so stupid crying about this when you're actually dealing with real pain, but I can't help it."

Rusty sighs, and then I'm startled by the feeling of a big, warm hand patting me roughly on the back. I glance up at him in surprise, catching the uncomfortable look on his face as he tries to console me, and my tears are brought to an abrupt halt as I burst into laughter.

He immediately withdraws his hand, but I keep laughing even as his eyes narrow at me.

"Why are you laughing?"

"Because..." My words come out in chunks as I continue shaking. "That was...the most awkward...consolation...back pat...to ever occur."

Rusty rolls his eyes and sits silently as I finish laughing, and when I finally trail off and wipe my eyes—this time from laughter and not from crying—I let out a long sigh and sag back into my seat.

"At minimum, thanks for the laugh. I needed it."

He makes some sort of sound that's reminiscent of a grunt of affirmation.

I grab my purse off the floor and push the door open but then turn to look at Rusty before I hop out. "I'm sorry if I ruined your evening, your plans to go..." I wave my hand, gesturing vaguely as if that can encompass *anything* about what his plans were tonight.

He shrugs a shoulder. "It's alright."

Nodding, I reach out and place my hand on his where it sits on the stick shift and give it a squeeze.

"See you around, Rusty."

The man bobs his head once and gives me a tight smile, and I take that as my cue to get the hell out of his car and out of his hair. I head into my dark house and up to my childhood bedroom, and I cry myself to sleep.

chapter two
rusty

"It looks great."

My eyes scan the structure, impressed by the work that has been accomplished in just the past six weeks. The rotting wood panels on the exterior have been treated and repaired in a way that preserves the look and feel of an old barn without the worries that come along with an antiquated building. The concrete flooring has been poured and finished, the interior re-insulated, and the windows and doors replaced. She looks brand-new but still beautiful and classic in a way that preserves the older vibe.

It's the one thing Jackson has nailed down that's of primary importance: we need to keep as much of the original structure as possible. Apparently old things are much more attractive than new things in the brewery space.

It speaks to the hipster soul.

My eyes nearly rolled right out of my head at that, but I just went with it because my business partner is nothing if not knowledgeable about this kind of shit. I, on the other hand, am focused almost exclusively on the product, on the actual beer we brew. It's been my baby for the past ten years and is where I tend to focus the majority of my time and energy.

I don't care what Jackson says about the fact that people will buy anything if you market it right. If I don't believe in what I'm selling, I'm doing something wrong, and I know without a shadow of a doubt that Cedar Cider is a top-notch, quality craft beer.

"I'm glad to hear that," says our contractor Nick, a smile on his face as he leads me around to the front again. "We've been pushing to make up for the time we lost in March."

I nod. We had an unexpected dumping of snow in early March that took a few weeks to melt off, and that delayed the project start date. I know construction jobs always come up against hiccups and delays, but I wasn't expecting to face such a big one right from the jump.

Thankfully, Nick is the kind of guy who *also* isn't a fan of delays, and I've been pleased to see just how aggressively he's tried to recoup the lost time.

"What's the timeline for installing the brewing equipment?" I step through the open doorway to the main space, looking at the long wall where the majority of the distillers will be lined up as a backdrop for the bar.

"By July at the latest. We're going to stick with setting up the interior in phases, like we discussed, and we need to get the kitchen elements in first before we bring in such large equipment. Otherwise it'll be a game of 'will it all fit', which is just a waste of time for everyone."

I cross my arms, mulling it over. I communicated that the brewing equipment needed to be in as early as possible so we could begin using it. Ideally, I'd have liked three months with it before we open in September, but I guess two will have to do.

"Alright, well, keep me posted about how things progress."
We shake hands. "Always."

I head back to my Chevy, leaving Nick and his crew behind to continue the final window installation that's happening today. I hop into the driver's seat and pull out my phone.

Me: Things are going good. We'll be able to finalize the equipment order in the next few weeks.

Almost instantly, I see the bubbles that mean Jackson is responding.

Jackson: Awesome. I'll set up the meeting with Harold.
Boyd: Harold's the guy from BruWorks?
Jackson: Yeah.
Me: And you're still sure BruWorks is who we should work with? Because I've been using Master Brewer for ten years.

We've had this discussion a few times, and I've asked for him to confirm and reconfirm the reasons behind why he thinks Bru-Works is the better company to purchase our new, much larger brewing equipment from.

Jackson: Yes. I am.

I can almost hear his irritation through the text, but I can't help it. I'm not great with change. I'm not the kind of guy who jumps on the new hot thing that's changing the game. I'm the guy who sticks with one thing for decades.
Deodorant.
Cereal.

Windshield wiper fluid.

Brewing equipment is no different, and I've been using Master Brewer since I first started brewing in my garage, though with a much smaller setup. I did it as a way to distract myself after I moved back to Cedar Point, and now their machinery is so intrinsic to me that switching manufacturers feels like a punch to the gut.

But Jackson is more than just my roommate and college buddy. He's one of my business partners for a reason, and I trust him. I trust not only his knowledge and experience but his intuition as well. So if he says it's the right move, I need to trust that, too.

Me: Sounds good. Just let me know when.
Jackson: Will do

I drop my phone into the cup holder, pulling out of the gravel lot and down the dirt road that's just off the end of Main Street and heading back into town. Today is a lot busier than I thought it was going to be, and I still have quite a few deliveries to make, both here in Cedar Point and throughout several of the small mountain communities nearby that keep Cedar Cider stocked in their convenience stores and restaurants. Nobody told me how much driving would be involved in keeping a small brewing business afloat. Most days I feel more like I'm delivering pizza than crafting beer.

I back my car into a spot behind One Stop Shop and pop the trunk, where I have ten cases of beer waiting to be unloaded. Thankfully, I was able to partner with a distributor who manages all the restocking down the mountain at the locations that keep our beer on the shelves, but for all the little businesses up here in the mountains, the cost of hiring someone else is just too great, so I handle those deliveries myself, including our local grocery, One Stop.

I push through the back door and prop it open then grab a dolly and begin unloading the first five boxes.

"Hey man."

I look over my shoulder and grin when I spot Andy Marshall, clipboard in hand, standing in the doorway.

"Happy Monday."

I snort. "Mondays are never happy."

He flashes me a smile and moves out of the way as I wheel the dolly into the stock room in the back of the store.

"I love Mondays."

"That's because you take off Tuesday and Wednesday," I reply. "I'd love Monday too if it was the start of my weekend."

He laughs and follows behind me as I head into the main store and over to the beer fridge. "Yeah, okay. I guess that makes sense." He pauses. "I was thinking about you yesterday."

I glance back at him just as I yank the fridge door open, unsurprised when I see the sympathetic look on his face. Andy's always been a softy at heart, and he tells me some version of the same thing every year at this time. He knows I don't want to talk about it.

Nodding, I don't address what he said, making quick work of hoisting the cases onto the appropriate shelves.

"What did you get up to this weekend?" I ask once I emerge and see that he's waiting for me. "Did Briar have that thing?"

He shakes his head and follows me as I head back to my car for the second load. "It's this coming weekend. We're heading down to Sacramento tomorrow for a few days, gonna make a little trip out of it."

"Sounds fun."

"I hope so."

Andy's girlfriend Briar is an exceptional florist, and she's competing in some kind of regional bouquet contest. She's been talking about it for months, sharing all the things she's been doing to prepare.

It's wild to me the things people find interesting. The idea that there are enough people into putting together vases of fancy flowers to the point that there are regional competitions... ones that lead to state and national competitions...it's just mind-blowing.

That said, I'm sure there are things I do that other people are shocked by. Well, things I *would* do if I had time to have any hobbies. Right now, nearly every minute goes into my business, whether it's day-to-day ops or working on something for the opening. Besides one or two other responsibilities, I just don't have time for anything else.

Besides, I'm not really a joiner, not a hobby kind of guy. I mean, I can't even imagine what I'd look like doing...something else, like playing tennis or collecting coins.

A huff of laughter falls from me as I finish up with the delivery and sign the paperwork with Andy that reflects the quantity of items I stocked up.

"I was thinking about heading into The Mitch tonight, grabbing a beer. You interested?"

I close the trunk of my car, considering. I'm a regular there, but I'm not really in the mood for being friendly.

It's almost like Andy can read my mind.

"We do this song and dance every year, Rus. You don't have to talk to me. You can just be a grump, but you shouldn't be alone right now."

I grind my teeth together a little bit, considering. He's right. I know he is.

So I nod. "Yeah, just text me what time."

Andy slaps my back and gives me that stupid smile again. Sometimes I wish I could be a happy man like Andy is, someone who sees the positives in things and stays optimistic, but I just don't have it in me.

I'm not sure I ever have.

When I walk into The Mitch later that evening, I pause in the entry like I do nearly every time, allowing my eyes to adjust to the dim lighting. This place is the quintessential dive bar, complete with a dart board, a pool table, a juke box, and a hazy quality that makes it seem like people still smoke inside even though that's been banned since before I was legal to drink.

Once I can see, it only takes a second to scan the room and realize Andy hasn't arrived yet. I cross to the bar and slip onto a stool, ordering a whiskey neat from the bartender—Emily, I think?—a cute blonde who's wearing the employee shirt that says *Mitch Bitch*.

She gives me a look I know well—one that tells me I can have more than just the drink if I ask—before striding down to the other end of the bar to attend to other patrons. If Emily were on *this* side of the counter, I'd be taking her up on whatever that look might promise, but I've learned well enough not to mess around with locals.

What's that old saying? Don't dip your pen in company ink? It's like that, but with the town, which is why I don't flirt or fuck with people who live here. Not anymore. The last thing I need is some sort of drama when I ultimately don't want anything more than a good time.

I *used* to hook up with fellow townies, but my sister begged me for years to stop sleeping with people we know, and after one particularly bad experience involving a woman who wasn't as single as I assumed, I decided she was right. Who needs a black eye anyway? Besides, it's much cleaner to sleep with people who aren't planning on sticking around.

My phone vibrates on the bar, and when I glance down, I see Andy's text on the screen.

Andy: Sorry, man. Got tied up. Be there in 20.

Twenty minutes isn't that long, but it's just another chunk of time for me to wish I were back at my own house, where the whiskey is significantly cheaper. I pick up my Woodford and take a sip, enjoying the burn as it coats my mouth and runs down my throat, before staring blankly into the glass.

Has it really been ten years?

I seem to ask myself that question every year on the anniversary of their death. Each one seems almost unbelievable, but ten is a milestone. A decade. The idea that it's been *a decade* since I've talked to them is just…

A laugh catches my attention, pulling me from my memories and the emotional place I almost slipped into. I glance over to where Emily is talking with Bellamy Mitchell, the latter tying an apron around her hips, a wild smile on her face. When Bellamy's eyes catch mine, her laugh fades, replaced almost immediately by a look of embarrassment. She says something else to the blonde and then heads my way.

Another perk of drinking at home alone—I don't have to worry about bumping into people I don't feel like talking to in the exact moment I don't want to talk to them. It's not that I have anything against Bellamy, exactly, but the last thing I want is for her to rehash whatever that was last night, aka the weirdest hour I've ever experienced.

"Hey, Rusty," she says, planting her hands wide on the bar top and leaning forward. "About last night…"

"Don't worry about it," I tell her, because I don't want to talk about it.

"But I've been feeling awkward about it, and I just wanted to say I'm sorry."

"You already apologized. No need to do it again."

Her nose scrunches up. "I get that, but I still feel like an absolute ass. I mean…" She sighs. "You were going through something, and I was—"

"Bellamy."

Her warm chestnut eyes, which always seem far too trusting for her own good, blink a few times at my interruption.

"It's fine."

She nibbles on her lip and, begrudgingly, bobs her head a few times.

"Alright. If you're sure."

"I'm sure."

"Well…thank you again. For the ride home and the…consolation."

At that, she gives me a real smile, and I fight the urge to do the same as she begins to giggle. Her mouth opens slightly, like she's about to say something else, but a look of…I don't know, something uncomfortable overtakes her for just a moment. Then a big fake smile stretches wide on her face.

"Hey there, Bells."

Connor Pruitt walks up to the bar and hops onto the stool next to mine.

"Hi Connor. What can I get you?"

My eyes scan over Bellamy, taking in the stiff way she's standing, her hands twisting together in front of her even as she pretends she's happy to see him.

"Just a Coors would be good."

Lifting my glass to my mouth, I fight the urge to sneer at him. Two dozen beers on tap, and he goes with Coors?

Bellamy makes quick work of snagging a glass and tilting it under the tap, her eyes zeroed in on where it slowly fills the pint.

"Hey, listen," Connor starts, and I already have a bad feeling about whatever is going to come out of his mouth just based on his tone. "I hope I didn't upset you the other night. With Stace."

Bellamy blinks a few times but keeps her gaze on the beer as she finishes pouring, sets a coaster on the bar, and thunks the glass down on top of it.

"What do you mean?" she asks, that same saccharine look on her face.

"Oh, you know, just…" He pauses and glances at me for a second but still continues. "…I know you've had, you know, a crush on me for a while…"

My eyebrows rise, and I watch as Bellamy's jaw drops just slightly.

"…and last summer was a bit of fun, for sure. But I just wanted to make sure you didn't take the news too hard. About the engagement."

A beat goes by. And then another one.

Suddenly, Bellamy breaks into laughter, but it's not her real laugh. No—her *real* laughter is that barely-breathing, gasping-for-air thing she did in my car last night, or the little giggle she just gave me a second ago.

This laugh is high-pitched and uncomfortable and draws the attention of just about everyone around us.

"Connor, you are so funny," she says, planting her hands on her hips. "I am not at *all* upset about you and Stace. I'm very happy for you."

I glance at the man next to me, and I can tell he's anything but convinced.

"Besides, I'm not sure my boyfriend would be happy to hear about this supposed crush," she continues, laughing dramatically again. "He'll get a hoot out of this story when I tell him."

Connor watches Bellamy with amusement, and it really pisses me off. Clearly, she's had feelings for this guy, and he's sitting here *enjoying* how uncomfortable she is about the whole thing, his engagement and whatever.

What a prick.

"I didn't realize you were dating someone," he replies, tilting his head and examining her. "Is it serious?"

She nods. "Very."

"Funny…I feel like someone would have mentioned if another one of the Mitchell girls got into a serious relationship. You should have heard my mom going on and on about Briar and Andy last year." He chuckles. "Drove Keegan nuts."

That's because your sister was trying to make a play for Andy, you dumb shit. That's what I want to say, but I keep my mouth firmly closed.

"Yeah, well…we've been keeping it under wraps, wanting to make sure it's real before we talk to anyone about it."

Connor nods, but it's clear he doesn't believe her. I don't envy her with this hole she's digging, and I can't imagine how she's going to climb her way out of it without making herself look…

"But I guess it's finally time to tell everyone, Rusty."

Her words cut my thought off in the middle, and I blink a few times, trying to understand what she just said.

"He's been so cautious," she continues. "Not wanting to upset anyone because of, you know, the fact that he's friends with my brother and everything. But, yeah…"

There's a beat of silence from Connor, and I just keep staring at Bellamy, who is looking at me with a hint of desperation clouding her eyes.

"*You're…dating…Rusty.*"

There's a thick layer of disbelief in Connor's voice, and when I finally turn to look at him, I see a completely different expression on his face than was just there a moment ago. Gone is the cocky, incredibly arrogant prick who was sitting next to me, and in his place is, well…still a prick, but one who looks a lot more uncertain. Almost like he doesn't like the idea of me dating Bellamy.

Well, I don't like the idea either, but I *do* like the idea of putting this little shit in his place. Before I can think better of it, I'm muttering two words I'm almost certain I'll regret.

"She is."

chapter three
bellamy

Ohmygod. Ohmygod. Ohmygod.

What the hell did I just do?

My throat feels thick and my head is pounding at a rate that matches the speed of my heart. Surely there is some kind of rewind button, backspace or erase or delete or *something* I can hit to go back to five minutes ago before I said the most stupid, idiotic thing I've ever said in my life.

Holy fucking shit.

"Really? Well, that's…" Connor clears his throat, his eyes glancing between the two of us. "…great. For both of you."

"Thanks, Pruitt."

Rusty sounds so calm, as if I didn't just pull the rug out from under him in the most asinine way.

"Well, now that the cat's out of the bag, how about we double-date soon? We're gonna be here in town for the summer, and I'm sure Stace would love to get to know you both."

Before I can even think about how to respond, Rusty is

speaking again. "Sounds great."

Connor raises his beer glass to us both then heads off toward the back deck that faces out to the water, where I can see Stace standing at a high top table looking out into the distance.

I look back at Rusty, and I'll be honest, he looks a lot more chill about this than I would have ever imagined. He steeples his hands and rests his chin against his fingers, letting out a long, slow breath, his eyes staring at the wall behind me.

"Rusty, I'm so sorry. It just…came out of me. I wasn't even thinking."

"No, you weren't," he says, lifting his barely touched glass of whiskey. "But neither was I."

He downs the entire thing. I can only imagine how much it burns.

"Hey man, sorry I'm late." Andy Marshall hops up onto the stool Connor just vacated, a smile on his face. "Had an issue with the front door lock and had to wait for Gene to come help me sort it."

Rusty nods but doesn't say anything.

"Can I get the Cedar Cider IPA?"

I drag my eyes from Rusty and look at Andy, giving him a thin smile and nodding. "Sure. Just a sec."

I spin around and take a deep breath. I still have a shift to work, so I take a few seconds, trying to push away any thoughts about what just happened, then grab a pint glass. I turn back to the bar with a new smile, pull the beer from the tap, and set it in front of Andy on a coaster.

"Have you wished this guy a happy 32nd birthday yet?" Andy asks, flicking a thumb at Rusty.

Surprise spreads through me. "Today's your birthday?" I ask him.

"Nah, it was yesterday," Andy responds before Rusty can say anything. "But he never celebrates, so I always drag him out for a drink."

My heart pinches, and something inside me wells up tight. If yesterday was Rusty's birthday, that means... Did his parents die on his birthday? How did I never realize that before?

Shit, no wonder he doesn't want to celebrate.

"Happy birthday, Rusty," I say, reaching out and squeezing his hand. Then I clear my throat. "How about another glass of whiskey? On me."

His eyes finally meet mine, and I can already see him preparing to decline, so I pull out a bottle of Woodford before he can answer me and pour him three fingers.

Andy slaps him on the back. "Now *that* looks like you're going to have a good birthday."

I wait for a second, until Rusty nods at me, before making my escape.

"I'm gonna go help..." I start, my head tilting in the direction of where Emily is pouring shots for a group of women wearing matching pink shirts. "We'll talk later?"

I turn, heading over to help make margaritas and tropical drinks while Emily prepares a full tray of shots. Apparently these ladies are planning to have a pretty wild Monday evening.

Unfortunately, apart from the group of women getting wasted, it's a fairly calm evening at The Mitch, leaving my mind free to wander through the murky discomfort of my thoughts and my mortifying declaration that I'm in a very serious relationship with Rusty Fuller. Clearly I was having a stroke, because that was an absolutely outlandish thing to say.

Ever since seeing Connor and Stace at bonfire night, I've been thinking about how much more convenient it would be if I had a boyfriend. Maybe what happened with Connor last summer wouldn't hurt so much if I had moved on to my own perfect relationship.

But through all those thoughts, it never even occurred to me to lie about it. I'm not the type of person to keep secrets or be dramatic or create a bald-faced lie.

I never lie about *anything*.

When Connor said what he said, about me having had a *crush* on him…as if last summer was nothing, as if my feelings are some kind of joke or anecdote to laugh about with friends—I mean, how could I *not* scramble for a way to make myself seem less foolish?

Because that's exactly how I feel: like a fool. My feelings for Connor were large and overwhelming from the start, stretching all the way back to sophomore year of high school, and there hasn't ever been any going back.

Not when he dated Jeanette Kingston junior year. Not when he would visit from college and began stopping in to see me at work. Not when he moved home for the summer last year and I started tutoring him in math because he'd failed a core business accounting class. Not when things between us finally became intimate.

Last summer was the best summer of my life, and when Connor left and went back to finish his senior year, I thought… Well, it doesn't matter what I thought, because I was wrong.

I was so very wrong.

Connor and Stace take off a little while later, promising to reach out about a double date soon. Eventually, Rusty and Andy leave as well, and it's hard not to notice the long look Rusty gives me before he walks out the door.

I don't doubt he's upset. I would be if someone had just made a claim like that about me in a public place where I felt pressured and unable to deny it, which is why I find myself parked outside his house once my shift has ended, mentally rehearsing my apology and trying to determine the best way to get us out of the mess I've caused.

Rusty's frown is more than apparent when he answers the door, but he also looks like I've woken him from sleeping, and it only then occurs to me that I've stopped by his place at two in the morning.

"I'm sorry, Rusty."

He sighs, his eyes rolling slightly before he turns away and retreats back into his house, leaving me standing in the open doorway.

"Okay…am I supposed to follow you?" I ask, calling after him.

When he doesn't say anything in response, I decide to just assume yes, and I step in, closing the door behind me and making the short trek from the entry into the living room. I find Rusty there pouring the second of two glasses of whiskey, and he turns, wordlessly extending one in my direction. I take it and tip back the entire thing in one go, grimacing at the way it burns my throat all the way down into my chest.

"You know, if you're going to wake me up in the middle of the night, you could at least pretend you appreciate good whiskey and sip it slowly."

"Sorry," I mumble, handing the glass back to him.

He takes it and turns back to the liquor cabinet, grabbing a bottle of Maker's Mark and refilling the glass about halfway.

"If you're going to drink it like a monster, at least don't waste the good stuff."

I nod, accepting the new glass and taking another big sip, coughing a few times from the burn.

"I'm really sorry."

"It's just whiskey, Bellamy. It's not that big—"

"I mean about the Connor thing." I stare at the glass in my hand. "I don't know what came over me, I was just…"

"You were upset." Rusty leans back against the counter, setting his glass next to him before crossing his arms. "People do dumb things when they're upset."

I shake my head. "Not me. I never do dumb things."

He pins me with a look that says *clearly* I do.

"But really, I'm not…" I shake my head. "I'm not the girl who blurts out weird things or lies or tries to be anything she's not. I'm just me. I've always been just me." I take another big sip. "Maybe that's the problem."

Rusty sighs. "It's not a problem to be you, Bellamy."

I snort, the warmth of the liquor beginning to slither its way through my system and making me feel a little more loose. "It is when I'd rather be Stace."

"You don't want to be Stace."

"They're *engaged*," I cry out, striding across the room and angrily setting my glass down on the counter. "Engaged! I mean, really, he probably barely knows her. I didn't even know he was dating someone and now he's engaged!?"

The striding feels good, so I turn and storm across the space in the opposite direction.

"After everything we've been through, he's just going to act like I'm some girl he knew in high school, like we're not…"

My voice fades and I slow to a stop, my emotions bubbling up again as I burst into tears.

"I feel like an idiot. I slept with him, and he comes back less than a year later with a fiancée? I thought we meant something to each other, but I was clearly very wrong."

When I look at Rusty, he looks angry, but I don't have the mental capacity to try to understand him when I feel so emotionally stretched thin. I drop down onto the sofa, suddenly feeling all-consumingly tired.

Lying takes a lot out of a person.

Apparently, so does crying hysterically.

I wipe my eyes and stare up at the ceiling, willing myself to stop the theatrics…but the whiskey is making me too honest.

"Maybe the sex was horrible and he couldn't wait to find someone better," I blubber.

Suddenly, Rusty's face is in my line of sight, hovering over me where I'm in repose.

"Why don't we call it a night, huh?" he says, bracing an arm on the back of the couch. "Abby's room is upstairs, nice and clean. Let's get you up there so you can sleep some of this off."

I mull it over for a minute, eventually deciding he's right. Pulling myself up off the couch, I wobble slightly, the liquor in my bloodstream suddenly surging to the forefront of my focus and highlighting just how drunk I am from downing nearly a glass and a half of whiskey in a few seconds. When I trip going up the stairs and need Rusty's help, any remaining thoughts about Rusty or Connor fly out the window, replaced by my sudden desire to curl up in a ball and go to sleep.

Rusty shows me to Abby's room, and my eyes lock on myself in the mirror above her antique dresser.

"The heater's been out for a few weeks, so I'm gonna get you another blanket."

Rusty disappears and I continue staring at my reflection, my shaky vision taking in my red eyes and running mascara. I never look like this kind of mess. I'm always put together, physically and emotionally, which is why looking at myself right now feels so startling.

For the first time in my life, I don't recognize who I see.

chapter four
rusty

This is the last thing I thought would be happening tonight.

After the absurdity of what transpired at the bar, I thought I'd come home and get a good night of sleep. I didn't want to think about Bellamy, or Connor, or this wild lie that has now roped me into something I want no part of.

I came home, watched the last inning of the A's game, then climbed into bed—not that I fell into a dreamless sleep or anything. Instead, I lay awake for quite a while, staring at my ceiling, unable to shut off my mind.

Surprisingly, there was a part of me wondering if maybe offering to help out a little bit with this Connor thing wasn't too bad of an idea. The guy seems like a prick, and I love nothing more than making assholes eat their words.

I mean, he's back for the summer, right? Then he's off to… somewhere else, I'm assuming. I could be a stand-in boyfriend for Bellamy. A dinner here, a bonfire there. Doesn't sound too terrible.

Until I consider the celibacy aspect. I wouldn't be able to take Bellamy Mitchell, Cedar Point's favorite daughter, out to dinner and then still go home with someone else.

Then, when I finally *did* fall into a fitful sleep, she woke me in the wee hours, standing a mess at my door, and it only highlighted just how little I actually want to be involved in this drama. It's not my style to *get involved*. I normally just try to keep to myself. It makes life a whole lot easier, and the last thing I need is some weird lie like this complicating anything.

Not to mention how Boyd would take it. I mean, I'd have to call him and give him a heads-up, absolutely. Make sure he knows the whole thing is a ruse.

I groan at how ridiculous it all sounds then snag a blanket from the linen closet where I've been standing and staring blankly for a minute or two. Hopefully, I can tuck away Boyd's little sister into Abby's room, let her sleep off the embarrassment of the night, and she'll be back to her senses by tomorrow.

Pushing the door open, I'm prepared to hand over the pink and white quilt to a drunk and tired Bellamy. Instead, I nearly swallow my tongue. Bellamy is in the middle of the room in nothing but her underwear and socks, in the process of tugging her shirt over the top of her head, her tits visible through the nearly transparent lace of her bra.

I swallow thickly, my mouth going dry as my eyes trace over her body, taking in her lightly tanned skin and gentle curves, the little ways her body dips and swells. It's her ass, though, that has me hypnotized, pert and round and covered by nothing but a tiny scrap of that same see-through lacy material.

She smiles once her shirt is off, chucking it on the floor as if she's completed a marathon.

"Time for sleep," she says, her voice soft.

Then she turns and crawls into Abby's bed, that ass sticking up in the air, before she collapses and lets out an exhausted sigh.

I clear my throat and avert my gaze, reminding myself that this is Boyd's sister.

"I'll be down the hall. Just knock if you need anything," I say, holding up the blanket between us, refusing to look at her again until I've tossed it gently over her nearly naked form.

I quickly click off the lights then stride to my own room and firmly shut the door, but when I climb back into bed and close my eyes, it's like the outline of Bellamy's shape is burned into my retinas. You can't go back once you've seen someone in their panties. You can't unsee them.

I groan and roll over, shoving my face into my pillow. Not once, in all my years of knowing Boyd and his family, have I ever looked at any of the Mitchell daughters with anything but a friendly gaze. Maybe an irritated one, but definitely not…this.

Whatever this is.

It firmly resolves for me that offering to help Bellamy with Connor is not something I should be doing. When Bellamy wakes up in the morning, I'll just tell her she needs to come clean to Connor, period. Then I can wash my hands of this mess.

When I wake and glance at my alarm and see that it's past nine, I bite out a curse knowing I don't have time to get in a morning swim. Waking later than seven is unusual for me, but it's not wild considering the fact that I was up for an hour in the middle of the night dealing with an emotional, drunk woman.

I roll out of bed and hop straight into the shower, hoping the rush of water against my skin will flood my system and wake me up. Eventually, when I head down into the kitchen, I'm surprised to find Bellamy up and cooking breakfast—thankfully, fully dressed.

She blushes when she sees me and gives me an embarrassed smile that says she either remembers last night or, at the very least, remembers enough to warrant the flush on her cheeks.

"Morning." She tugs a pan off the stove and dumps a batch of scrambled eggs onto a plate. "I made you breakfast."

I nod and take a seat at the island. "I can see that."

"I wasn't sure what time you go to work, so I started once you got in the shower," she continues, setting the eggs in front of me, followed by a plate of bacon and some roasted potatoes. "I'm…"

"Don't apologize again."

Her shoulders droop.

"It is what it is, and I don't doubt it will all get resolved. Soon, right?"

My eyes lock on hers, waiting for her confirmation, waiting for her to say, 'Yes, Rusty, I'll definitely fix it all and get everything squared away with Connor.'

But she doesn't. Instead, she gives me a look I'm not sure I like, one that says she's maybe thinking the exact opposite.

"I actually wanted to talk to you about that."

I stab my fork into a potato, keeping my eyes on hers as I do, but she doesn't take the hint. Or perhaps she just ignores it completely.

"I was wondering if there's any way you'd consider playing along for a little bit."

I shove the small potato in my mouth, my eyes narrowing as I chew.

"Just for a little while," she continues. "I was thinking about it last night, and I just really think it could be a good idea."

"Please tell me how the hell this could be a good idea."

She opens her mouth to reply, but I cut her off.

"And for that matter, please tell me all about the thoughts you had last night. When exactly did you do all this thinking? When you were sobbing on the couch or when you were passing out drunk in Abby's room after your little striptease?"

Bellamy blushes again. It makes her eyes bright in a way I've never noticed before, and that makes me even more irritated.

"I just don't want Connor to think I sat around all year waiting for him," she says, ignoring my previous statement entirely. "I *need* him to believe that."

I stab another potato. "Why? Why does it matter so much?"

She winces. "It just does."

"Well that's not good enough. I'm not trying to jump into some big, complicated lie I have to explain to my sister, or to Boyd. And I *definitely* don't want to put my own personal life on hold to cater to whatever this absurd idea would require of me."

Bellamy's fingers tap lightly on the counter as she listens.

"So the answer is no. I don't care what you do or what you tell him, but the idea that we're dating needs to be firmly stomped out. For good."

She keeps her eyes on the counter for a beat or two, eventually turning away without looking at me again, instead focusing on scrubbing the dishes from the breakfast she just made.

Of course, I feel like an asshole. There was no reason for me to be that rude or aggressive, no reason for me to shut her down like that.

But there *is* a reason for me to not go along with this boy-friend farce. Several reasons, in fact. I don't like to lie, first of all. I might not have impeachable character, but lying isn't in my repertoire. Life is always easier when everything deals with the truth. I'm also friends with her brother and far too old for her, so the idea that we would actually date in real life is not only incredulous but would cause very real problems. Then there's my unwanted reaction to her inadvertent striptease last night.

No. Cutting this off at the head is the best decision.

For everyone.

I finish off the breakfast she cooked then head into my home office, hoping if I just disappear, maybe Bellamy will take the hint and do the same.

"I could trade you something."

Sighing, I turn and look at where she's standing in the doorway.

"Trust me when I say there is nothing you have that I'd want to trade for."

I ignore the tiny voice in the back of my mind saying that's not entirely true.

"I could work for you. I'm not an accountant yet, but I'm still really good with numbers."

I scrub my hands across my face.

"Bellamy."

"Rusty."

Standing, I walk toward her. She smiles, possibly thinking I'm going to agree to her trade, but her expression shifts when I take her by the arm and walk her to the front door, grabbing her purse from the back of the couch on the way there and thrusting it into her arms.

"Figure out how to tell Connor," I say, yanking the front

door open. "By tomorrow."

Her shoulders sag and she steps out onto the welcome mat, watching me with a look that makes me wish I could give her what she wants.

But I can't.

"Good luck."

Then I shut the door, ignoring the lump in my throat as I leave her behind.

"I can't believe there are only a few months left until you open a frickin' pub!"

My sister bounces on her toes next to me as we stare at the boxes of pasta and jars of sauce on the grocery aisle, trying to narrow down what we want to make for dinner.

"I hope you know I will be taking advantage of the 90% family discount."

I scoff. "Because that's a thing."

Abby bumps me with her shoulder and winks. "I mean, if you're taking suggestions, I would definitely drop that one in the box." She pauses. "Along with my previous offering of my name to go on one of your drinks."

Rolling my eyes, I retrieve a box of farfalle from the shelf.

"Don't act like it's a bad idea. You *know* everyone wants a good, old-fashioned Abbysinthe."

At that, I actually laugh. "Where did you come up with that?"

"My own mind." She taps her temple. "I've got a bunch of incredible ideas up here that I'd be willing to share." Abby shrugs. "All you gotta do is ask."

Shaking my head, I snag a jar of vodka sauce and set it in my basket next to the pasta. "You're a menace, Fuller, you know that?"

She just beams at me. "I learned from the best."

We get to the end of the aisle and split, Abby heading to the produce section to grab some garlic and fresh tomato for me to add to the sauce, me off to the liquor aisle to select a bottle of wine. I've got plenty of bottles at home, but I usually get a few new ones before heading to the little house Abby and Briar share on the other side of the lake for our Tuesday-night family dinners.

It's partially because I know any wine Abby would pick would be a poor pairing for whatever I'm cooking—she just doesn't have a knowing palette—but also partially because I'm her big brother and it's always nice to have a sibling with more money pick up the tab for little luxuries like nicer bottles of wine.

It's been fun, doing these dinners at Abby's, though I'm always hyperaware of being the fifth wheel. Abby's dating my friend Jackson, and her roommate Briar is dating my other buddy, Andy. It's a good time for sure, all of us usually drinking too much wine and ending the night with a card game or, as the weather has gotten warmer, sitting outside for a campfire. But there is a touch of discomfort in wondering if the two girls would rather just have dinner with their boyfriends instead of inviting me to tag along.

I've been my sister's only family since she was in high school, so I never know if she's looking at me for brotherly comfort or fatherly advice, and sometimes I wonder if that bleeds into what role I take in her life. Tonight, though, it'll just be me and Abs. Jackson is an investor in a few companies and is in Washington meeting with a potential new partner, and Briar and Andy are out of town for that bouquet thing. I'm looking forward to a little quality time with my sister, something I used to take for granted when she lived with me.

"Hey, man."

I turn, one eyebrow rising at the sight of Connor and Stace strolling toward me, hand in hand. It feels impossibly unfair that I keep bumping into this guy when I can't even remember the last time I saw him before the past couple of days, but I guess that's just how life works.

"Hey."

I give them what I think might be a friendly smile then return my attention to the wall of wine, hoping Connor will take the hint and leave me alone.

He doesn't.

"Grabbing wine for dinner?" he asks, eyeing the basket I'm leaning against.

"Yup."

"So are we."

I bob my head then reach out to snag the nearest Syrah, not even pausing to read the label. I just want whatever I can get quickly so I can wave goodbye and head in the opposite direction.

"Got the tomatoes, but they're out of garlic."

Abby drops a bag of red and orange heirlooms into my cart then grins and says a friendly hello to the couple standing a few feet away. I'm not sure if Abby knows Connor at all since he's a bit younger than she is, but I don't want to risk the two of them striking up a conversation, so I begin to walk away.

"Alright, well, I guess we'll see you around."

"Oh wait," Connor says, halting my movements. "We need to talk about the double date."

I wince, dread filling me.

"Stace and I were thinking maybe Thursday night? If you and Bellamy are free."

I sigh. Clearly Bellamy didn't tell Connor she lied to him. When I turn around, trying to find the words to explain to him that the entire thing was made up, I can't do it. Something inside me just refuses to expose Bellamy like that.

Unlike the other day in my house, I don't have a bristling desire for Connor to know the truth. That irritation with Bellamy has subsided and is instead replaced by a nagging desire to help her place Connor in her past. Where it comes from, I'm not sure, but it's there all the same.

"Yeah, I'll...talk to her about it. Does she have your number?"

Connor nods. "She does."

"Great. Well...we'll be in touch soon, then."

Before he can say or do anything else, I spin back around and grip my sister's bicep, tugging her down the aisle and around the corner. I can feel her eyes on me, wide and curious, the ripple of surprise a tangible thing radiating off of her. I studiously ignore it as I lead us down the bread aisle for a loaf of sourdough.

"Are you seriously not going to say anything?" she finally asks.

"About what?"

Abby's head dips to the side and she looks at me, unamused. "About what," she repeats. "About the fact that you're taking Bellamy Mitchell on a double date? When did this happen?"

I sigh. "Will you keep your voice down? You're practically shouting."

"Are the two of you dating? Because I'm trying to remember even a *hint* of there being something mentioned about this. Ever. There's nothing." She grabs my arm and stops me from continuing down the aisle. "How long has this been going on?" Her eyes widen even more dramatically. "Does Boyd know?"

"It just…happened," I finally reply. "And no, Boyd doesn't know. I need to talk to him about it."

I make a mental note about that, because there's no way I can fake date Bellamy and not give my best friend a heads-up.

"What do you mean it *just happened*? Like…" She leans in and dips her voice lower. "Did you hook up with her? Not that I want the details, but I thought we'd agreed you weren't going to poach the locals."

Gritting my teeth, I pin my sister with an irritated look, not liking the way she's looking at me, not liking the way it makes me feel.

"I don't *poach* locals."

"So then…what's the deal?"

"We're dating."

"Dating." She thinks it over, staring at me with a pinched expression. "Bellamy Mitchell…is dating *you*."

My head jerks back at the implication in her tone. "Is that so hard to believe?"

"Actually, yes. It is."

"Why?"

"Because. She's Bellamy Mitchell, and you're…" She eyes me up and down.

"I'm *what*?"

I don't know how we got to this place, arguing in the middle of the grocery store about a relationship I'm not even actually in, my sister giving me another once-over with that look. I don't like how it feels.

The idea that my sister thinks something not so nice about me...it stings, and while I might not normally worry about what this town thinks of me in any way, I at least assumed my sister had my back.

My sister who I raised.

My sister who I sacrificed my entire life for.

"You're not the dating kind" is what she ends up saying.

Even though I get what she means—because it's true, I'm *not* the dating kind—I still can't help the way it thickens something in my throat to know it's how she sees me. Suddenly, there's something within me that is desperate to prove her wrong, to convince her I'm not only the dating kind, but the kind someone like Bellamy Mitchell would date since Bellamy Mitchell is apparently the barometer my sister is using to determine the worth of men around town.

"Well, apparently Bellamy disagrees with you," I rebut, pushing the cart down the aisle and toward the front checkout, desperate to leave the conversation behind us, as if physically moving away from it can relieve this pressure in my chest.

My sister is persistent, and it only takes her a few seconds to catch up to me.

"Hey, I'm sorry," she says, putting her hand on my forearm and pressing gently, pulling me to a stop next to the jars of pickles. "I didn't mean to sound so surprised. I was just..."

"Surprised," I finish for her when she trails off. "I get it."

She watches me for a long minute before a soft smile stretches across her face. "Bellamy Mitchell, huh? You're really dating?"

I nod.

After a few seconds of considering the idea, Abby claps her hands together a few times, her earlier attitude transforming into excitement. "Oh my gosh, this will be so great. You can bring her to the next family dinner!" Her eyebrows dip. "Does Briar know?"

Shaking my head. "Nobody knows. Nobody *knew*," I correct. "Not until last night."

"Well, give it a day," she jokes. "In this town, news travels fast. You know that better than anyone."

I can't help the way a little thread of panic flickers through me at that thought, and I know the first thing I have to do when I finish dinner with Abby is call Boyd and tell him what's going on.

I have a feeling our friendship will be at stake if I don't.

chapter five
bellamy

It's hard to hide my surprise when I step into the parking lot after I finish waitressing at Dock 7 and find Rusty leaning against the back of his Blazer, eating peanuts and chucking the shells on the ground. By the amount scattered in the gravel beneath his feet, I'd wager he's been out here for a while.

I know he's here to ask me about Connor, to make sure I've told him the truth…but the reality is I haven't worked up the nerve. How do you tell someone *I was so blindsided by your relationship I fabricated my own* without sounding like a total nutcase?

Knowing I can't avoid Rusty's questions, I head in the direction of where he's parked next to my CRV, resigning myself to my fate. I'll have to dig us out of the lie I crafted, no matter how embarrassing or uncomfortable it may be.

When I'm just a few feet away, I stop, tucking my hands into my sweater.

"I haven't told Connor yet."

"I know. He cornered me at One Stop to ask about our double date."

He says the words like they're the most foul he's ever spoken in his life. But then he lets out his own dramatic sigh and cracks open another peanut, chucks the shells to the ground, and tosses the nuts into his mouth, chewing them thoughtfully as he watches me for a long moment.

"What if I agreed to do it?"

My head jerks back. "What?"

He just keeps staring at me.

"Seriously?"

Rusty nods, the cracking peanut shell the only sound in the darkness of the parking lot as we stare at each other.

I shift where I stand, glancing around aimlessly while I try to think up an answer. What I *should* be saying is 'Hell yes! You can absolutely be my fake boyfriend.' But I still need at least a moment of hesitation because…what?

"Why the change of heart?" I finally ask, wanting to hear his reasoning. Maybe that will make it make more sense.

I can tell almost immediately that he's not going to share based on how his head moves, his jaw jutting just slightly forward as his head tilts back. He's gone on the defensive.

"Do you want help dealing with your *little crush* or not?"

I bristle at his reference to what Connor said at The Mitch.

"Of course I do, but that doesn't mean I can't want to understand why you'd be so adamantly against it just this morning and then suddenly change your mind. What am I missing?"

"You're missing someone to play your fake boyfriend, Bellamy." His tone brooks no argument. "Yes or no."

"Fine! Okay, jeez. You don't have to be all"—I wave my hand around—"Grumpy Pants McGee about it."

His face pinches. "Grumpy Pants McGee? Really?"

"Well. You *are*."

Rusty rolls his eyes. "Connor suggested a double date," he says, moving the conversation along. "He told me to check with you about Thursday."

I cross my arms, trying to imagine how that conversation went. Part of me doesn't like the idea of Connor talking to Rusty when I'm not around. Who *knows* what this man said about me—not that it really matters, I guess. The only thing that matters is that Connor believes I have unequivocally and undeniably moved on from last summer, and if that means Rusty helps me convince him, I guess it also doesn't matter what his reasons are.

"I work Thursday, but I can probably switch with Danielle."

Rusty hops down from where he's sitting and brushes the little crumbs off his black jeans. "Okay. Will you text Connor and let him know once you get that sorted?"

I nod. "Yeah. I can do that."

He shuts the trunk and gives a shrug. "Alright, well…I guess I'll see you Thursday."

"What?"

Rusty pauses his movements toward the driver's side door and glances back at me. "What do you mean what?"

"I mean…we can't just meet up on Thursday. We need a story. If we're going to make it seem like we're dating, we have to actually seem like we're dating."

He lets out a dramatic sigh. "Fine. Just…meet me here tomorrow night. We can have dinner and talk."

I blink a few times, weighing the idea in my mind: meet Rusty at my place of work to have dinner and come up with our fake story to convince Connor we've been dating and that this is not just a big fat lie.

I must be too slow to respond, because Rusty speaks again.

"If you're worried about people seeing us together, news flash, the whole town is going to think we're dating." He seems to brace himself then as he crosses his arms. "Do you have a problem with that?"

I shake my head. "No, I just…"

How do I explain this without sounding so much younger than I am?

"…I've never been on a date before."

Something about Rusty seems to short-circuit, as if I've said the exact thing I shouldn't have said. It's the truth, though, and I'm already doing enough lying.

"What do you mean you've never been on a date before?" he asks, almost like the words themselves are foreign.

"I mean," I say, my shoulders rising as I refuse to let him make me feel bad about it, "I've never been on a date before." I pause for a minute, waffling on what to say. "It's not like *everyone* finds dating and hookups to be a collector's sport like you do."

Rusty's face sours. "Clearly."

We stare at each other, me feeling vulnerable and exposed and Rusty looking irritated in many ways.

Eventually he sighs again and digs out his phone. "What's your number? I'll text you tomorrow."

I'm almost surprised that I don't already have his number, considering how long we've known each other. I rattle it off, and a few seconds later I feel my own phone vibrate in my back pocket.

"I just texted you, so now you'll have my number, too."

With those as his only parting words, he hops into his Chevy and fires up the engine. I take that as my cue and hop into my CRV, following Rusty out of the gravel lot, but when he turns left and heads toward town, I turn right, deciding to take the long route home, hoping the extra time around the lake will help to clear my head.

Tomorrow, I'm going out on my first date—but it's a pretend date with my fake boyfriend.

How exciting for me.

When I originally decided to push myself to graduate early, I envisioned collecting my diploma then jumping right into full-time employment. However, I hadn't taken into consideration the fact that most accounting firms tend to hire in the summer and fall, leaving me with few options, none of which felt like the right fit.

So, back in January, even though I had just finished my degree, I dove right back into studying, deciding a better use of my time would be to focus on banging out the Uniform CPA Exam as quickly as possible.

My mom encouraged me to take some time off, give myself a chance to enjoy the accomplishment of completing my bachelor's degree, but that's not my style. I spent most of the winter with my nose in a book, and so far, I've completed three of the four required exam sections in record time and with flying colors. I'm hoping to take the final—and most difficult—section in July or August.

Then, I'll be searching for full-time work and likely leaving my jobs waitressing at Dock 7 and bartending at The Mitch behind. I've worked at the former since high school and the latter for over a year now. Because I went to college online, I never had to bounce around and get short-term work during winter break or the summer, and those places feel more like family now than employers. I'm sure once the day comes when I have to move on, it will be filled with emotion.

Thankfully, most accounting work can be done virtually, so while I might leave my current jobs, there won't be a huge pressure to leave Cedar Point to find something related to my degree. Even so, part of me is still nervous about how everything is going to play out.

I don't want to leave my hometown, even if that means it takes me a while to figure out exactly what my next step is going to be. Many people leave small towns for college only to decide later on that they want to move home because they miss the community feel a bigger city can't offer. Often, they at least wanted the chance to see if life somewhere else might be a better fit.

That wasn't something I needed. I love Cedar Point, always have. Do I think it's the best place in the world? Probably not. But is it the best place in the world for me? I think so, and I'm not someone who needs to see all my other options before being happy.

I'm the only one of my siblings who decided to stay. Boyd left for college on the east coast, and Briar moved down the mountain. My twin brother, Bishop, took a full ride playing baseball, and my younger sister, Busy, liked being away so much she got a job at a summer camp instead of coming home last year between semesters.

Then there's me, the 22-year-old who hasn't ever moved out of her childhood bedroom and still plays cards on the deck with her mom on Sunday mornings. I'm just happy here. It's a special place, and I don't ever want to leave.

Eventually, I'd like to open my own accounting business. George Sterling has been the only licensed CPA in Cedar Point for years, and he's been talking about retiring soon and moving to Florida with his new wife. It will leave a CPA-sized hole in the Cedar Point infrastructure that I'm hoping to fill, as long as someone else doesn't do it first.

For now, I'm just biding my time, working and studying and ruminating on different pathways to what's next, and wrapping up these exams this summer cannot come soon enough. I desperately want a chance to get a job doing more than slinging drinks. It's not that I hate being a bartender or a waitress. I actually really enjoy them both, but I also really enjoy using my mind for work. I mean, I got this degree for a reason, and I want to use it.

After I've finished up a few hours of studying on Wednesday morning, I change into some shorts and a ratty tee then head out to the back yard where my mother is working on her brand-new vegetable garden. It's bittersweet, doing yardwork alongside my aging mother. I love spending time with her and digging my hands into the dirt, but it also makes me hyperaware of the fact that she's moving a little bit slower, needing longer breaks.

Like now, as she cuts open the last bag of potting soil, she stops before dumping it into the bed, like she has to brace herself in order to be able to lift it enough to dump it out.

"Here, I've got that," I tell her, wrapping my arms around bottom of the twenty-pound bag and pouring it on top of the mixture of filler and dirt that is already spread throughout the wooden boxes.

"Thanks, sweetheart." She grins and tugs off a glove then

snags her water bottle and takes a big swig. "You know, if these vegetable gardens work out, it might be fun to set up a booth at the farmer's market."

I laugh. "With our six carrots and two heads of lettuce?" I tease. "It'll cost more for the fee to grab a table than what you'll end up bringing home."

Mom laughs. "Yeah, maybe that idea is a bit far-fetched. I'm just excited. I've wanted to do this for so long, and I want to share it with everyone."

That's such a mom thing to say. Patty Mitchell is nothing if not a person who enjoys sharing: her time, her energy, her resources. She donates constantly. Volunteers everywhere. Invites everyone to everything.

It's one of the things I admire the most about her, her 'we're all in this together' attitude. Everyone in town loves her, and not just because she's part of Cedar Point's founding family. It's because of her heart.

And her smile.

I'm the only one out of her five children who got her smile, all the way down to the slightly crooked way it sits on my face and the tiny dimple on my right cheek, and it's my favorite thing about the way I look.

"Well, hopefully we'll get there," I tell her, using my gloved hands to spread the soil out evenly.

"Not *hopefully*," she corrects. "Definitely. We'll *definitely* get there."

I grin. "Definitely, we'll get there."

We dive back into it, hauling over additional large sacks of potting soil to cover the tops of the remaining four beds before giving each a thorough watering. Mom has a layout etched into a notebook, accounting for things like shade and how long different sections will get direct sunlight at certain points of the year. She's always been into gardening, but her interest in a vegetable garden is only recent, so she has been taking copious notes and meticulously reading information about veggies and their preferred environments. It's one of the other ways we're so alike, each of us very organized and methodical about how we approach things.

The day is nearing the end and we're both exhausted, so the steps to plant all the seeds in the right spots will have to wait until tomorrow. Now, it's time to go get ready for my date with Rusty.

Something unfamiliar ripples through my belly.

"Shower then jammies and a movie?" Mom asks me as we kick off our dirty shoes on the back patio before entering the kitchen. "I bought Cherry Garcia ice cream."

"Actually, I have plans tonight."

Her eyes flick to mine, and something about my expression must give me away because she gives me a shit-eating grin that says she thinks she knows what I mean.

"Plans?" she asks, drawing out the word for far longer than she should.

A little part of me panics inside. The last thing I want is for my mother to begin imagining me falling in love and getting married soon. I might have thought that would be a possibility before Connor dropped the bomb that ripped me apart, but it isn't anymore.

"Yes, plans." I walk through the kitchen and over to the stairs off the entry, and I can feel her following in my wake.

"Like...*romantic* plans?"

I blow out a breath then spin around, pinning her with a look.

"Maybe."

I barely have the word out and my mother shouts out with joy, her arms in the air, as if she just won the lottery.

"Oh, honey, I'm so excited for you. Do you want my help getting ready?"

Shaking my head and letting out an embarrassed laugh, I turn and continue up the stairs. "Thanks, but I've got it."

"Alright, well I'm here if you need anything!" she calls as I hit the landing and walk down the hall to the bathroom.

"Thanks!" I call back before shutting the door firmly behind me.

And locking it.

The entire time I'm in the shower, I try to decide how I feel about tonight, about this faux date…with Rusty, my faux boyfriend.

Part of me is grateful. We get the time together to concoct a story that feels real and believable, something that will convince Connor I'm happily dating—even in love. But the other part of me is feeling some pretty big emotions I don't know what to do with.

I'm still reeling from Connor's engagement announcement. I'm nervous about trying to pull this off. I'm worried about how people will react to this idea of me and Rusty being together, especially my family.

I'm also irritated at my own self for allowing my feelings for Connor to convince me the best solution was to fabricate an entire relationship to the point that I've now dragged a mostly unwilling victim into the fray.

Resting my forehead against the cool tile, I try to imagine how tonight will go. I tend to feel less stressed about things if I can plan them out in my mind ahead of time. It's why I always read spoilers about movies before I see them, why I check menus online before eating anywhere unfamiliar.

Known is best.

Maybe that's what's actually stressing me out the most. As much as I know Rusty, as many memories as I have of him and Boyd rambling around the house over the years as far back as I can remember, I still don't really *know* him, so I don't know what to expect.

And I don't like it one bit.

chapter six
rusty

"This is Boyd. Leave a message."

When I hear the beep, I clear my throat. "Hey, Boyd. It's Rusty." I clear my throat again. "Just wanted to chat about something. Gimme a call whenever you have a few minutes. Later."

I disconnect and slip the phone into my pocket then cross the gravel lot of Lucky's and tug open the front door.

I've always loved this restaurant. Dock 7 has been around for a long time but went through a complete transformation when I was in high school that gave it a much more youthful edge. It's turned into the place to be for tourists, which is how it got its nickname among locals. We call it Lucky's because if you're looking for a chance to score with someone just passing through town, this is your best bet.

Bellamy's not supposed to meet me for another 20 minutes, but arriving early was intentional on my part, and I step up to the bar and order a whiskey, hoping to take the edge off whatever these nerves are.

Clyde, the bartender who's been working here since I was too young to sit at this bar, immediately pulls out a bottle of Woodford, my go-to and what I typically order when I come in on a weekend night.

"Not used to seeing you here during the week," he says, giving me a friendly smile.

"Yeah, I'm…just mixing things up."

Clyde seems like an okay guy. I know he's been around for a while, but part of me thinks at least half of the rumors that pick up around town start with things Clyde sees, and I don't want to give him anything that might spread with a quickness.

He takes my statement for what it is—an indicator that I'd like to sit in silence—and turns to continue working on unloading a case of recently washed glasses. I'm left to my thoughts, which is what I believed I wanted, but now that I'm here, staring into my glass like I wish it had some kind of explanation for why I feel so stressed about tonight, I'm kind of wishing Clyde would come back and distract me.

This dinner is going to be interesting, that's for sure. I wish I could have just turned my mind off to this whole thing and focused on work until our double date with Connor and Stace tomorrow night, but I get why Bellamy thinks this is important. At least connecting about a backstory is a good idea.

I think back to the way my sister looked at me in the grocery store, like I was growing a second nose on my face. Maybe an origin story will make everything seem a little more believable.

I take a long sip then turn my head and look out through the massive glass doors that get slid to the side during good weather to give an indoor-outdoor feel to the large restaurant. We'll be sitting on the patio tonight. I even called and made a reservation, and I can't remember the last time I did something like that. The hostess sounded surprised when she took my name down, but at least for the summer, that kind of stuff will be the new norm—calling in reservations, hanging out with Bellamy around town.

Who knows? Not getting laid aside, maybe it won't be so bad. I can't imagine spending time with Bellamy will be too much of a hardship. She's kind of always been around, actually. Maybe not the two of us spending time together alone, but she was definitely there in the background.

That gives me pause as I flick through my memories of Bellamy when we were younger. Mostly I remember her always in a corner, doing homework. I don't have a lot of specific recollections of her after I came back to Cedar Point. There's a ten-year age gap between us, and I've been pretty focused on my own shit. I know she has come out of her shell quite a bit, even if she's still fairly studious. She has always been like that, very focused on her education.

Light from the front door opening draws my attention, and I turn in time to see Bellamy walk through, the sunlight illuminating her figure before the door shuts behind her and I take her in. She's grown into a knockout, that's for sure. I hate myself for even thinking it, but it's the truth.

She's wearing a pair of snug jeans that accentuate her long legs and a loose maroon top that shows off her tanned shoulders, and when she sees me, she smiles. It feels like I've been socked in the stomach, and I clench my jaw at the discomfort I feel as I watch her approach.

"Hey."

"You're early."

Her brow furrows, and she glances over at the clock behind the bar.

"By five minutes."

I grumble an acknowledgment and turn, taking the last sip of my whiskey.

"I guess we should get this over with then."

I feel like a prick when Bellamy's smile dips, but it lifts back up after a second and she spins, heading toward the hostess.

"Hey Nicole."

"Hey! I didn't know you were coming in tonight."

Bellamy smiles. "I'm on a *date*," she whispers conspiratorially. "Can you believe it?"

Nicole laughs, but it fades and her eyes widen when I come up next to Bellamy.

"With...Rusty?"

I tuck my hands into my pockets and glare at her. "We have a reservation."

She glances at Bellamy for a second before tugging two menus from the holder and clicking a button on her screen, then she leads us through the slightly busy dining room and out to the patio. I catch a few eyes from familiar faces and give a thin smile I hope is at least a little friendly, then we both take a seat at a small table right up against the railing overlooking the lake.

"Your server will be right with you," Nicole says, handing us our menus before turning to head back inside.

I flip mine open and begin perusing it but pause when I see Bellamy just staring out at the water, her menu remaining closed in front of her.

"You're not going to look at the menu?"

She glances at me with an amused look. "I work here. I know the menu."

Something sour tugs at my stomach, and I feel a little bad for taking her on her first date at the restaurant where she works.

I could have thought of something nicer.

But I shake away those thoughts. I don't need to do something nicer. We're not really dating. She'll get another *real* first date someday, and that guy can be super thoughtful and do something creative.

Tonight, we're just ticking boxes: be seen together, sort our story. Tomorrow, more boxes: double date with Connor, begin convincing the douche that someone like Bellamy would *never* concern herself with who he is or isn't dating or engaged to.

I still don't fully understand her interest in the guy. He seems like a prick, but I guess there's no accounting for taste.

I return my eyes to my menu then snap it closed and set it down.

"I don't know why I'm looking at that when I can just ask you your opinions."

She looks surprised, and I can't help but notice the way her shoulders go back just slightly.

"Well, my favorite is the fish and chips. It sounds like it's going to be all greasy and cheap, but it's actually incredible."

"Is that what you're getting?"

She shakes her head. "I'm in the mood for a boujie burger tonight."

"Alright, then fish and chips it is."

Bellamy beams at me. "You're gonna love it. It's *so* good."

The server arrives, a guy named Dennis who is just a little too friendly with Bellamy considering the fact that she's clearly here on a date. He takes down our orders and heads off to help other tables.

"Okay, well…I guess it's time to start talking, huh?"

I take a deep breath and nod. "I guess."

"So, I was thinking we could say we've liked each other for a long time, but we were always worried about Boyd."

"How long is a long time? Because if you don't remember, I'm a bit older than you."

She scrunches her nose. "Oh. Yeah. Okay."

For whatever reason, she looks dejected, and part of me wants to know why.

"How about you tell me why that was important, and we can try to find another way for it to work."

Bellamy looks back out at the water, a bit of a blush coloring the apples of her cheeks in a way that tells me she's a little embarrassed to tell me this story.

"I've liked Connor since high school. I guess I was just trying to figure out a way that I could make it seem like he was just some guy." She shrugs. "Maybe if he believed I was always crazy about you instead, I don't know…" She trails off.

"Maybe if he thought it was always about me, he'd start to rethink all the things that made him believe you were always mooning over him?"

Bellamy nods but then shakes her head. "It's stupid. It was a stupid idea."

"It's not a stupid idea," I tell her. "But when you were in high school, I was in my mid-twenties. We just have to find a different story."

Dennis returns with our drinks—another whiskey for me and a glass of wine for Bellamy—then leaves us to our story searching. We bat around a few ideas but end up agreeing we don't have anything concrete enough.

We can't say we met somewhere because we've known each other most of our lives. We can't go back too far if we want things to be legal. We have to make it sound plausible enough that people will believe it, so it can't be some outlandish tale about saving her life or…

"What if we say I was helping you with financials for Cedar Cider," she suggests. "I mean, the idea that we'd spend long hours together while I'm doing some bookkeeping or something…that sounds pretty normal, right?"

I think it over, trying to make it work in my head, and it sounds like our most realistic option.

"I like it. The idea that we fell for each other over months of working together…sounds very Bellamy."

She laughs, and it slams into my chest, the sound rich and genuine and beautiful.

"Sounds very Bellamy?" she asks, picking up her wine glass. "What does that even mean?"

I grin and shrug a shoulder. "It just seems like you to fall for someone slowly instead of an instant attraction, you know? You seem like the type of person who is measured about the decisions she makes."

Her lips tilt up. "Measured. Huh." She takes a sip of her cabernet. "And how was our love story for you? Because I wouldn't say a slow-growing attraction would be very Rusty."

Chuckling, I lean back in my chair. "Well maybe that's why it was different for me than how I normally am. We'd known each other our whole lives, but I never really knew you, and then once we started spending time together, once I got to know you, it changed me."

"Good girl changes the bad boy, huh?" she asks, giggling.

"I mean, the movies use that because it works, right?"

She shakes her head, but her smile is still there. "But that's the only place it works. I'd bet you a billion dollars a good girl could never convince Rusty Fuller to be a one-woman kind of guy."

Dennis appears then and sets up his little tray stand, quickly and efficiently getting our food set on our table before disappearing back inside, but my mind stays firmly rooted on what she just said: that nobody could ever convince me to be a one-woman guy. Is that really how people see me? As a manwhore only interested in getting into bed?

I look out to the water, digesting the concept until it sits like a rock in the pit of my stomach. I don't know why I'm that surprised. It's mostly true. I *do* sleep around. I *do* prefer one-night stands and casual sex to relationships. I have for a long time, mostly because the last time I thought about something more, it nearly destroyed me.

I feel like I've reached my capacity for pain and loss at this point. Simple is better, easier. Less complicated, and less likely to blow my world apart again.

We spend a few minutes digging into our dinners, me lost in my thoughts and Bellamy in hers. All the while, I wonder if I'll be able to convince anyone this relationship is real. If everyone sees me the way Bellamy does—as a guy who isn't capable of committing—maybe we're screwed before we even start.

"So, I'll pick you up tomorrow at six?"

She nods. "Yeah. Connor said to head over by six-thirty and we'll cook out on their deck."

Because it didn't take too long for us to come up with our backstory, we spent the rest of dinner reminding each other of details we already vaguely knew about each other. Bellamy told me about her CPA Exam and her online degree and her penchant for Cherry Garcia ice cream. I told her about my enjoyment of swimming and hiking, and some of the simpler details about how things are coming with the new Cedar Cider site.

Overall, it was a pretty nice dinner, and the part of me that used to go on dates when I was younger was reminded that they can actually be fun. With the right person, of course.

"Do we need to bring anything?" I ask.

"No, but I might stop to get wine or something."

I grin. "I've got you covered. I have a bottle I can bring."

"Great. Well, then I'll see you tomorrow."

"Yeah. See you tomorrow."

We both stand there for a long moment before she sticks her hand out like she's going to shake mine.

I laugh. "I thought I was the awkward one."

She rolls her eyes and drops her hand.

"How about we start with a hug?"

Bellamy beams at me. "Oh, I like hugs. That sounds great."

Then she's tucking herself against me, her arms around my waist and her head pressed against my chest. Slowly, I wrap my arms around her as well, the sensation different than I was expecting, the warmth of her seeping into my skin in a way that makes me realize how cold I was before this moment.

It unsettles me.

Swallowing thickly, I step back, releasing her as quickly as I can.

"I'll see you tomorrow," I say again, then I stride quickly to my Blazer, hopping in and pulling out of the gravel lot as fast as I can manage without kicking up rocks and dust.

I have this feeling skittering beneath my skin. I can't figure out what it is, but it makes me uncomfortable. It makes every emotion feel bigger, sharper, last longer. It's easy to see that somehow, Bellamy is responsible for it, that her existence is enough to cause...whatever this is. But I can't risk allowing this tiny spark of attraction a chance to grow into anything else.

I have to snuff it out before it catches.

chapter seven
bellamy

I lie flat on the dock, staring up at the stars, enjoying the cool night breeze as it wafts lightly around my body, tickling me gently as it grazes the fine hairs on my arms.

For as long as I can remember, this spot on the dock, staring up into the heavens, is where I've come to clear my mind. It doesn't matter if there are other people around, if it's quiet or noisy, night or day, rain or sun. There should be a little crime scene outline spray-painted on the ground right where I'm lying with how frequently my body is in this exact spot, in this exact position: flat on my back, eyes up, palms to the wood of the dock beneath me.

Something about feeling the planks against my hands is grounding and always brings me a sense of calm, which is why I'm here. I desperately need some calm.

My mind is a jumble after my dinner with Rusty, and I keep replaying our conversation on a loop—or rather, every interaction since the bonfire, from the drive out of Cedar Point on the anniversary of his parents' death to his reaction when I said he was my boyfriend in front of Connor to the night I got drunk and fell asleep in his sister's old room.

It's hard to believe all of that has happened in just a few days, hard to believe I went from seeing Rusty around town to going out to dinner with him and planning a fake beginning so we can spend even *more* time together convincing Connor we're dating. I worry I'm creating a bigger mess than I'm trying to clean up, but that's lying for you. Once you start, it's hard to stop. The hole just gets bigger and bigger until you feel swallowed up and can't see where you came from and don't know how to climb your way out.

My fingernails scrape lightly against the wood beneath me, and I close my eyes for a minute, trying to think through how tomorrow night will go. The real test. The first time Rusty and I will really be on display.

Though I guess our dinner tonight was a bit like our coming out party. I saw more than a few curious glances from people I know from around town, surely wondering what the hell Rusty and I are doing out together. My best guess is people are dismissing it outright, assuming it's some sort of familial closeness since Rusty has always been somewhat a part of our family, especially after his parents died.

I can't imagine the type of impact that would have on someone. I'm very close with my parents, but I'm also ridiculously close with my twin brother. Bishop and I have been inseparable since birth. It's hard to explain the closeness you feel with someone when you shared a womb. Even the knowledge that I might exist on this earth without him someday fills me with so much emotion I can't allow myself to dwell on the thought.

A soft tone fills the air, and I smile, knowing instinctively it's

Bishop on the other line. This happens all the time. I'll be thinking about him and he'll call, or vice versa. It's our twintuition.

Grabbing my phone from where it rests next to my head, I
hit connect, then speakerphone, my smile growing when I hear
his voice.

"I hate it here."

I giggle. "No you don't. You're just mad you couldn't go to
Europe with Eliza."

Bishop groans. "Well, fine. I'm mad I'm not in Europe with
Eliza."

"There, see? Doesn't it feel better when you actually say how
you feel instead of bottling it up?"

"No. I'd rather say I hate it here than admit my girlfriend
went on a two-month trip without me."

I hum, feeling the ripple of unease in his words and knowing I shouldn't have brought up his original summer plans.

"How's camp?"

Bishop makes a noise that sounds precisely like a shoulder
shrug, and I have to stifle my laugh. My brother has been talking
nonstop about this baseball camp since his coach first told him
about it last year. He's been there for a little over a week and texts
me pictures constantly, so I don't buy this *meh* vibe he's trying
to give off.

"Oh, come on. There's no way you're not having a total blast.
Five weeks of camp to prep for the combine? I'm almost jealous."

At that, he laughs. "Bullshit. You hate baseball."

"But I love you, and I love imagining you getting ready to
go after your dream."

He sighs. "It's pretty great, alright?"

I laugh. "See? What's been your favorite part so far?"

Bishop launches into a story about meeting a player from

the Dodgers, a name I recognize as someone whose posters he had on his wall when we were younger. Apparently this guy is friends with his coach and will be at the camp intermittently to help out. He complimented Bishop's performance today. He says it like it was God herself reaching out and patting him on the back, and I love it for him.

"So, how's things around town? Who's back?"

My mind scrambles for something to say, but I must be silent for too long because I can hear the suspicion in my brother's voice when he speaks again.

"Bellamy," he says, drawing out the end of my name. "What's going on?"

I've never kept anything from Bishop before—nothing important, at least—and the idea of keeping what's going on with Connor and Rusty from him doesn't sit well with me at all.

So I spill.

I start with Connor's return to town and end with my dinner tonight with Rusty, leaving no stone unturned. I even share the hug after dinner and the fact that I've never realized Rusty could be so huggable.

When I'm done, I can tell my brother doesn't know what to say. When he finally does say something, it's not at all what I expect.

"Don't let him break your heart."

I roll my eyes. "He already did," I mumble.

"No, not Connor. He's a little shit who isn't good enough for you. I've never liked him. I'm talking about Rusty."

My mind trips over the fact that Bishop hasn't ever liked Connor—that's news to me—but then comes to a complete halt on his comment about Rusty.

"What? You heard the part about this being fake, right? I

don't actually like Rusty."

"Sure."

"What do you mean, *sure?*" My voice sounds as incredulous as I feel about whatever point he's trying to make. I push myself up into a sitting position and grab my phone, taking it off speaker and putting it up to my ear.

"I mean…emotions are complicated, and Rusty is a good guy. I can see someone like you falling for a guy like him."

"Someone like me?" I hate that I keep repeating his words back to him, but I continue to feel like I must be misunderstanding what he's saying.

"You know, it's that whole 'good girls who want to fix up a bad boy and take him home all for herself' thing." He pauses, then he begins to sing poorly into the phone. "Tale as old as time…"

"You're an idiot," I say, unable to keep from laughing at how tone deaf he is. "And I'm not trying to *fix* Rusty. I'm not interested in him."

"Sure."

I let out an irritated sigh.

"You're trying to tell me, in your whole life, you've never looked at Rusty with any kind of interest?" Bishop asks. "The guy who sacrificed his entire life to take care of his younger sister. The man who donates his time and energy to the seniors at The Pines. You don't find anything about him attractive?"

I snort. "Sounds more like *you* think he's attractive."

"Come on, I'm serious."

I make the mistake of pausing. I've never actually considered it before.

Objectively, I've always known *other* people find Rusty attractive. Clearly that's the case or else he wouldn't be jokingly referred to as Cedar Point's most attractive tourist destination. Every joke, even if it's in poor taste, has at least a little bit of truth behind it, right?

So, while Rusty might not be *my* cup of tea, he is certainly a perfect cup for others. He's got that slightly burly mountain man thing going on with a full strawberry blond beard and an obsession with flannel. His eyes are nice, the green of them something I've always thought was beautiful.

Sure, he's handsome. But do *I* find him attractive? Definitely not.

Though even as I think it, part of me can't help but admit how nice it was to be wrapped in his arms tonight, even just for a minute. And when his eyes were on me, listening as I shared more about myself than I ever thought he'd be interested in knowing, I loved what it felt like to keep his attention.

"Earth to Bellamy."

I blink. "What?"

"See? Told you."

"Told me what?"

"Don't let the guy break your heart, Bells. That's all I'm saying."

I let out a long dramatic sigh and decide to just agree so we can move this conversation on to something else. "Fine. I promise. I won't let him break my heart. Happy?"

Bishop pauses. "I'm happy as long as you are."

My shoulders fall, and I pull my knees up and wrap my arms around them, putting the call back on speaker. Our conversation goes on for only a little while longer before my brother says he has to go. Apparently this camp has a firm lights out policy and he doesn't have much time before he has to call it quits for the night.

"I love you, Bells," Bishop says, his voice warm. "Let me know how things go with Pruitt and Rus."

I nod. "Yeah. Love you, too."

We disconnect, but I stay out on the dock for a little while longer, thinking over my brother's words. Maybe I should look at them more like a warning...a warning against allowing myself to develop any kind of feelings for Rusty, though I can't help thinking that's laughable.

My heart has only ever belonged to one man, and that man is the one we're trying to convince that I've moved on. *He's* the one who broke my heart.

And I don't know if I'll ever fully recover.

I'm thankful that my parents had plans with another couple on Thursday night so they're not home when Rusty shows up to collect me for our double date with Connor and Stace. My mom was quite surprised when I came home last night from my date with Rusty, having heard about it from a friend of hers who was also dining at Dock 7 while we were there.

"Rusty?"

She said his name like it was a question, and I told her I wasn't ready to talk about it yet then headed down to the dock. When I returned, she had gone to sleep, not that I wanted to talk to her about it anyway.

I try to be a lot of things for my parents. I strive to be an honest, helpful daughter as often as I can, but that doesn't mean

I want to tell my mom everything. If anything, I keep a lot to myself so I don't burden her, and this whole story of what happened with Connor last summer and what's going on with Rusty now…it would just upset her.

I smooth out my dress in the mirror of the entryway then tuck my keys in my purse and head outside to wait for Rusty. I'm nervous about tonight, about going to Connor's house and essentially performing for him. There's a part of me that thinks it's not worth it, thinks I could just avoid him all summer until he and Stace leave to go do whatever is next for them in their happy married life.

But then I try to imagine the lengths I'd have to go to in order to avoid them. I mean, I work at two of the busiest places in Cedar Point during peak tourist season. Connor and I share plenty of overlapping friends who I'm sure are also returning to town for the summer. The reality is that, for most of the people from our graduating class at Cedar Point High School, this might be the very last summer they return home before beginning their real-world jobs. The last thing I want to be forced to do is hide away at my parents' house for three months.

No. This thing with Rusty should be great. He can be my emotional buffer, and in a few months, I hopefully won't have to see Connor on a regular basis ever again.

When Rusty pulls up out front and I hop into his Chevy, I'm immediately assaulted by the warmth of his cologne, a delicious scent of honey and hops and something else I can't place. It stokes feelings of comfort and makes me want to snuggle up in a big overstuffed armchair with a cup of tea and a good book.

He barely looks at me as he turns around in our large front drive, but my eyes do a perusal of him while he's focused on something else. It's his signature look—black jeans and a long-sleeved flannel—but the vibe looks different tonight. The pants look more crisp, and his shirt looks like it received an extra tumble on a wrinkle-free setting.

"You look nice," I say as he turns left onto the main road, heading toward the Pruitts' large property tucked into the hills in the northeast part of town.

He glances at me, his eyes doing a quick flick up and down over my outfit then back to my face. "Thanks" is all he says before returning his eyes to the road.

I look out the window, ignoring the niggling feeling of disappointment that he didn't have anything to say about how I look as well. It's not a real date, so…I guess it doesn't matter.

My stomach dips as we pull onto the dirt drive that leads up to the Pruitt house, memories assaulting me from the last time I was here. It was the best night of my life, one I thought was the start to an incredible future.

I was wrong.

When we come to a stop behind Connor's BMW, I swallow my feelings down. Tonight isn't about me continuing to pine for Connor. It's about me proving to him that I've moved on, just like he was so easily able to do. I might not have much of an ego on most days, but everyone has their limits, and the idea of Connor continuing to look at me with pity about my *little crush* is enough to make me sufficiently desperate to pull something like this off.

"You ready?" Rusty asks, his voice quiet and gravelly.

I turn to look at him, prepared to say yes, but for whatever reason, the word gets stuck in my throat when I find his green eyes watching me. They really are such incredible eyes.

Rusty reaches out, places his hand on mine, and gives it a squeeze. "We're gonna be fine," he says, mistaking my silence for nerves. "Connor's an idiot for letting you go, and tonight, we're going to show him what he's missing."

I want to tell him I'm not so sure and maybe I just wasn't enough, but instead, I give him a small smile and nod then slip out of his car. We approach the front door, and once he knocks, Rusty slips his hand in mine and gives me one more gentle squeeze. A shiver runs up my arm and down my spine, and when I look to Rusty, I find him watching me with a curious expression on his face. His lips part like he has something to say, but before he can say it, the door opens.

"Hey, guys." Connor grins. "Glad you could make it."

Rusty offers his hand and the two shake.

"Come on in, let's get you two a drink, huh?"

We follow Connor through his entry and into the kitchen, where Stace is slicing tomatoes at the island. She beams and rounds the counter, wrapping me up in a hug I'm not expecting. My eyes connect with Rusty's, and he looks just as surprised as I do.

"I'm so glad you're both here! I've been dying to get to know some of Connor's friends from home." Stace pulls back and looks at me. "Gosh, you are so pretty." Then she looks at Rusty and Connor. "Isn't she pretty?"

Connor nods, but he looks a little uncomfortable.

"She's stunning."

My eyes flick to Rusty's, the sound of him speaking those words sparking something in my chest.

"Ooooh," Stace croons, giggling. "A man who tells it like he sees it." She winks at Rusty and moves back to the island to continue cutting her tomatoes. "So, how did you two meet?"

"They've known each other for a long time," Connor interjects, tugging a few beers from the fridge. "Though I *am* curious about how you started dating because I'm sure that's a wild story."

He sets the bottles on the counter then starts popping the tops off, one after another.

Suddenly, I'm hyperaware of Rusty behind me, the warm wall of his body pressed up against mine and his hands coming up to gently rub up and down on my biceps.

"Not wild, really," he says. "I'm sure you know we're expanding Cedar Cider."

Connor nods. "To that spot off Main?"

"Yeah, and Bellamy has been helping with some financials. Things are getting a lot more complicated, and with all the extra numbers, we thought we'd bring in someone who knows what they're doing. We ended up spending a lot of time together and I just…started falling for her, you know?" His arms wrap fully around me, and his head dips down so his mouth is right by my ear. "I mean, how could you not?" he says, his voice soft, almost like what he just said is only for me.

It sends something delicious skittering underneath my skin, and I can't help the way I lean back into him, allowing the solid strength of him to hold me. My eyes rise to find Stace watching us with a smile but then connect with Connor's; he's watching us in a way that's more assessing than I would have expected.

"I guess Bellamy helping people with math is kind of her thing," he says. "I mean, it's all thanks to her tutoring me last summer that I passed my business accounting class in the fall."

I feel Rusty tense just briefly behind me, but he drops a kiss to the crown of my head.

"That's my girl. Smartest woman I know."

Stace is leaning forward on the island, her tomatoes forgotten as she watches Rusty with a gaze that is a little too dreamy for my liking.

"I'll take a beer, if you're offering."

Connor seems to snap out of whatever little funk he's in and passes one of the open bottles to Rusty, then one to me.

"How about you two?" I ask, not really wanting the answer but also desperate to know at the same time. "How did you two meet?"

"Oh Connor and I go way back, too," Stace says, finally finishing up with her tomatoes and moving on to slicing onions. "We lived down the hall from each other freshman year."

My stomach turns over, and my eyes shift to Connor's, wanting to light him on fire where he stands. Did he turn me into a woman who sleeps with a taken man?

"But we didn't really connect until we saw each other again at a party at Connor's fraternity in the fall."

I feel my shoulders sag, the weight of regret falling by the wayside and leaving me with an overwhelming relief.

But then I realize that still means Connor returned home two times over the course of the school year—once for Thanksgiving, once for his mother's birthday—and never said a thing about this relationship. He still visited me at work. Flirted with me. Tucked my hair behind my ear like he wasn't dating someone else.

"I think we just knew it was different than when we met freshman year, you know?" Stace continues. "When you're young, you think you know so much about love and the world, but when you get a little older you have so much more knowledge about how things work." She turns and looks at Connor. "We had both grown into different people, more in tune with ourselves and what we wanted...more honest about life in general." She pauses. "Sorry, I totally dominated that. Con, why don't you tell it from your perspective."

He chuckles. "Aww, babe, I think you did a great job." He wraps his arm around her shoulders and looks at us. "It's basically like she said: bumped into each other at a party and knew immediately we were meant for each other."

I grit my teeth and take a long pull from my beer, trying to tuck away my irritation. Part of me wants to tell Stace about Connor and me, tell her we slept together right before the two of them started dating and he never communicated to me that he started seeing someone.

But my emotions feel too fragile, too brittle, like they might snap apart in my hands if I handle them without care. So I do what I'm good at—what I've always been good at: I stuff them down deep. Don't cause any problems, don't make waves.

Instead, I smile along, listening as Rusty asks more questions and Stace and Connor share more about themselves and their senior year. Eventually, we make our way out to the patio and cook burgers, and Connor and Rusty start talking about the brewery and how the construction is coming along. All in all, it goes a lot smoother than I expected.

Connor and Stace seem happy.

Rusty and I seem happy.

But beneath it all, everything feels like a lie.

Because it is.

chapter eight
rusty

When I see Boyd's name on my caller ID, I groan.

I know exactly why he's calling, and it's my own fault that I've let it get this far. I should have called him as soon as I agreed to this whole farce, but I've been allowing myself to get distracted. Part of me is tempted to let it go to voicemail, but instead I tilt my neck from side to side and answer.

"Hey, Boyd."

"Why am I getting text messages that you're dating my sister? This is some kind of joke, right?"

His voice is tight, and I can just picture my best friend on the other end of the line, his dark brow furrowed and his eyes ablaze. Boyd is a loyal friend *and* brother, so it isn't surprising that he's calling me.

"It's not a joke, but I'm *not* dating Bellamy."

There's a pause, and I take advantage of it, launching into an explanation I hope will appease my friend.

"It's why I left that message yesterday. I wanted to give you a heads-up. We're just...*pretending* we're dating. Apparently there's a guy and she told him we're dating for reasons that are too ridiculous for me to say out loud, so I agreed to be her boyfriend while he's in town."

More silence.

"It's really just to fuck this guy off, Boyd. I promise, it's not a big deal."

He sighs, and I know what remains unspoken is what's running through my own mind right now: if it *actually* wasn't a big deal, I wouldn't be needing to tell Boyd that. My hope is he understands I'm not poaching on his sister, to use my sister's terminology.

Bellamy is beautiful, without a doubt, and maybe in another life that would be enough to cloud my judgment, but there's a line you don't cross with friends. You don't date their sisters.

That thought makes me laugh.

"I'm failing to see the humor in this."

"No, I'm...I'm not laughing at you, I'm just...I really do get what you're going through. How you feel is how I felt when I found out about my sister and Jackson."

He hums but doesn't say anything else. That's Boyd; he's not quick to speak. He's an internal processor and usually takes a bit more time than I do to think through the important parts of things and come to a conclusion. I'm more impulsive. It's been my greatest strength and my greatest weakness in equal measure.

"I'm gonna need more information than just 'we're pretending to date,'" he finally says.

I blow out a long breath and explain the whole thing, about Bellamy and Connor and his fiancée and what she said at the bar. I don't tell him about seeing her naked, though.

Well, *nearly naked*—like that's so much better. I figure that's one of those details friends don't need to share.

"Okay well, if it's really all fake, I just want to make sure you treat her with respect. Bellamy is one of the best people I know, and I don't want you corrupting her."

I chuckle. "Corrupting her? Boyd, we're gonna go on a few dates, and I'll rub how awesome she is in this guy's face. That's really it."

"Alright." His response says it's not an issue, but his tone says otherwise.

We talk for a few more minutes about nothing important—apparently he and Ruby are moving into a new space soon, and I share the progress on the site for the brewery even though he already knows that information—then get off the phone.

Though not without one final warning shot from Boyd.

"Be careful with my sister, Rus. She deserves someone special, and I don't want whatever this weird situation is to mess something up for her."

I sit at my desk for a while after we end the call, trying to shake off the feeling that crept up the back of my spine while we were talking: the idea that Boyd might think I'd have a negative influence on Bellamy's life.

There's a small part of me that gets where he's coming from. I mean, I had similar feelings about Abby and Jackson when I found out about them, and Boyd probably doesn't really understand just how shitty this Connor guy is or else he'd be shoving me in his sister's direction. Still, the idea that spending time with me might screw her up in some way or negatively affect her ability to date in the future? That seems a bit much, no?

I click around, sorting emails and staring blankly at our budget spreadsheet, though my mind barely takes in any of the information I'm seeing. Instead, I'm still ruminating on Boyd's parting words over an hour later. We've been best friends since junior high, me, Boyd, and Andy, so to know he thinks I could possibly ruin something for Bellamy—or worse, hurt her in some way—it just sucks.

Eventually I give up trying to make my brain focus on work, and I head into my bedroom and change into a loose pair of shorts and a plain tee. There's only one thing that comes to mind during periods when I'm angry about something I haven't fully processed, and that's heading out on the trails.

Sometimes a bit of sweat goes a long way.

There are about a dozen different hiking trails scattered around Cedar Point that I tend to hit on a fairly consistent basis, but over the past few months, with my mental energy focused almost entirely on the brewery, I haven't given myself the time or permission to set the busyness aside and disconnect to be in nature.

For whatever reason, today feels like the right moment to release myself from the guilt of taking a break from work. The stress of the brewery, this thing with Bellamy, my recent conversations with my sister and Boyd…I just need some space to quiet all the noise and think things over.

It doesn't feel good, knowing my sister and my best friend might see me differently than I thought. Part of me wants to forgive Abby a bit more than Boyd. She's young and looking at me through the lens of someone who misses her parents. Abby wants me to be the father she lost.

Nobody can replace our dad, though.

God, everyone in town loved Everett Fuller. He was a mechanic at the small garage in town and was one of the most honest, hardworking guys I've ever known. He was there for us when we needed him and showed up for everything, whether it mattered or not. Both of our parents were that way, which is why their death felt like such a cruel and pointless tragedy.

I tug on my backpack and slam my car door where I'm parked at the foot of the trail leading to Whistler Peak. It's a four-hour roundtrip hike up to a lookout that straddles the mountain between Cedar Point and two other neighboring towns, Belleview and Spencer Creek.

I've done this particular trail more times than I can count. It's the perfect length to sort through whatever is on my mind, and it's rare to come across another person, even during the peak of tourist season. The mixture of fairly flat trails and periods of steep incline are also a good level of intensity to make it interesting.

My mom used to hike this trail with me and Abby when we were younger. She said Whistler Peak was her favorite, and by sharing it with us, she hoped we'd love it, too. I took to it immediately and begged Mom to take us hiking as often as possible. Abby, not so much. She'll get out here every now and then as long as I pick one of the beginner trails like Sutter View or Washburn Trail, both of which mostly just weave in and out of residential neighborhoods on the western border of town. I'm the one who knows all these paths like the back of my hand.

Fuck, I miss my parents.

It's rare for me to give myself permission to sit and think about them like this, and after 10 years, you'd think the pain would have eased more. But every time they come to mind, it doesn't just sting with the pain of a long-ago loss. The agony of losing them rips through me afresh, as if I just found out about their deaths.

Maybe I should have listened to Patty Mitchell when she told me I should go to therapy. Back then, though, I had too much on my plate. I came home after they died, spent the summer trying to take care of everything that needs handling after people pass. For a while, I thought I would go back to school and finish out my senior year. Patty and Mark had agreed to let Abby move in with them for a while until we figured things out.

It only took a week of being back to know Cedar Point was where I needed to be, so I basically dumped my entire life and moved home to take care of Abby, to make sure she had support and be entirely certain she wasn't shoved into the system as an orphan when I knew I was perfectly capable of being there for her.

I don't regret it. I don't, but every once in a while, I'll allow myself just a moment to think about what my life might have been if my parents hadn't come to visit me for my birthday, if their love for me wasn't the reason they died.

Would I have stayed with Hailey? Would we have stayed together if I hadn't needed to leave college and move home? If I hadn't had to choose my sister over my girlfriend?

What kind of job would I have if I'd finished my degree instead of dropping out of school? Would I have gone on to graduate school like I'd thought about?

The easy assumption is that I wouldn't be living in Cedar Point, that I would have pursued my other dreams and found somewhere else in the world that made me happy. I don't hate this place by any means. I loved the small-town life as I was growing up, knowing my neighbors and having a really connect-ed group of friends, the supportive environment where everyone pitches in.

But I knew it was where I had grown up, not necessarily where I wanted to live forever, so having to return home in the wake of everything I had to give up…in the midst of the pain I was experiencing after my parents' death and during a time when I was essentially filling a father-like role in my sister's life… well, I might not have hated this place, but it was hard not to resent it.

Even knowing this was the best place for us to be consider-ing the circumstances. Even while feeling thankful for the love and care that flooded into us from friends and people who loved my parents. Even though I've been able to see Abby truly create the life for herself that makes her happy and feel loved and like she has purpose.

In some ways, I've done the same, though I can't help but harbor some anger that I'm still here. It's a weird place to be mentally, but that's life, and my options were to either sit in my misery indefinitely or figure out a way to distract myself from it.

One way I do that is Cedar Cider, the little home brewery that has now become a successful operation and is in the process of transforming into a legitimate, storefront business. I started it in our garage when I didn't know what to do with myself after moving home, and now it's a thriving company that I spearhead. Jackson and Boyd are investors and have been since the begin-ning, but Boyd has a job in Boston, and Jackson likes to dip his investment pen into many different company inks. For me, though, it's my main priority, my main focus, the most import-ant thing in my life besides my sister.

The other way I distract myself is women, as often as I can

make the time. I'm a frequent flyer at Lucky's, enjoying the bar during the peak points of tourist season, and I rarely go home alone, although I don't bring women to my house anymore. I got out of that habit at the insistence of my sister, though I guess now that she has moved out, I could resume my old ways.

Surprisingly, I actually enjoy the separation of my home from my one-night stands now that I have my routine down. The ability to slip out of hotel rooms rather than do the see-you-never song and dance is much cleaner, much easier. Plus, there's no chance of the drop-by to get something that was forgotten 'on accident.'

I can only assume my interest in the many women who visit Cedar Point throughout the year is what has Boyd disgruntled about this whole Bellamy thing. When Jackson and Abby started dating, I had a really tough time with it because Jackson was a lot like me.

But I'm not *really* dating Bellamy, and that's why Boyd's displeasure stings a bit more than I was anticipating. Under these circumstances, it feels more like he's upset that I'll be spending time with her, as if who I am is a bad influence in some way.

Boyd knows better than most the sacrifices I've made in my life, the hard decisions I've been faced with, and on more than one occasion, he's told me I'm one of the most incredible people he knows. I've always held his high opinion of me close to my chest as something important, not to be squandered.

Now that his sister's involved, is that in question?

I mull this over for as long as I can, perusing every element of my irritation and frustration, until the fatigue from hitting the final incline up to Whistler Peak has exhausted my mind to the point that I can only focus on my steps.

This is always my goal, this blissful silence in my head that only physical exertion can provide, the kind of nothing space I have to seek in order to be able to truly reflect on anything.

It's why I swim several times a week and hike as often as I can. I've always figured if I exhaust my body, if I push myself so hard I don't have the strength to be irritated or frustrated anymore, I'll be able to look at things from a more logical perspective—or from a more neutral one, at least. It's how I dealt with my anger after my parents died and I had to leave my life behind. It's how I dealt with Hailey breaking up with me for reasons outside of my control. It's how I calmed myself when Abby was acting like a petulant 16-year-old and it felt like too much for my 22-year-old skills to handle. And today, it's how I'm letting go of my anger at my sister and Boyd for thinking less of me than I thought they did.

When I break through the clearing at the end of the trail, I step out onto the wide-open space known as Whistler Peak. The wind up here blows in much stronger strokes, unfettered by the thousands of trees covering most of the mountain ranges. To my left, I can see Cedar Point, the lake, and the length of Main Street and downtown. To my right I can just barely see some of the houses scattered in the trees in Spencer Creek, as well as the bustling small town of Belleview in the distance.

These mountain communities, among many others, are beautiful and special and wonderful places to live. As angry as I can get about the shitty hand life decided to deal to me and my sister, I'm so thankful we had somewhere soft and familiar to land, a place that was safe and filled with love. After what we went through, we needed it.

I lie down in the grass and stare up at the sky for a good twenty or thirty minutes, my fingers twisting into the blades beneath me as I try to sink into the calm of my mind. Maybe what

I'm feeling isn't actually anger with my sister and Boyd. Maybe it's disappointment instead, but not in them—in myself.

There was a time when I saw a future that was filled with more than just nameless, sometimes faceless women. There was a time when I wanted a serious relationship, when part of my imagined future included a family.

With my parents' death and then Hailey ending things, I just turned that part of my mind off, deciding it wouldn't be worth the pain, but maybe it's time for a change. Maybe this thing with Bellamy is coming at the perfect time.

I mean, being in a relationship with the town's favorite daughter *has* to win me some brownie points, right? Set me up as a different kind of man than what people normally think of when they hear the name Rusty Fuller?

When I first agreed to fake date, it was mostly out of a complete dislike for Connor Pruitt and wanting to help Bellamy put the little shit in his place. Now though, I'm wondering if maybe there are other positives that could come from it as well.

chapter nine
bellamy

"Hey, Bellamy!"

I turn at the sound of the unfamiliar voice, internally wincing when I see it's Stace walking toward me, a wide smile on her face.

It never once occurred to me that I'd need to be on guard at work, that the man I pined after for years would be engaged and his fiancée would come into my place of employment. Clearly it was naïve of me to assume Lucky's would be a kind of safe haven, a place where I wouldn't have to worry about seeing either of them.

"Hi, Stace." I tuck my tray under my arm. "You here for dinner tonight?"

If the two of them are coming in for dinner, I will literally give Nicole all my tips for the day to seat them in another section. The last thing I want to do is wait on Connor and Stace and get snippets of them planning their wedding or talking about the future.

No thanks.

"No, I'm actually just stopping by to see you."

My eyebrows rise, surprise evident on my face. "Oh, yeah? Well, what can I do for you?"

At that, she blushes and tucks her chin-length hair behind one ear, and that's when I realize she looks a bit unsure.

"Well, it's actually kind of embarrassing," she says, confirming my suspicions. "I'm wondering if you want to get coffee or something this weekend."

My entire body freezes as shock ricochets through me. I could have been given all the guesses in the world, and not in a million years would I have assumed Stace would be asking me to…hang out.

"Connor needs to spend part of our summer in town helping his dad at work, and that's going to leave me kind of on my own. I just had so much fun at dinner last night and…I don't really know anyone else here, so I was hoping you might have some time? Like I said, we could get coffee or maybe hang out at the lake." She shrugs. "I mean, I don't really know this place at all, and when Connor said you've also lived here your whole life, I thought maybe you could be my tour guide."

There's a brittle voice inside my head saying I should tell her to fuck off. I'm working two jobs and studying for my CPA Exam, not to mention the fact that I should be trying to figure out what's next for my life. *That's* what I need to be doing with my time, not carting Connor's fiancée around Cedar Point.

I don't want to know her.

I don't want to spend time with her.

I don't want to hear about her relationship with Connor and pretend to care.

But I also know how it feels to be lonely, to wish you had

some sort of confidant, somebody to talk to, even about things that don't matter at all.

Staying in town for college, as great as it can be, has been really difficult from a relational standpoint, and I've spent many months wishing I had someone local to hang out with and do exactly what Stace has been brave enough to ask of me.

So even though there's that bitchy part inside me saying I should tell her I'm too busy—or, hell, just tell her about my history with Connor—instead, I swallow my irritation and do the exact opposite.

"You know, there's a vintage music store on Main Street, and I was thinking about getting a coffee and flipping through their old records. Do you want to come with?"

Stace beams. "That sounds awesome. Yes, I'd love to."

"Alright, well…let's meet at Ugly Mug at 10 tomorrow? Does that work for you?"

"That's perfect." She slips her hands into her back pockets. "I'll let you get back to work, but thanks in advance for taking pity on my lonely self."

I laugh and give her a wave as she heads back toward the front door and out to the parking lot, my shoulders sagging once she's gone.

Ugly Mug really does have fantastic coffee, and I *do* like checking out the vintage records on Saturday mornings, so it isn't like this is going to be a complete hardship. In a worst-case scenario, we hit those two spots and I tell her I'm busy once an hour has passed. That's a reasonable amount of time for a friend-ly get-together, right?

I sigh and turn toward the bar to put in a drink order for table 12. Entertaining Connor's fiancée…

At the very least, this should be interesting.

When I push through the doors of Ugly Mug the following morning at just before ten, the place is packed to the gills. The line isn't out the door or anything, but it's clear from the many unfamiliar faces that summer is officially here and families and vacation-goers are already making their way to Cedar Point.

Living in a town that somewhat revolves around tourist seasons has its ups and downs. The inconsistency of business is something most people have to account for, with entire months of the year going by with few customers. Some shops on Main Street are seasonal boutiques, only opening during busier months.

It's nice when the pace of things is a bit slower, but I know for the sake of this town and the businesses owned by people I care about that it's better for everyone when things are busy. So, even though there are mornings like today when I'll have to wait longer than normal for a cup of coffee, I do it gladly, knowing it's a positive for Cedar Point and the community.

"Hey!"

I turn, smiling when I see Stace.

"Hey, good morning. Find it okay?"

She nods. "It's hard to miss the only coffee shop in town, especially when it has a big sign with a steaming mug outside."

I laugh as we step into the line. "I'm assuming there are more places to pick from for coffee where you live?"

"I'm from Seattle," she tells me, "so yeah, you could say I

have my pick of coffee places."

"Oh, wow. Seattle. From the city? Or somewhere smaller?"

"I'm a city girl, through and through. Grew up in a twenty-story high-rise only a few blocks from the original Starbucks." She shrugs. "I might be a bit of a coffee snob."

"Well, I can't speak for other places because I've lived in Cedar Point my whole life," I say as we step forward, "but I'd say Ugly Mug isn't exactly dirt in a cup."

She snorts. "I'm glad to hear it, because the fancy espresso machine at Connor's parents' house makes exactly that."

"Oh, that sucks."

"It really does. You know, I'm not one to complain, though, so I've used it every day since we've been here with a smile on my face."

"Yuck. Well hopefully today you'll find a new morning routine."

She grins. "Fingers crossed."

It only takes a few minutes to get to the front and we put in our orders quickly—an iced mocha for me and an espresso for Stace—then step over to the side to wait.

"This place is really cute," she says, her eyes scanning the space and taking everything in.

Even though I've been coming here since it first opened, I glance around as well, trying to see it through fresh eyes. Ugly Mug is a place people on TV would say has 'character.' Big couches are mixed in with café tables and chairs to accommodate various seating preferences. High ceilings are open to the wooden beams. One massive brick wall is covered in tchotchkes and antique signage acquired over the years, including the original, hand-painted Main Street sign from Cedar Point's earlier days.

Because I did almost my entire degree online, I used to come in here several times a week to study. Basically, anything that was math-related I could do here. The hustle and bustle can't break through my mental focus when I'm working with numbers.

For all my general education courses, however—literature, history, communication—I wore noise-canceling headphones in my bedroom and flipped a sign on my door so my parents would know not to bother me. It might sound childish, but it took all of my mental energy to complete a research paper about social issues facing Americans during desegregation or put together a presentation on the impact of Shakespeare's works on modern literature. I couldn't afford any distractions.

"It *is* pretty cute." I point to a bulletin board next to the door covered in flyers. "You should check out the Bored Board, especially if you're gonna be around for a while and want to do something fun. There's info about group yoga classes and hiking trips, and people advertise for their businesses doing craft classes and boat excursions."

I hear my name called from the counter, and I quickly grab my iced mocha.

"It's a great way to meet people and find things to do," I continue, slipping my sunglasses on as we step back out to Main Street.

Luckily, even with the busy season already begun, we're able to grab a table on the sidewalk under the awning, giving us just the right amount of shade from the bright morning sun.

"I'll definitely look into that, thanks."

We sit in silence for a few minutes, me chewing on my straw and Stace's eyes surveying everything and everyone we can see. It's surprisingly easy to talk to her, not that we've hit on any real, important topics or anything. Some people just have that energy, that kind of positive, friendly sense about them, and Stace is, for better or worse, one of those people. It would be a whole lot easier on me if she wasn't, but I'm starting to learn that life rarely gives you what you're expecting.

"So, are you and Connor the same year? Did you graduate, too?"

She shakes her head. "Technically, I could have graduated, but I still have one more year left. I'm doing a 4-plus-1 nursing program that gives me both my bachelor's and master's in five years."

"That's so cool. What do you want to do with that?" I laugh. "I mean, I know you want to be a nurse, but...you know what I mean."

Stace leans back in her chair, holding her coffee with both of her hands in front of her chest. "I really want to work as a women's health nurse practitioner, hopefully in a free clinic or family planning center. Women face so many issues and *so* many people don't have access to healthcare." She shrugs. "The pay will be horrible, but I'm just hoping to do something that helps people."

My lips tilt up. "That's really awesome."

She grins. "Thanks. What about you? You mentioned the whole"—she waves her hand between us—"helping with financials thing at dinner, but I never asked."

"I want to be a CPA, open a little business here in town. I just love numbers, and math is definitely a skill I have so it seems like a natural choice."

"And how romantic that it brought you and Rusty together." Her head tilts to the side, and she gets those hearts in her eyes again, the ones she had when she was looking at me and Rusty the other night at dinner. "He seems like a great guy."

I nod and shift my cup of coffee around on the table, the condensation leaking down the sides, dripping through the openings of the wrought iron, and dropping down to my bare legs beneath.

"Rusty is a great guy. He's…" I pause, thinking it over. "He's one of those people who wants the people he loves to be happy, and that's what guides most of his life. He's very thoughtful and always puts family first."

"Wow. I wish someone would give *me* that kind of rave review." Stace giggles. "Sounds like he might be the one?"

I take a deep breath and give what I'm sure is an awkward smile. "Oh, I don't know. I feel a little young to be making a statement like that."

Even as I say it, I want to snatch the words from the air and pull them back. Not only because just days ago, I was so sure Connor was the man for me, but also because Stace and I are the same age and I don't want that to sound like a judgment.

"Not that it's wrong or anything," I'm quick to clarify. "I think everyone finds love at a different time, and for you and Connor, that's great."

The words feel thick in my throat, and I'm sure she can feel my lie like a palpable thing, but instead of shutting up, I just keep talking.

"I've just been wondering recently if I really know anything about love or relationships."

Stace eyes me thoughtfully. "Do we ever really know anything about love, though?"

The question catches me off guard. "What do you mean?"

"Well…I think the idea that we have to know a lot about love before we can truly experience it is like, I don't know, it doesn't make a lot of sense, at least not to me. Love isn't some tangible thing that has to look perfect in order to mean something. You just have to feel it."

I purse my lips, thinking it over. Before I can say anything in response, Stace's smile grows and she looks past me, waving.

I turn, looking over my shoulder, my eyes widening in surprise when I see Rusty walking down the street in our direction. His hand freezes mid-wave when he sees me, and I can only assume he's as surprised to find me sitting at a table with Stace as I am to *be* sitting at a table with her.

"Hey, Bellamy," he says, coming to a stop next to us.

There's a brief pause, then he leans toward me, dropping a gentle kiss on my forehead, his palm warm on my shoulder. My brain short-circuits as I try to process each component: the proximity of his face to mine, the softness of his lips on my skin, the tingle traveling up my arm at his touch.

I clear my throat, trying to refocus my attention.

"What are you ladies up to?"

"Just a little coffee date," I answer, finally finding my bearings. "We're headed to The Vault after this. Stace said Connor is going to be kind of busy this summer working for his dad, so she asked me to show her around a bit."

Rusty's eyes stay on mine and his lips tilt up slightly. "How fun for you both" is all he says in reply, and I don't miss the implied meaning only for my ears.

"And I so appreciate it," Stace says, her voice bright and enthusiastic. "Being in a new place where I don't know anyone is harder than I thought it would be. Sorry for stealing her away from you, though."

She directs the last part at Rusty, and he steps infinitesimally closer. "Nah, I know it's important for Bellamy to get time doing her own thing. Besides…"

My eyes rise up to look at his, and something dips in my stomach.

"If she's out here enjoying herself, that means I'll appreciate it all the more when I get her alone later." His voice sounds deeper at the end of his statement, and I swallow thickly as Rusty leans down and presses his lips against my temple. "You two have fun." His voice is low enough to seem meant only for me but loud enough for Stace to hear. "Call me when you're done."

He bids Stace goodbye before heading off in the direction of whatever errand brought him to Main Street in the first place. My eyes follow him until he disappears into a store at the other end of the block, my mind scrambling over our interaction, trying to figure out what that was—not only the way Rusty whispered in my ear, but my own reaction to it...to the whole thing. I can still feel his hand on my arm and his lips against the crown of my head.

"Damn, girl. You've got it bad."

I blink a few times, giving Stace a small smile even though embarrassment races through me at having been caught staring after Rusty—not that I have a reason to be embarrassed. I mean, we're supposedly dating, right? It's only natural for me to watch him with longing, to eye him up and down as he walks away.

Even so, I feel caught, because watching Rusty's retreating form wasn't for show. It wasn't for anyone else.

We finish up at Ugly Mug not long after that and mosey down to The Vault, but my mind doesn't absorb any of the records as I distractedly flip through the cases. Instead, it stays firmly on that interaction with Rusty.

I guess I finally understand the appeal. It's a heady thing to have his focus placed on you, to be the direct recipient of the charm that has gotten him into the pants of many a lady. Something within me doesn't like that thought, and I groan as I get into my car later, headed for home to change before I have to go into work at Lucky's.

As I drive out of town and up the east side of the lake, I make a promise to myself to nip any shreds of attraction in the bud before they can grow into anything other than amusement at being the subject of his attention. The last thing I need to do is allow myself to confuse Rusty's very fake interest for anything real.

chapter ten
rusty

"You're what?"

Jackson could not look more surprised if I told him I was moving to Hawaii to work with sea turtles.

I get it. I'd be surprised if I were in his shoes, too.

"I'm inviting Bellamy to family dinner this week."

He shoves his hands in his pockets and leans back against the wall, almost like he needs the support.

"No, I heard that part. I'm just…confused as to why."

"Because we're dating."

I say it like it's not a big deal, like it's nothing to tell one of my closer friends I have a girlfriend for the first time in ten years, as if Jackson should just smile and say 'That's cool' and move the conversation back to the wall paneling options we've been staring at for the past hour.

But it *is* a big deal. I know it is because it took me that entire hour of staring unseeing at different wood types and stains to work up the nerve to tell him.

I've never intentionally lied to anyone, and I'm quickly realizing this thing with Bellamy is going to require me to fudge the rules a bit. The way I'm getting around it is telling myself we actually *are* dating. We both agreed to it; it's just there isn't any romance involved, and to be honest, do other people really need that information? With this logic, telling Jackson I'm dating Bellamy is not an outright lie. It's just omitting information that isn't anyone's business anyway.

Ignoring how all that sounds like bullshit even to me, I turn and look at the blueprint that's laid out on the pop-up table.

"I feel like I've been hearing that shiplap is overdone. If we *are* going to use it, we should do it sparingly."

Jackson laughs. "The guy tells me he's dating someone and then starts talking about shiplap."

When I glance back at him, I find him shaking his head with a smile on his face.

"Well, that's why we're here, isn't it? I mean, we've been staring at this shit for an hour."

He crosses his arms and clears his throat. "Alright. If you want to pretend it's nothing, it's nothing." He kicks off the wall and walks to the other side of the table, staring down at the blueprint as well.

I sigh.

I guess it was foolish of me to think I could tell Jackson this kind of information and have it be a super quick, simple thing. I mean, the guy was there when I started dating Hailey, and even though he was still at school once I moved back to Cedar Point, he saw the hit I took when she called it quits. For Jackson, hearing that I'm dating someone, that I have a girlfriend, is a really big deal.

And this is where the lying part comes into play, because it feels horrible to talk to Jackson about someone I'm dating when, in reality, the whole thing is a farce. I feel like I'm manipulating my friend when that's not the intention at all. If Bellamy and I are going to lean into this relationship—if we are really going to convince people it's real—inviting her to a family dinner is a surefire way to prove a point, to prove things aren't just real, they're serious.

"Fine." I cross my arms. "What do you want to know?"

Jackson laughs again and rubs at the back of his neck.

"What do I want to know?" he asks. "What do I *not* want to know? I mean, how did this even happen? When have the two of you been spending time together? How did I not know? How does *Boyd* feel about it?"

I let out a long breath at his string of questions and remind myself to be careful about how I answer. The story we gave Connor and Stace about how we started dating won't make as much sense to Jackson, who has quite a hand in our company's finances, so I have to figure out how to give him the same story without making it sound too much different than what we said at dinner.

"Well, she just got her bachelor's degree in accounting, and she asked if she could look at our budget and past tax documents so she could get an understanding of a real business's finances, rather than a hypothetical one from her exam books. We just… started spending time together."

"And you, what…realized she was the one to get Rusty Fuller to commit? To give up his playboy ways?"

I roll my eyes. "I guess."

"And Boyd? You told him already, I'm assuming."

"I did," I reply, nodding. "He was a bit irritated at first, but he came around." I lean across the table and poke Jackson in the chest. "Somebody else showed me the importance of talking to a friend when you're going to start dating his sister, showed me it makes a big difference."

Jackson smiles and shakes his head again.

"What?"

"Nothing, man. I'm just surprised is all."

"Yeah, me too," I answer honestly. "But it's a good thing. For both of us, I think."

"And it's serious?"

I pause before I speak again. "Yeah."

This time it's Jackson who leans across the table. He slaps me on the shoulder twice, a wide grin across his face. "I'm stoked for you, man. Really, I am."

I nod but don't say anything.

"You know, I'm not sure if I should be saying this to you considering the fact that you're Abby's older brother, but I've always had doubts about relationships. For a long time, I didn't think monogamy or commitment were things that had a place in my life."

"Trust me, I remember," I tell him, my mind recalling all the days when he would tell me the single life was the only kind of life he wanted.

"But I guess the real truth of it is that, for the right person, anything is possible. Anything can be true. Abby is that person for me in a way I never could have expected. I mean, when I think about her, I can't help but think about the future. And who knows? Maybe Bellamy is that person for you."

I give him a tight smile. "Maybe. I guess we'll just have to wait and see, won't we?"

"Nah. I think this is it, man. I think Bellamy is your person. I mean, I wouldn't have come to you about Abby if I wasn't absolutely sure things with her felt different than they'd ever felt with anyone else. I'm assuming the same is true for you and Boyd." He pauses, seeming to consider his words before he speaks again. "You know, after what happened with Hailey, I was really concerned for you, man."

I scratch at the back of my head, not wanting him to dredge this up but knowing he's going to.

"I never thought the two of you were right together. Something just never really…fit, you know? And the way she dropped you when everything happened with your parents…it only confirmed for me that she wasn't your person. I think this thing with Bellamy is proof of that, you know?" He lets out a sigh…a happy one that sounds like he has all the optimism in the world bolstering his confidence in me. "Like I said, I'm stoked for you."

Jackson returns his attention to the panel samples leaning against the wall behind him, seemingly having decided he has finally gotten enough information from me to feel satisfied.

All I feel inside my chest is turmoil. It's been there for a long time, and now it's beginning to leak into my personal life as well, everything feeling amplified by this relationship with Bellamy. It's like I'm on the precipice of something, like everything I've worked so hard for might slip through my fingertips if I make one wrong move.

I try to shake it off, attempt to focus my attention back on the work in front of us.

Instead, the little voice telling me I should be worried about what's to come doesn't quiet, and the turmoil rages on.

It's after 10pm when I finally drop down onto my couch with a beer and a sigh of relief, wanting nothing more than to chill out with both my mind and the A's game on mute—but I still need to talk to Bellamy about family dinner, so I pull up her number as I take a swig of our summer pale ale and hit call. It only rings twice before she picks up, her voice quiet.

"Hey, what's up?"

"Everything okay?"

She pauses, but just for a second. "Yeah," she replies, drawing the word out. "Why wouldn't it be?"

"Just…sounded like you were trying to be super quiet. Wanted to make sure you weren't hiding from a serial killer, is all."

Bellamy giggles, and the sound brings an unexpected smile to my lips.

"No, I'm just out on the dock, and I've heard enough times from Mrs. Garley that the sound carries."

"I'm surprised she can hear you over the sound of her own self-importance," I toss back, and Bellamy laughs again, the sound muffled like she's trying to stay quiet.

"Have you ever seen the way she walks through town with her dog in her purse like she's in Hollywood or something?"

"Yes, and she lets that little rat out to poop on the street and doesn't pick up after it," I add, causing Bellamy to launch into laughter again.

"Don't call Mr. Gregory a rat," she begs between breaths.

"Its name is *not* Mr. Gregory."

"It *is*. It totally is. And her cat's name is Lady Bernadette."

At that, I start to laugh too, and it sounds like an old car coming back to life, like something in my chest has loosened slightly. It's like clearing out my lungs after a bad cold, the tightness beginning to dissipate.

Eventually our laughter begins to fade, the quiet settling into something easy.

"You're just sitting out near the water?" I ask, picturing Bellamy on the familiar wooden dock that extends out from the Mitchell family back yard.

"Mmhm. I come out here a lot, lie flat on my back, and stare up at the stars."

"Sounds a bit too daydreamy for me." But I know I'm full of shit. I love those quiet moments too and seek them out whenever I can.

Bellamy's quiet laughter wafts through the phone again, and I realize just how much I actually like the sound of it.

"Well, if you're ever in need of an escape, you are welcome to use our dock," Bellamy says. "I can personally assure you that many problems have been resolved during my time lying on it, and I don't doubt it will do the same for you."

"What, like math problems?" I tease.

"No, you goof," she answers, and I can't help but picture Bellamy, her head of thick, dark blonde hair spread out around her face as she stares up into the sky. "Like real problems. Deciding whether or not to do college online, or how to tell my mom I'm ready to move out…how to handle this Connor thing."

I ignore the comment about Connor.

"You want to move out?"

"Yeah, well…someone recently told me I wouldn't know the true value of money until I moved out of my parents' plush house, so…it got me thinking."

I wince, having forgotten I said that to her at the bonfire.

"I didn't mean…"

"It's fine, Rusty. I know you were having a shitty day, but

there was some truth in what you said. It's just been on my mind."

There's a beat of silence before Bellamy speaks again.

"So, what's up?" she asks, her voice still low. "I thought an old man like you would definitely be in bed at this hour."

I snort. "Says the woman who came by my house at two in the morning last week."

She giggles again.

"Well first, I wanted to ask how your girl day with Stace went on Saturday."

Bellamy groans. "Don't say 'girl day' like that—like we're best friends."

"That's sure what it looked like."

She lets out a long sigh, and I hear a thump on the other end of the phone. The sound of her voice is closer now, like she took it off of speaker.

"It was okay. It was *weird*, but okay. She's really nice, which is annoying."

I laugh. "Why is that annoying?"

"Because I want to hate her." Bellamy's voice grows tight, and the mood of our phone call changes on a dime. "She's marrying the man I thought I was going to end up with. And *of course* she's lovely and friendly and funny instead of evil and bitchy and easy to loathe. It's infuriating."

I don't say anything in response, because really, there isn't anything *to* say. Instead, I just let her keep venting; she clearly needs it.

"She's going to be a nurse who helps people at a free clinic, did you know that? So on top of all the other wonderful qualities she has, she's also gorgeous and generous. And today was just the worst because we actually had fun together and I don't want to like her."

"It's not a bad thing to meet nice people, Bellamy."

"I thought we were perfect for each other," she whispers, and I know she's talking about Connor now. "And now I have to rethink…everything."

"Hate to break it to you, Bells, but there's no such thing as perfect." I huff out a humorless laugh. "Trust me."

"Sounds like you know from experience."

I pause, thinking briefly of Hailey and how *perfect* things were before she destroyed me.

"Maybe I'll tell you about it another day."

"Selfish. Listen to me make a fool out of myself and then don't reciprocate with your own foolishness."

I grin. "There's plenty of foolishness for you to revel in. No need for me to share it all right at the jump."

She hums in acknowledgment.

"Speaking of foolishness," I continue, "on Tuesday nights, I have family dinner. It's a thing I do with Abby. It's her, Jackson, Briar, and Andy. Dinner and drinks and sometimes card games. Abby told me I should invite you, now that we're dating."

"You know, that actually sounds like a lot of fun, but I'm working tomorrow night."

"Yeah, I figured." I'm a little disappointed, though I try not to think too much about it.

"Maybe next week? I usually work on Tuesdays, but I can ask someone to switch."

I shrug, though I know she can't see me. "It's not a big deal. If you can make it, you can make it. If not, don't sweat it."

We're quiet for a long moment, and I can feel our conversation coming to a close. Something inside me starts flicking through things we could talk about, and the unfamiliar desire to stay on the phone with someone surprises me.

"I think I'm gonna head in," Bellamy says, though, making it clear she's ready to bring our call to an end. "I'm exhausted and I have to help my mom with her garden in the morning."

I grin, imagining the two Mitchell women out mowing and weeding and whatever else they're planning to get up to.

"Alright, well…have a good night."

"You, too, Rusty."

We end the call, and my eyes scan over to the TV, where I see the game highlights are running. I had the last inning of the game on mute and don't remember watching a single minute of it.

I sigh and click it off then finish my beer before flicking the light switch and heading up to bed, where I dream of a tiny dog in a purse and lying on my back on a dock, staring up at the sky.

chapter eleven
bellamy

"Thanks so much for picking me up." Emily hops into the passenger seat of my CRV and chucks her purse on the ground. "I swear, this car is going to be the absolute death of me if I don't get it figured out."

"Glad I could help," I reply, waiting until she's buckled her seatbelt before pulling away from the small wooden cabin Emily lives in with her grandmother. "And I'm sorry about your car. Is it going to take a while to fix?"

She shrugs and rolls down her window, allowing the slowly warming summer air to filter in as we turn out on the main road.

"No idea. Gam said if it's too much, we can always share her car, but she uses it to get to bunco with her friends, and I don't want her to be any more stuck at home than she already is. I'd rather walk."

One of the things I love about Emily is how much she cares for her grandmother. It's been just the two of them since Emily's mom left when she was a toddler, and she's always said her Gam is the only mom she's ever needed.

"Hey, would you mind swinging by the resort really quick? I was hoping to pick up my paycheck and get it cashed before the weekend so I can try to sort this shit out."

"Yeah, no problem."

The South Bank Resort and Marina is the only hotel in Cedar Point and the largest employer in town. It's been the site of some of my favorite memories—high school prom, multiple marriages for friends and family, and a variety of seasonal events. Emily is one of several bartenders from The Mitch who pick up shifts at the resort when the number of guests rises during the summer.

I've worked a few nights there in the past alongside Emily, usually when our friend Elijah asked if I could serve as extra hands for a banquet or special event. He used to be our manager at The Mitch, working for my uncle for as long as I could remember before becoming the events manager at South Bank.

"You get to see Elijah at all?" I ask as we cross Temple Bridge and turn onto South Bank Road.

"Hell yeah I do," she replies, smiling wide. "Who do you think I'm going to beg when I go in there asking for my paycheck early?"

I laugh. "I miss having him around. Celine is okay, but…I don't know."

"Celine is a boss. Elijah was family."

Nodding, I flip my blinker and pull into the resort parking lot. "You are absolutely correct," I tell her, rounding to the back of the hotel and coming to a stop in one of the few dozen spaces reserved for employees.

"I'll only be a few minutes." Emily rolls up her window and pushes her door open.

"I'm actually gonna come in, too," I tell her, stepping out of the car as well. I close my door and move to the front, meeting Emily at the bumper. "It's been a while since I've seen Elijah, and today feels like the perfect day to remind him of that twenty bucks he owes me."

Emily laughs as we walk inside. "From what?"

"He bet me I couldn't memorize a brand-new drink list in one night."

She scoffs. "Seriously? Did he not know about your memorization skills yet?"

I shrug. "Who knows, but what I *do* know is he still owes me twenty dollars, and every time I see him, he somehow manages to get out of paying me. Not today, though."

She laughs as we turn down a wide hallway that leads to the hotel lobby. There are two young women helping guests at the concierge desk, and Emily steps behind the counter and dips into an open doorway that I'm fairly sure is Elijah's office.

Before I can follow her, I hear my name, and when I turn, I smile at Sean Pruitt's approaching form.

"Hey, Mr. Pruitt."

He opens his arms wide and gives me a big hug before leaning an elbow against the counter, a smile on his face. "Hey there, sweetheart. Haven't seen you in…wow, a few months at least."

"I know. You and Tricia haven't been in for dinner in forever."

"Yeah, you know how it is. The months leading up to summer are filled to the brim with all the prep work getting ready for the influx of guests. How are things for you? Get that CPA license yet?"

I roll my eyes. "Still finishing up the last section of my exams, then I have to get some work experience under my belt

3

before I'm eligible for a license. But I'm hoping it'll be sooner rather than later."

Mr. Pruitt nods. "Well, keep me posted. You know we use George for all the resort financials, but I heard he's retiring soon, and we'd like to stay local." He chuckles. "None of that online tax mumbo jumbo."

I stifle a laugh and nod. "I'll definitely let you know once I'm able to start working."

He snaps his fingers. "Hey, not sure if you know, but Connor is back in town, and he brought his fiancée with him. We were thinking about doing a little engagement dinner celebration soon. Maybe we'll come to Dock 7."

I've never had a poker face, and it requires all my effort to keep smiling.

"That sounds…great."

His phone starts ringing, and he glances at it. "Ah, speaking of my son…" He puts it up to his ear. "Hey, Connor." Pause. "Yeah, I'm actually in the lobby right now with…" Mr. Pruitt turns, his words trailing off as he looks over my shoulder.

My heart sinks, and I glance behind me, spotting Connor approaching us. I don't know why it didn't occur to me that he'd be here, too, but of course it makes sense. Stace mentioned that Connor came home for the summer to begin working for the family business, and the Pruitt family owns the resort.

God, I want to kick myself. I should have just stayed in the car.

"Hey, Bellamy." He gives me that same charming smile that used to make me swoon and now just makes me angry.

"I'll let you two kids chat," Mr. Pruitt says, patting me on the shoulder. "It was good to see you, sweetheart. We'll see you at Dock 7 soon for that engagement dinner." He looks at Connor. "Find me once you're done chatting."

He heads off through the lobby, leaving me behind with Connor.

In the past, I was only able to imagine a run-in with Connor Pruitt happening so seamlessly. Accidentally seeing his dad, Connor showing up out of nowhere, his dad leaving the two of us behind to talk—it's all so perfect.

Now, though, my skin itches with the need to get out of here.

"You here to see me?" Connor asks, stepping closer, his smile growing smug.

I take a step back, trying to maintain a bit of space between us. "I actually came in to see if Elijah is here."

Connor nods, but it's apparent he thinks I really *am* here to see him, regardless of what I tell him.

"Elijah doesn't work on Thursdays," he supplies. "But he'll be here tomorrow if you want to come back to see him."

"Cool, well…thanks for that."

Before I can turn and walk off to grab Emily and get the hell out of here, Connor speaks again.

"You know, I never would have guessed you two were together. You and Rusty, I mean."

I lick my lips.

"Yeah, well, opposites attract, you know?"

He bobs his head, his lips pursed, like he's thinking something over. "I mean more because, the last time I was in town, you seemed pretty single, at least to me. And so did Rusty."

"That was what, three months ago?" I shrug, trying to seem more confident than I feel. "We were still figuring things out."

I don't mention the fact that Connor *also* seemed very single, though it feels like a very big and obvious elephant in this conversation seeing as how he's *engaged.*

"And now you're so serious that you're telling everyone? Friends, family…" He trails off.

Something inside me snaps, and I'm suddenly less concerned about maintaining my lie and more exasperated by his unusual nosiness.

"What are you getting at, Connor? Why does it matter to you? You're engaged."

His eyes narrow just slightly before he affects that charming smile. "Look, Bells, I'm just worried you're wasting your time on a guy like Rusty—who we both know doesn't have a monogamous bone in his body—because you're upset about me and Stace."

"You know what? Rusty might not be *your* idea of a great guy, but he certainly is mine, and that's all that matters. So why don't you keep your thoughts about our relationship to yourself." I pause. "And don't call me Bells."

Thankfully, I spot Emily emerging from behind the concierge desk.

She beams at me. "Guess who got her paycheck early!" she says, waving a check in the air. Her hand freezes and her smile drops when she sees my expression, her eyes flicking to Connor and then back to me.

I say nothing, storming past her and down to the exit to the employee lot.

"What happened?" she asks, her voice quiet as we both settle into my car a few minutes later. "You look like you want to strangle someone, and I don't think I've ever seen you look more than mildly constipated."

I choke out a laugh, thankful for Emily's go-to tactic of using humor to defuse situations.

"It's just wild when you realize people aren't who you thought they were" is all I say in response.

She hums her agreement and rolls down her window again. "Well, if you want someone to talk to about whatever it is, I'm here for you, girl. Lord knows you've listened to me ramble on and on about enough of *my* drama to grant you as many vent sessions as you need."

I glance at Emily, finding her watching me with gentle eyes. "Thanks, Em. I might take you up on that someday."

We're silent for the last few minutes of the drive to work, and I try to force myself to let go of my irritable attitude and just enjoy the breeze and the country music playing on low from my radio.

I try, but my mind continues to tear apart my interaction with Connor. There's a small part of me that doesn't want him asking questions about me and Rusty because I don't want him to find out we're lying. If that happens, his ego will grow even larger upon finding out I concocted this story to try to convince him he's less important. He'll take it as confirmation of my feelings for him.

But the larger part of me just wishes he would fuck off entirely, wishes I didn't have to deal with him *at all*. Because something tells me Connor is going to continue to surprise me, and not in a good way.

It really is true: you have to take off your rose-colored glasses to see all those red flags.

Thankfully, my shift passes quickly. That's how most days are as summer begins to pick up. Tourists swarm the resort and the marina and downtown and the restaurant, pushing all the locals who want a mostly-tourist-free space over to The Mitch.

I'm surprised by the relief that runs through my body when Rusty takes a seat at the bar later that night, but it's swallowed by nerves when Andy and my older sister Briar sit down next to him. Briar rarely comes into The Mitch, and based on the way her eyes focus entirely on me, I'm immediately suspicious that she's here to ask me questions, or at the very least, to observe our interactions.

"Happy Thursday," I say, tossing down coasters in front of all three of them. "What can I get you?"

"A vodka cranberry."

"A pale ale."

"A whiskey and a kiss."

I actually laugh when Rusty says it, my surprise overriding any other potential reaction. Then he leans forward, his hand coming out to slip behind my neck, and he tugs me gently across the bar, planting his lips against mine. It's just a simple kiss—a smooch, really—before he drops back down on his stool.

I, however, feel frozen in place. Where the hell did that come from?

Clearing my throat, I pull out the vodka and cranberry juice to start making Briar's drink, using the time to try to unscramble my mind.

"You know I can't kiss you when I'm working," I finally reply, but then I laugh again. Thankfully, I'm pretty sure my laughter can be perceived as giddiness over Rusty's kiss and not the frazzled ends of my nerves bubbling up with nowhere else to go.

Though part of me feels like maybe I *am* a little giddy about that kiss.

I set Briar's drink on the counter in front of her, and that's when my eyes connect with hers. Her eyebrows are raised, but there's a small smile on her face.

"That was so weird," she tells me, her voice quiet, but not so quiet that Andy and Rusty can't hear her.

"Trust me, it was just as weird for me to have you here to see it," I reply honestly. I grab a pint glass and pull Andy's beer from the tap then put a rocks glass out and pour in two fingers of Woodford for Rusty. "Be right back," I say, giving them a smile before moving down the bar to help other customers.

Technically, this is Emily's side of the bar, but she's busy helping a woman at the far end, and I feel a desperate need to put a few feet between me and the man who just kissed me. I move through a simple order—three shots of tequila and three bottles of Bud—almost unseeing, my mind fixated on that kiss.

It was a nothing. A peck. So then why does it feel like someone is tightening a cinch around my chest? Why did the feel of his beard on my skin send threads of desire simmering through my body? Didn't I *just* tell myself any level of attraction to Rusty is a no-go, full stop?

And yet here I am, feeling flustered by a kiss that, to Rusty, was surely about as platonic as they come.

After I help a few people, I dip out from the bar and take a quick bathroom break, hoping to shake off whatever this is, but when I step back out a few minutes later, Rusty's leaning against the wall, his arms crossed and that inscrutable expression on his face.

"What was that?" I ask, feeling slightly mortified by the way my voice squeaks. "A little warning would have been nice."

"I did warn you. I said, 'A whiskey and a kiss.'"

"I thought you were joking."

"Well, I wasn't." He uncrosses his arms. "But clearly it was an issue, so I won't do it again."

I can feel him bristling, and I reach out and put my hand on his forearm, halting him before he heads down the hallway.

"Look, it's not…" I sigh. "It's not a *problem*, it just caught me off guard, okay? It's not something I have a lot of experience with."

He huffs out a laugh, like he thinks I'm joking. "What, kissing?"

"Yeah."

Rusty's eyebrows pull down in the middle. "What's that supposed to mean?"

"It means…" I pause as someone comes around the corner and down the hallway, greeting Rusty with a nod before stepping into the men's room. "Can we just talk about this later?" I ask, not wanting to discuss my lack of experience in the bathroom hallway at my work.

He watches me for a long beat before nodding, and I take that as my cue to head back out to the bar. Rusty follows and slips back onto his stool just as I get back behind the counter.

"Sneaking off for a little smoochy where nobody's looking?"

I pin Andy with a look. He just grins and takes another sip of his beer.

"Abby said you're coming to family dinner next week." Briar watches me with a thoughtful expression. "That should be fun."

I nod. "Yeah, as long as I can get someone to cover my shift here."

"You need someone to cover you? When?"

My head turns to the left, where Emily is filling a pint glass from the tap.

"Oh, um…on Tuesday? We have a dinner thing."

"Apparently, these two started dating a little while back—can you believe that?" Andy says, waving a hand between me and Rusty.

Emily's eyes widen. "Oh my god, you two are dating?"

I've never been in one of those situations they show in the movies when someone says something loudly right when the music stops and everyone hears it, but I can imagine it feels something like this. Emily's voice carries through the entire bar—or at least it seems that way—and when I glance around, I can see many eyes focused on us.

I laugh, unable to help myself. I guess if anyone in town didn't know before, they definitely do now.

"Yes," I say. "We are."

Something devious races through me in that moment, and I just can't help myself. I follow Rusty's lead and reach across the bar, placing a hand behind his neck and tugging him in for a kiss.

chapter twelve
rusty

When I pull up in front of the Mitchell house on Sunday evening, Bellamy is already outside, sitting on the little bench next to their front door. I've noticed she does that, sits outside instead of waiting inside for me to come to the door and knock. She did it the night we went on the double date with Stace and Connor, and she's doing it tonight.

"How come you don't let me come up to the door and knock?" I ask once she's climbed into my passenger seat.

She raises an eyebrow. "I just figured we're not really dating, so it's an extra thing you'd have to do when you're already doing a lot."

I take a second or two to turn my car around then head down the driveway and out to the main highway. "Well, it's something I *would* do, so just let me come to the door, okay?"

Bellamy thinks about it for a minute then nods. "If you want to."

We drive in silence, neither of us addressing what feels like the baby elephant riding in the car with us.

At least, *I* feel like there's a baby elephant, and its name is 'Bellamy's Kiss at The Mitch.'

I mean holy *shit*. My throat feels tight just thinking about it.

She said she doesn't have a lot of experience—which we still need to talk about, along with her other mention of having not been on a date before—but you'd never know it from the sexy way she reached over to plant one on me. This wasn't a somewhat friendly kiss like the one I gave her. Sure, I enjoyed the feel of her lips pressed against mine, but that was the extent of it.

When Bellamy kissed *me*, I felt it in my fucking toes. Her warm hand on my neck, the mischievous look on her face as she leaned toward me, the gentle way her teeth nibbled on my lips—I was a half second away from yanking *her* across the bar so we could continue that kiss in private. God, even now, just thinking about it, I'm having to will away the pulse of desire growing thick and hard between my legs.

Of course, after that, I wasn't able to stop thinking about Bellamy for the rest of the evening—hell, for the rest of the weekend—which can be the only explanation for why I texted her saying we should go to the bonfire tonight. In my head, I tried to justify the invitation with the idea that it's a chance for Bellamy and me to go to something public. Now that it's common knowledge we're 'dating', it would seem a little weird if we were never actually seen together.

Of course, there's also the voice I can't seem to quiet telling me that's not the real reason, saying maybe I enjoy Bellamy's company a little more than I should. My eyes glance in her direction briefly, taking in her pouty lips and long neck before I return my attention to the road.

The reality is that I haven't gotten laid in a few months.

That's probably what this attraction is. It's animal need, clawing its way out and latching onto the only person I'm giving any of my attention.

I look at Bellamy again, this time finding her eyes on me.

"How are things coming with the brewery?"

Her question catches me off guard. Here I am, thinking about her plump lips, and she's over there wondering about my business. I'm grateful for the subject change, though, as a reprieve from my thoughts.

"It's going well. Construction has been going on for about a month, and they're almost done with the renovation aspect of shoring up the building's foundation and replacing the elements that weren't salvageable. They'll be starting on all the electrical and plumbing this week."

"Are you excited? About how it's all progressing?"

I nod. "I am. It's a dream realized."

She pauses. "But?"

"But…there's a lot riding on this, too."

"Like what?"

I blow out a breath and flick my blinker, preparing to turn down the dusty road leading to Forks, the closed campground I'm fairly certain only remains so because townies have commandeered it for Sunday bonfire nights during the summer.

"Well, Boyd and Jackson are investors, and there's the pressure of making sure they feel like their investments were worth it."

Pressure doesn't even begin to describe how I feel about it.

"I mean, I've always been thankful for Boyd helping me get off the ground and then Jackson buying in once he'd found his own success. I couldn't have gotten Cedar Cider to where it is today without them, but even though they've made their investments back, now we're investing even more into it with this brewery." I shrug. "It's a big project with a lot of overhead, and if we make a mistake, we might go under really quickly. My mind is constantly thinking about finding success and whether or not we have it in us to create a company that can last the long haul."

My Blazer wobbles on the dirt road as we transition off the paved street.

"Then there's the personal hit I take any time something goes wrong, because I always feel like it's my fault, whether that's true or not. We were supposed to start construction in March but we had a snow delay, so I've been wondering if I could have done more to avoid that."

It's easy to say weather can't be controlled, but at the same time, could I have done more research on weather patterns and picked a different date to start construction? Maybe I didn't do anything wrong, but it still *feels* like I did.

"And then there's the town."

"What do you mean?"

I chuckle as we pass by cars parked along the side of the road.

"You know what I mean," I reply, pulling over when I spot a space and shifting into park. "This town isn't a big fan of me, you know? So it feels like everyone's watching me, just waiting for me to fail."

Bellamy turns in her seat to face me, a fierce expression filling her features.

"Rusty, that is *not* true."

I give her a slightly embarrassed smile. "It *is* true."

"No, it's *not*." She leans forward, her brows dipped as she glares at me. "This town *loves* the Fuller family."

"They loved my parents, and they love my sister." I shake my head. "I know it's unfamiliar to you. Everyone has always loved you, Cedar Point's favorite daughter."

Bellamy rolls her eyes. "That's a ridiculous nickname and it's categorically false." She moves even closer, placing her hand on top of mine where it rests on my knee. "You might have some bad history with a few people, and yeah, there might be a bit of gossip about how often you head to Lucky's during tourist season…"

I laugh under my breath, and Bellamy gives me a small smile before her face turns serious, as do her words.

"…but everyone knows who the real Rusty Fuller is. He's a man who has sacrificed so much to take care of his sister, a man who has worked his ass off to create a thriving local business." She squeezes my hand. "You are an incredible brother and friend, and anyone who thinks otherwise doesn't really know you and shouldn't warrant your concern."

My heart thunders in my chest, the overwhelm of her esteem filling up a well I didn't even realize had run dry. Bellamy Mitchell just knocked me on my ass, and she did it while building me up.

Without allowing myself to think too much about it, I lean forward and press my lips to hers, wanting nothing more than to be close to her. I can tell I've surprised her by the way she freezes, but it only lasts a few seconds before her mouth opens almost tentatively.

The taste of her explodes on my tongue, and I reach forward, slipping my hands to either side of her face. My tongue twists with hers, and I can feel myself growing hard as she moans softly. She does that nibbling thing, like she did the other night at the bar, and I groan, sliding my hands into her hair and deepening our kiss, tilting her head just how I want it as I lick deeply into her mouth. I breathe her in, feeling lost in everything about her, and for the first time in a long time, the storm inside me quiets.

I barely notice when there's a tapping noise on the hood of my ride, but Bellamy notices and jumps back, pulling away from me with wide eyes—though whether from the surprise of the knocking sound or the surprise of our kiss, I'm not sure. We look through the windshield, and I grit my teeth when I see Connor and Stace, hand in hand.

Stace is waving, a big smile on her face. She looks like she's laughing, and I can only imagine she's giggling at having found us making out like teenagers in my car before a bonfire night.

Connor, though, has a sour expression on his face. He looks at me and gives me a three-finger salute before wrapping his arm around Stace's shoulders, leading her off in the direction of the campground.

"Good call."

I quirk a brow and look back at Bellamy.

"I saw them when we pulled in but didn't even think about something like a kiss. Great idea."

She's panting, and her pupils are blown, and I want nothing more than to tug her toward me and continue what we started.

But then what she said hits me: she thinks I kissed her because I saw Connor. What's more, she kissed me back because *she* saw Connor.

I nod. "I'm glad you figured it out."

Turning off the ignition, I shove my door open and step onto the dirt road, my feet kicking up little clouds of dust as my shoes hit the ground. Bellamy follows suit and rounds the front, and we begin walking down the path toward the large campsite in the middle of Forks that serves as the main hub for bonfire night.

Now, the last thing I want to do is go to this stupid thing. I'm too old. Isn't that what Bellamy told me the last time we were here? I'm pretty sure she even accused me of selling beer to underage kids.

What I want to do is go home and drown myself in whiskey, because all my mind can think about is that kiss, and it's killing me to know she thought it was for show when it wasn't.

I startle when Bellamy slips her hand into mine, our fingers interlocking in a way that shouldn't feel as incredible as it does.

"We should hold hands, right?" she asks, looking up at me as we continue walking.

Swallowing, I nod. "Yeah. Of course."

Bellamy nods, too.

I try not to think about the kiss, about her hand in mine.

Or about the little thing inside of me saying this isn't at all what I expected.

"I shouldn't have had that much to drink."

I don't respond. Instead, I just reach across Bellamy and pull her seatbelt around her body to click it in.

Then I start my car and begin pulling out of my spot on the side of the road.

"But I just hate looking at him, you know?" She pauses. "How can love turn to hate so quickly?"

It's a surprisingly intelligent question for such an inebriated person.

"I think love and hate are a lot more closely intertwined than you'd think," I tell her, pulling out onto the dirt path and beginning the long, slow drive toward the main road. "Because you still love the person, you just hate the way they hurt you."

"Yeah."

I glance over at her in the dark, and the light from a passing lamp post illuminates her face enough for me to see she's crying.

"He doesn't deserve your tears," I tell her, my voice gentle even though I'm boiling inside. "He doesn't deserve them."

"Yeah, I know." She leans her head back against the seat. "I'm not actually crying over him, I'm just...mad at myself."

"Why?"

She sighs, and instead of answering, she rolls down the window and leans her head against the edge, closing her eyes and letting the warm evening breeze waft across her skin and through her hair. How did I never notice how beautiful she is? She's crying, and I still think she might be one of the most beautiful people I've ever seen.

I come to a stop, preparing to turn right toward her house, then she surprises me.

"Can I stay at your place tonight?" she asks. "I don't want to go home."

She looks up at me with sad eyes, and for whatever reason, I can't say no. I turn my car to the left instead, heading to the southern part of the lake where the home I grew up in is tucked into a short, wide lot.

I'm not surprised when we walk through the front door and she walks straight to my liquor cabinet, tugging out some crappy tequila gathering dust and pouring herself a shot. I know I should head to bed and leave her to her own demise. I've had many nights where tequila seemed like the answer to all my problems and many mornings when I realized I'd been wrong. I feel at least partly responsible for Bellamy, so leaving her to whatever demons are working their way through her mind right now while I go get cozy in bed feels wrong.

"You never answered my question earlier," I say, taking a seat on the couch.

She tosses back a shot then gasps at the burn, her eyes closed. "About?"

"About Connor." Bellamy pours another shot. "You said you were mad at yourself. Why?"

"Because I believed him."

It's all she says, and I wait, hoping she'll finish telling me what happened. Instead, she sets down her still full shot glass, takes a swig straight from the bottle, and leans back against the liquor cabinet. She's not super plastered, but I can tell she's a bit wobbly based on the glassy way she watches me.

"I never understood what all the fuss was about," Bellamy says a minute or so later.

"What do you mean?"

"About you. All the women who wanted you...I never got it." She nods. "Now I do. I get what they all see when they look at Cedar Point's most attractive tourist destination."

Bellamy pushes off the cabinet and saunters toward me, and before I can ask what she's doing, she crawls onto my lap, straddling me, and presses her lips to mine. I'm shocked at first, but it's easy to get lost in the kiss. After our make-out session in the car earlier, my libido is eager to continue things, and I moan into her mouth when her tongue tangles with mine. My hands rest on her hips, then slide back, grabbing her ass and grinding her down on me, and she yanks her mouth away and whimpers when she feels how quickly I've grown hard for her.

"Fuck," I whisper, tugging her mouth back to mine.

Never in a million years did I think I'd be in this spot right here with Bellamy Mitchell. How do you fall for your best friend's little sister? Bellamy, whose ass feels amazing in my hands. Bellamy, whose hands are reaching for my jeans. Bellamy, who smells like strawberries and tastes like tequila.

That's a douse of cold water, and I pull back, reminding myself that she's had a lot to drink tonight.

"Bellamy, we need to stop," I say, bringing our foreheads together as I try to catch my breath. "You're drunk."

"It's fine," she tells me, leaning down and kissing my neck. "It doesn't matter."

"It *does* matter," I tell her, lifting her off of me and setting her on the couch. "It matters because I want to make sure you know what you're doing."

She scoffs. "Like you don't go drink and then get laid with random people at Lucky's."

"Not when I'm this drunk—and not when they are, either," I reply. "You might not feel like it right now, but you will to-morrow."

Bellamy glares at me, and I can't help how it makes me smile.

"Let's get you to bed," I tell her, feeling like it's that night from two weeks ago all over again.

She begrudgingly lets me lead her upstairs and down to Abby's room then falls almost immediately into the bed, which is still outfitted with the bedding from the last time she was here. Instead of naked and face down, this time she's curled up on her side, looking at me.

"Is the idea of sex with me so off-putting that you'll sleep with thousands of tourists but not me?"

I grin. "I haven't had sex with thousands of tourists."

"Hundreds, then."

I shake my head. "Not hundreds, either, but my number doesn't matter, just like yours doesn't."

"So it doesn't matter that I've only ever had sex with Connor?"

My surprise is evident, and I scratch at my chin and then the back of my neck, trying to decide what to say. When Bellamy told me she didn't have a lot of experience, I thought she was just comparing herself to me. The idea that she's only ever been with Connor…I mean, she really is inexperienced. It makes me feel even worse, the way I've been thinking about her.

Not only is she far too young for me, she's far too innocent as well.

"You can't say it doesn't matter. I can see on your face that it does."

"It doesn't matter, Bellamy. I'm just surprised, is all. I mean, I would have assumed all the boys would have been after you in high school, at least. Or that you'd have had a boyfriend over the years."

"Well, they weren't, and I didn't. And now I hate that he's the only one I've been with."

I grit my teeth as I slowly realize what she means.

"Is that why you jumped me downstairs? Because you don't want Connor to be the only person you've had sex with?"

Bellamy just stares at me, a slightly sheepish expression on her face, and I clench my fists.

"Don't ever do that again. I've worked too hard and sacrificed too much to throw my friendships away just because you're filled with regret."

I leave the room and head down the hall, irritation boiling like acid beneath my skin as I stomp downstairs and over to my liquor cabinet. How could I not have seen what was really happening? Obviously it's because I've foolishly allowed myself to develop feelings for her.

Fuck.

I pull out shitty whiskey, the stuff I use when I want to get good and fucked up, and take a long drink straight from the bottle. I know Bellamy is drunk, and people do stupid things when they've been drinking, but still. That would have been a huge mistake.

Really, I'm not even that mad at Bellamy. I'm mad at myself. What I said to her was true—my friendships *do* mean too much to me to throw them away for a drunken hookup with her.

Taking another long swig of whiskey, I try to remind myself that things with Bellamy are supposed to be fake. They're not supposed to become physical or emotional like this.

Somehow, I've let myself lose sight of that.

Somehow, I've fabricated some kind of connection with her.

I need to remind myself of what we're really doing and let go of the rest.

chapter thirteen
bellamy

I shut the medicine cabinet, wincing as it closes with a loud snap.

Normally I'm a wine drinker, so last night was rough for me, and now I'm reaping the consequences of my very stupid mistake. Mistakes *plural*, I guess. It began with too many beers at bonfire night then steamrolled into me doing shots of tequila at Rusty's and trying to get him to have sex with me.

Ugh.

I wince again, but this time at the memory. Mortified doesn't begin to describe how I feel.

Squirting toothpaste onto my toothbrush, I aggressively try to scrub the taste of stale tequila and regret from my mouth. I'm also in desperate need of a shower, and the idea of standing underneath the hot spray of water sounds incredible.

I finish up with my teeth then reach into the shower and slap the handle, turning it on to max heat before stripping out of the clothes that still smell like smoke. The water feels incredible when I climb in, and I sit on the floor, letting the water just rain over me.

Rusty was livid when I got up, which I know because he barely looked at me and only spoke about three sentences. He just told me he was taking me home and drove me silently back to my parents' house, hardly saying a word.

My foggy, hungover brain feels confused. Didn't he kiss me first? In the car?

It was incredible. I've never been kissed like that before. But then Connor and Stace arrived, and that was the reminder that Rusty had only kissed me because they were there.

It's wild to me that his kiss was a ruse. I might have only kissed a few men in my life, but it sure felt real to me. The way he touched my face and gripped the back of my head…I shiver just thinking about it, even under the heat of my shower. I was drunk on the high of that kiss long before I got drunk on tequila and jumped him in his living room.

Closing my eyes, I try to remember what he said while I was straddling him. Did he say something? Or was it just those deep moans that make it hard to regret what I did?

All I know for sure is that he was angry this morning, back to his grumpy, bear attitude, the 'keep away from me' vibes I've always gotten from him prior to the past few weeks. And I'm more upset about it than I thought I'd be.

I've begun to enjoy being around the Rusty who teases me on the phone and listens to me vent. I can't remember the last time someone listened to me, really listened, like they cared about all the little pieces of why something had upset me or excited me. He was becoming my friend, and now I've gone and fucked it up because I can't keep my emotions in check when it comes to Connor and the past.

I pull myself up to standing and go through my shower routine. Shampoo. Conditioner. Body wash. Shave. When I'm done and I've turned off the water and dried my body, I really do feel like a new woman. Showers will do that.

But I feel like my insides need to be cleaned, too. My mind feels…mucky. Not just because of the hangover, although the fog from that is still lingering for sure, but also because I feel terrible about the way Rusty and I left things. He was so upset, and the one thing I really remember him saying was that he didn't want to throw his friendships away because I'm filled with regret.

I wish I could tell him that, yes, there is a part of me that doesn't want to have only ever been with Connor, but I'm starting to think that wasn't the driving force behind my attempt at seducing Rusty.

It's all getting so jumbled in my head. The way I feel about Connor, the way I feel about Rusty, the way I feel about myself…

Clearly, I really need to figure it all out.

And I need to do it before I make any other horrible choices.

When I pull up to the construction site and park next to Rusty's Blazer, I worry he's going to be pissed when he sees me. There are about a dozen or so workers scattered around doing various construction-y things, and I wonder if maybe I should try to talk to him about this later, when he's not focused on work.

But then I spot him, rounding a corner and walking with Nick Waltham, both of them in hard hats, and I smile, thinking how cute he looks wearing that ever-present flannel and dark jeans with a neon piece of plastic on his head. I want us to stay friends, and the sooner I apologize and move him away from his irritation at me, the better.

I step out of my car, and when I close the door, the sound of it draws Rusty's attention, his head turning to look in my direction. He's too far away for me to see the minute facial expressions that always give away how he really feels, but I can imagine his lips are dipping down into a frown.

I wave a hand but stay where I am. He's seen me; he knows I'm here and that my only reason to be here is to see him, so he'll come over when he's free.

My eyes scan the construction site, taking in the location for Cedar Cider's new brewery and the old barn that has been given new life. It's a perfect location, up on a little hill and visible from Main Street, only a five-minute walk from all the shops that bring in so many tourists throughout the year.

Rusty's worried about how this place will do, but I have a feeling he's going to be blown away by the success on the horizon. I heard Boyd telling my dad about it when he was home for Christmas. "I never call anything a sure bet," he said as they sat at the dining room table playing cards while I stirred my soup. "But this? This is as close to a sure bet as I can imagine."

I doubt Boyd said anything like that to Rusty. He tends to be a little tight-lipped about his opinions on most things, unless he's talking to our dad or his girlfriend, Ruby. I wish Rusty could understand how much people really do believe in him and the decisions he makes. He might not be perfect, but he's a sure bet, and I wish he could see that, too.

It's about ten minutes before he breaks free from whatever he's doing and heads my way. Even though I'm a little nervous about apologizing, I can't help but scan him from head to toe, taking in his broad shoulders and long legs and the beard that tickles my skin when he kisses me.

I look away, clearing my throat. That's not why I'm here.

"Hey," I say as he makes his final approach, my voice soft.

"What's up?" He says it without really looking at me, and I get the feeling that what he would have liked to say instead was *What do you want?*

"I just wanted to come apologize. For last night."

He shakes his head. Takes a deep breath and lets it out, his eyes scanning the ground.

"You were right," I tell him. "I *am* dealing with regret... among other things, but I shouldn't have assumed you would be okay with what I did. And I'm sorry."

"Alright."

I blink. "Alright?"

Rusty nods. "I'm not one to hold a grudge, Bellamy. You apologized. That's enough."

I scratch at my cheek, his reaction unexpected. "Okay, well...thank you."

"You're welcome. Just promise me you're not going to try something like that again. Your brother is important to me, and I told him this shit with us was just to piss off this Connor kid. Don't make me a liar."

I nod. "I promise."

I don't tell him we're already liars.

"Family dinner still on for tomorrow?"

Rusty crosses his arms. "It is. You still coming?"

"I am."

"I'll pick you up at five-thirty."

We stand there for a beat or two, and I can't help but feel like, even though he let me apologize, even though he said he doesn't hold grudges, something is different. His words are stiff and short, and I get the feeling he's ready for me to leave the construction site. Whatever wall had come down between me and Rusty has been put back up, with fortification.

And it becomes my new goal to bring it down again.

"I'm so excited you're here!" Abby's enthusiastic voice envelops me in excitement, and I beam at her.

"Thanks! I'm excited, too." I kick my shoes off next to the pile near the front door and drop my purse on a little table.

After giving us both big hugs, Abby leads me and Rusty into the small living room where there's an L-shaped couch and a coffee table covered with several plates of snacks.

"Feel free to grab something to nibble on if you're hungry now. We're doing a taco bar, but I'm waiting on some last ingredients, so we won't be eating for another 30 minutes or so."

I glance around, looking for my sister. I've been here a few times to hang out with Briar since she moved in with Abby at the end of last year. In just six months or so, they've done a pretty good job making the small cabin feel like home.

There are touches of my sister's modern preferences mixed in with Abby's organic vibes, from the woven art hanging on the walls and the neutral color palette to the natural wood furniture

I'm pretty sure used to belong to Abby's parents. It's homey, the kind of place that feels like you can settle in and take your shoes off.

"Where's Briar?" I ask, taking a seat on a stool at the peninsula countertop that divides the small kitchen from the living room.

Rusty grabs a beer from the fridge and takes a seat next to me.

"She and Andy got done with work a little late, but they'll be here soon. Jackson's on his way, too." She tugs an old casserole dish from the oven and sets it on a cooling rack on the counter that separates us. "I hope you like brownies."

"Are these slutty brownies?" I ask, my mouth salivating at the thought.

"They are."

I pump my fist in excitement, and Abby laughs.

Abby works at Ruthie's, the bakery in town, so everything she makes is incredible, but her slutty brownies are what made her famous, at least with me. It's a cookie base and a brownie top with Double Stuf Oreos in the middle, and it is the most gooey, delectable dessert I've ever had.

"Can I have some right now?"

She giggles. "If you want, but we should let them cool a little bit first."

"Oh trust me, I want. Let me know when they're good to eat because I will literally down the entire tray."

"I didn't realize you had such a sweet tooth," Rusty says.

I lean to the side and bump him with my shoulder. "I'm dating you, aren't I?"

He rolls his eyes and takes a swig from his beer, but I can see the way his lips tilt up just the tiniest fraction. I know he's still mad at me because of Sunday night, but my goal is to make him smile. Rusty can be such a big grump, and there's something inside of me that's relished the way he has smiled in my direction over the past few weeks. I *know* those smiles weren't fake, because almost all of them seemed reluctant.

Those are the best kind.

"Are you guys going to become one of those nauseating couples who are constantly doing and saying adorable things to each other?" Abby asks, mid-laugh. "Because I'm not sure I can handle seeing my brother like that."

Rusty shakes his head. "You think it's easy for me to watch you and Jackson being all loved up?"

"Or for me to see Briar and Andy?" I add, leaning into Rusty's body and linking my arm with his. "Face it, sister—PDA is a-comin'."

Abby rolls her eyes. "I guess I can't gripe about it too much, huh? Apparently we landed in an exclusive club of sisters who date their brothers' friends."

"I better be the only friend you're dating."

I turn, spotting Jackson walking through the living room and into the kitchen. He places a kiss on Abby's temple then lifts a bottle of tequila for us to see.

"Grabbed this from the store. You were out," he tells Rusty.

I tuck my lips into my mouth and glance up at Rusty with a sheepish expression. He just chuckles under his breath and takes another sip of his beer.

"Sorry I haven't been around much lately. I've been—"

"I don't want to know," Rusty says quickly. "I'm happy to live in blissful ignorance and an empty house if that's how it's going to be."

Jackson smirks and tugs some margarita mix from the cabinet, setting it on the counter next to the tequila. "I figured if we were doing tacos tonight, we should *definitely* do margaritas. Who wants one?"

The reminder of my nasty tequila hangover from yesterday morning is enough to get me to pass, and Rusty declines as well, raising his beer. Abby wants one and so does Jackson, so he gets going mixing everything together.

We shoot the shit for a while, talking about nothing in particular until Briar and Andy arrive a little while later with the onion and cilantro for the tacos.

"Where's the cheese? And the sour cream and tomatoes?" Jackson asks, looking shocked at our minimal topping spread.

"We're doing street tacos," Andy says. "Onion and cilantro are all you need."

Jackson's eyes widen, then the two launch into a hot debate about the merits of different types of Mexican food.

"They're always like this," Briar offers, leaning against the counter next to me. "Heard you went to bonfire night and got a little tipsy."

I groan. "Yeah. I might have had a little too much, followed by a little *more* too much at Rusty's later."

"Everything okay?"

Smiling, I lean forward and wrap my arms around my sister's middle, and she follows my lead, wrapping her arms around my shoulders.

The closeness I've been developing with Briar is still new. She's not a very talkative person by nature, tending to keep her emotions and opinions close to her chest. Ever since she moved back to Cedar Point, I've been trying to get to know her better, spend more time with her.

At first, I could tell it was foreign to her, but something

clicked into place a while back. It's like she removed some of the barriers she had surrounding her, letting me see inside a bit more. Not entirely, because that's not Briar, but a little bit.

So, her asking me if everything's okay is her trying to keep that connection alive, and I appreciate it more than she knows. Her willingness to start opening up to me somewhat is probably why I feel so sure I can get Rusty to bring his own wall back down. I've already been around the block with my sister, and it worked.

"Thanks for asking," I tell her. "I'm good."

She gives me a soft smile and nods. "I'm glad."

A few minutes later, everything is laid out on the counter, and we each move through the kitchen preparing our plates before heading outside to the little grassy area that leads to their short dock and the picnic table I am almost certain must have been swiped from one of the campgrounds at Forks.

As we eat dinner, Briar shares about her recent participation in a floral competition. She took fourth and is very proud. Abby talks about her ideas for possibly creating a social media presence for her home baking. Andy briefly says things at One Stop are going well, then Jackson and Rusty discuss progress with the brewery.

When their eyes turn to me, I realize they're wanting me to share about my life as well.

"Um…I'm studying for my fourth and final CPA Exam section. That's the big deal right now, because it is notorious for being the hardest."

"I thought you already graduated." Jackson looks confused.

I nod. "I did. The CPA Exam is one of the steps for getting a license. You do it after you graduate."

"And what's the plan after you're done with your exams?"

Andy asks as he reaches across the table for salsa. "You gonna work for someone in town?"

I take a big breath and blow it out dramatically. "I mean, I want to start my own accounting business and do work primarily for local businesses. George is retiring, so it wouldn't be like I'm poaching his people to start my own firm." I take a sip of my water. "But I have to get in a bunch of work experience before I get licensed, so I have to figure that part out."

"You should ask George if he'll give you a job," Jackson suggests. "I mean, if that would count. I'm not sure how it all works."

I blink, realizing that in all of my extensive planning, I'd never even considered that idea.

"You know, I might actually talk to him about that," I say, smiling.

Jackson winks at me before the conversation breaks off into little side comments and questions about all the information we just shared. It makes me wonder if they do this every time they get together, share updates about their lives and everything they have going on.

I like this. I like it for my sister, and I like it for Rusty. It's great that they have each other to talk to, people to listen to them when they have something to say, who are curious and ask questions.

The guys get up from the table and head over to a little bricked-in hole in the ground surrounded by a bunch of mismatched chairs as us ladies clear the table and take the dishes inside. When I step back out just a few minutes later, they have the beginnings of a campfire going.

"Tonight is the perfect night for a fire," Abby says as she settles into a chair next to Andy.

I glance around, quickly realizing there are only five chairs.

"Oh, shoot. I'm sorry, Bellamy." She starts to get up. "I have an extra chair in my car. Normally it's just the five of us, so I didn't think to grab it."

"Don't worry about it," I tell her, walking toward where Rusty is seated on the only wooden chair around the fire. "I'd rather sit here anyway."

I see Rusty's eyes widen just slightly as I stop in front of him, but it only takes him a second to follow my lead and adjust how he's sitting to stick his knee out just a little bit. I take a seat and wrap my arm around his shoulders, trying to ignore the flutter I get when one of his hands rests on my hip, the other on my knee. His fingers flex, gripping and releasing a few times, like he can't decide what to do.

My original intent was to make myself physically close to Rusty, hoping it would contribute to breaking down his wall again. Even though I wasn't trying to make this in any way sexual, I now realize my mistake. For whatever reason, when he touches me, it lights me on fire. Rusty sets something inside me ablaze without even trying, and I can't help my desire to snuggle closer into him.

I stare into the fire, the sounds of the conversation around me turning into a distant murmur I can barely understand as I focus on the feel of Rusty's body surrounding mine, holding me. He says something, and I feel the vibration of it through his chest.

I close my eyes for just a minute.

"Let's just hope you don't embarrass the Fuller name any more than you already have."

I feel Rusty tense beneath me, and my head whips to the side, glaring at Abby, who has a smile on her face. I might have

144

checked out of the conversation for a few minutes, but I heard what she said with crystal clarity.

"What did you just say?"

She waves her hand like it's not a big deal. "Oh, I was just teasing. Rusty's got a history, you know? Now that he's dating you, maybe people will start to see him differently." She gestures between the two of us. "You're super cute together. I was just telling him not to screw it up."

"Well it's never easy to succeed at things when people are constantly reminding you of every mistake you've ever made." My tone reflects the irritation I feel inside. Now I understand why Rusty feels like people in town are just waiting for him to fail, why he shared that huge emotional weight he's been carrying around the other night in the car.

"Woah, Bellamy," Abby says, holding her hands up as concern flashes across her face. "I was just teasing."

"Hey, you don't have to defend me." Rusty squeezes my thigh.

"Rusty is an incredible person," I continue, ignoring them both. "I don't doubt you know that—you're his sister, so you probably know him better than any of us, but I can promise you Rusty is hard enough on himself about everything in his life. He is *constantly* worried about letting down the people he loves, so what he doesn't need is for the most important person in his life to add fuel to that fire."

Everyone is silent, only the crackling of the burning wood sounding around us.

Abby blinks a few times, and I can tell even in the dimming light that her eyes are growing glassy. Part of me feels bad about the fact that I might have made someone cry, but honestly, maybe she *needs* to cry about it. Maybe she *needs* to be reminded that she can't shit on people she loves, even as a joke.

While I'm sure she didn't have bad intentions, I doubt she realizes the impact her words have on her brother. I sat in the car the other day and listened to the worry in his voice as he told me he doesn't want to be a failure, told me he's terrified of letting people down, and if there's any chance I might be able to ease some of that fear, no matter how small a part, I'm taking it.

No matter what bridge I might burn in the process.

chapter fourteen
rusty

"You didn't have to do that."

Bellamy turns to look at me from where she stands at the end of the dock, her chin high, an expression on her face so stubborn I want to just kiss it right off.

"Yes, I did. I don't care if we're actually dating or not—I'll defend you to anyone who tries to talk shit. Whether it's your sister or someone in town…or even you."

I should be irritated at her for dampening the mood, but I'm honestly feeling a fullness in my chest that I wasn't expecting. This is the second time Bellamy has leapt to my defense, the first time being in the car on Sunday. Maybe I never realized how important something like that is to me until just now, that ride-or-die mentality. Hailey certainly wasn't ever that way, and it's been a long time since I've let a woman get close enough for it to matter.

With Bellamy, it matters. Even if we're technically just friends, having her on my team makes me feel like I could face anything and not get knocked down. Or, hell, even if I *do* get knocked down, I have someone there to dress my wounds and tell me to get back out there.

The more I spend time with Bellamy, the more I'm starting to realize that...developing real, true feelings for her is more than just a possibility. It's a reality. I keep telling myself I need to work on keeping a boundary so nothing happens between us, but that ship has sailed. It has sailed and crashed into a rock and sunk to the bottom of the ocean.

I'm falling for Bellamy Mitchell, and I don't know how to stop it.

And the truth is...I'm not sure I want to.

"Anyone ever tell you you're a little stubborn?" I ask, my voice teasing.

Even in just the moonlight, I can tell she blushes, but she lifts her chin again, only further proving my point.

"Maybe."

I laugh. "Alright, just checking."

We stand in silence together for a few minutes, just looking out at the water. I suspect she's trying to cool off or manage her embarrassment about having barked at my sister. Possibly both.

Regardless, I'm unable to help it when I reach out and wrap my arm around her shoulders, tugging her into my side. She looks up at me, surprise evident in her expression.

"Thank you," I tell her. "It's been a long time since I've had someone be so adamantly on my side. I didn't realize I missed it."

Whatever tenseness was left in her body melts away, and she sinks into me. I revel in her closeness for as long as I can, until I think we should probably head inside. I press a kiss on the crown of her head, and when she looks up at me again, it takes everything inside of me not to bend down and kiss her where I really want to.

"Ready to take off?" I ask her instead.

She nods, and I reach down, taking her hand in mine, and we walk up the dock and back to the house together.

When I open the door a few nights later, my sister is standing there with an uncomfortable smile on her face. She texted me earlier, asking if she could come by and drop off some banana bread she baked for me. It's my favorite, so I don't doubt she made it on purpose so she could come over to talk.

"How's work going?" I ask, shutting the door behind her then trailing her into the living room.

"Good. I've started creating the new summer menu, and people are really enjoying it."

I nod. "That's great. What goes on a summer menu at a bakery?"

"A lot of fruit-forward stuff. Strawberry pie is a big one. Cakes that are kept cold, lemon sweet rolls, blueberry bread."

Rubbing my stomach, I smile at her. "You're making me hungry."

She grins back and lifts the Tupperware she's carrying. "Then I came at the perfect time."

Abby steps into the kitchen and begins working, first tugging out a cutting board and putting the bread out, then slicing off a few pieces and handing me one on a paper towel.

"A peace offering," she tells me as I take a bite.

I pin her with a look. "We don't need a peace offering," I tell her, uncaring that I have food in my mouth. I swallow my bite. "I'm not upset with you."

"Well your girlfriend sure is."

I grin, remembering Bellamy's outrage on Tuesday. "Yeah, well…she's sensitive."

Abby snorts. "I'll say." She takes her own bite of the bread, swallowing before speaking again. "But she was right."

Before I can try to tell Abby she doesn't have anything to worry about, she holds up her hand.

"She *was*, Rus. You've done so much for me."

"Come on, you don't have to—"

"Let me finish."

I sigh and brace myself against the bar that separates the living room and kitchen.

"After mom and dad died, you sacrificed everything in your life for me, to make sure I didn't get separated from you, to make sure I didn't lose my life, too…and I don't think I've ever really thought about how that was for you. Sure, I thought about how it was for *us*, the pain and everything…but not about how it was for *you*."

She shakes her head.

"Rusty, I am the last person who should have ever judged you for the way you coped. I should have always had your back, especially if anyone in town ever had something to say about you. And I am so sorry that I didn't."

My chest feels tight. I didn't realize how much I needed my sister to say something like that until she was actually saying it.

"I appreciate it, Abs. I do. I hope you know I've never been upset with you about it. I know being part of this town has always been important to you, and I'm sorry I haven't paid more attention to how *my* behavior affected you."

Abby offers me another piece of bread, and I accept.

"Well, you might not have been upset about it, but Bellamy was upset enough for the both of you." She smiles at that. "I've gotta say, I didn't really get it when you first told me you were dating her, but now, consider me officially on board the Busty train."

I bark out a laugh. "What's a busty train?"

"You know, it's your two names together. Bellamy and Rusty—Busty."

Shaking my head, I laugh again. "Absolutely not."

"Oh, come on. Rellamy sounds lame."

"So don't call us Rellamy."

"Well, then what will I call you?"

"Bellamy and Rusty."

"How about Besty? That's better than Busty, right?"

I sigh. "This is not going to be a thing."

"Just you wait. I'm gonna get Bellamy on board and you're gonna be Besty forever!"

I roll my eyes and shove the second piece of bread in my mouth in one go. My sister is a nutball sometimes, but I love her more than anything.

We talk for a little bit longer, then she leaves, letting me know she and Jackson are going out of town to San Francisco for a quick weekend away.

"Be safe," I tell her as she walks out to her car.

"Will do, dad," she teases before dropping down into the driver's seat.

The first time she jokingly called me dad, I was upset. I know I sit in this weird middle place for her—partial father figure, partial brother—but I'm not her dad, and I reminded her of that back then.

Over the years, though, it's bothered me less and less, not because I think I *am* her father in any way, but because I do look at her as the most precious thing in my life. It's how I imagine our parents looked at us when they were alive, so now when she says it, I take it as a compliment, as an indicator that I'm loving her the best I can.

And how could that ever be something I let bother me?

On Friday mornings, after I go for a swim, I spend a few hours at The Pines, the elderly community in Cedar Point, playing cards with a group of men who are in their 70s and 80s. I've been doing it fairly consistently since I moved back to town after my parents passed, as a way to honor my dad.

He used to come here once a week for years just to watch movies with his mentor, the man who taught him everything he knew about cars. My father used to tell me the most beautiful thing we can do for the elderly is give them our time, because we have so much of it, and they have so little left.

He was a big softy.

Ever since we broke ground on the brewery project, though, I've struggled to make it to the 10am bridge game with Gilbert, Arthur, and Stan. So when I sit down Friday morning at the little card table set up on the back patio of The Pines, I'm unsurprised when Gil gives me the stink eye.

"Look who decided we're worth his time." There isn't any

real heat in his voice, but I don't doubt there *is* a tiny bit of hurt.

"I come with apology gifts," I tell them. "Stuff with the brewery has been kind of nuts, and I'm sorry for bailing. Hopefully this will make it up to you." I hoist a six-pack of beer out of a duffle, thunk it into the middle of the table, and then follow it with a second.

Stan grins and instantly plucks one from the cardboard carrier, popping off the cap with the opener he always has on hand and taking a long pull. I don't even contemplate pointing out the time to him. I figure he's old enough to make his own decisions.

"Consider yourself forgiven," Art tells me, leaning back in his chair, his fingers folded together and resting on his large stomach. "Besides, we know you've been working extra hard on your business."

His response is classic Arthur—very paternal, supportive, and without any drama.

Gil, on the other hand, eyes the beer like it's poisoned.

"A bribe?" he huffs. "I don't even drink."

I was waiting for him to say that, and I reach into my bag to pull out one final gift: a 12-bottle box of Mexican Coke. His favorite.

His eyes narrow.

"Come on, Gil. You know I missed you guys, and I promise I won't miss any more Friday-morning games for the rest of the summer."

Eventually, he grabs a deck of cards and begins shuffling, his way of telling me he's accepted my apology.

"Tell us about the brewery, Rusty," Stan says, lighting a cigarette and inhaling deeply before exhaling into the air above us. "Are we gonna live to see this place become a reality, or what?"

"It's coming along." I move the boxes off the table and set

them on the floor. "The barn's been refinished and cleaned up, and they're working on electrical now. Plumbing, too."

"I loved the Kelso Barn," Art says, and I know he's going to jump into the same thing he always tells us about the old barn that used to belong to the Kelso family. "When I was fifteen, I spent a few months helping Doug out by cleaning the stables." He shakes his head, a smile on his face. "Worst summer of my life."

He says it like that every time, and I know there was some kind of formative experience that happened back then. You can't call something the worst anything and talk about it with that kind of smile.

"You still in business with Patty and Mark's boy?" Stan asks, puffing out another cloud of smoke as Gil deals the cards.

I nod, smiling as I accept my cards and begin organizing them in my hand. They ask the same round of questions almost every week. It might have been about two months since my last time playing with them, but this information never changes, so it always makes me want to laugh.

"Yup, him and my buddy Jackson."

"The one who's datin' your sister."

I nod again. "That's him."

Gil shakes his head. "Your generation. Back in my day, if a guy went after his best pal's sister, there'd be fists exchanged."

"Oh, come off it, Gil," Art says, laughing. "Don't act like you weren't a fan of Peggy Orsen. We all were."

"Yeah, and she was Marty's sister, so we didn't do nothin' about it, did we?"

The three of them launch into a conversation about somebody named Marty and his sister from back in the day, and I just lean back in my chair and listen. Gil, Art, and Stan all went to Cedar Point School together when it was a K-12, before the town had a boom in the 70s that led to the need to split into primary and secondary.

It's like this almost every time I visit. Gil pitches a fit about something and Art grins and teases and they all trip over into memories about growing up. I usually listen to them pretty closely, but today the topic of conversation is pushing me into my own memories...about *my* best friend's sister.

I never thought I'd be in this position, and I *definitely* didn't think it would be with Bellamy. She's a solid decade younger than me, so the idea of her ever being someone I was interested in just...wasn't a thing.

But now, things are different. Even if it's wrong, I can't seem to help it. There's something about her that speaks to me, that speaks to my soul, a connection I didn't think I would ever have with someone again.

After Hailey, I was pretty sure I wouldn't ever want a relationship, period. She broke things off with me during what was the most difficult, trying time of my life, and you don't just bounce back from that.

With Bellamy, though, something tells me I'd never need to worry about that. She seems like the kind of woman who, once you're in with her, it's a ride-or-die situation. That loyalty is hard to come by because it requires an element of self-sacrifice not everyone is willing to commit to.

I shake my head and try to focus back on what the guys are talking about. I don't need to wonder about Bellamy's level of loyalty. She's Boyd's sister, and I already promised him things between us are just for show.

"I'm tellin' ya, he told me she's coming back to town to watch her grandson in the TBA Swim."

"Marty told you that?"

Stan nods. "Fred died fifteen years ago, and she hasn't remarried. Maybe you could ask her to dinner."

Gil gives him a sour look. "I'm not asking Peggy to dinner. We're almost 80. What am I gonna do, take her on a date?"

"Yeah. That's exactly what you could do."

He shakes his head. "A date to the cafeteria of this dump? You're a fool if you think that's what I'm gonna do." He glares at the cards in his hands, his expression making it clear he doesn't want to talk about it any longer.

But Art speaks again. "Well, there's still a few weeks before the TBA, so you should at least think about it."

Every summer, Cedar Point hosts the There and Back Again Swimming Competition to promote literacy. It used to benefit the local library, but after a horrible storm a while back, the building had to be torn down and the city sold the land to a developer who ended up creating a bunch of new storefronts on Main Street.

The city council has continued the TBA Swim every summer with the intention of having the money raised go toward the creation of a new library on a plot of land near the primary school just outside of downtown. They're expecting to break ground next year, and this year's swim event is larger than it ever has been in the hopes that they'll reach their target before they begin construction.

"Am I still taking you guys to the marina?" I ask, keeping with the topic but helping to shift things away from Art and Stan harping on Gil. "I bought seats on the finish line."

Stan nods. "I'm in."

"I'll definitely be going."

I'm unsurprised by Art's response. He used to be a librarian and was part of the original committee that created the TBA Swim back in the 90s. He told me the only thing he wants before he dies is to see a library reopened for the town.

"I might be busy this year."

"Oh yeah? Busy doing what?" Stan says to Gil. "Because how I see it, the only thing we're busy doing right now is counting our meds in the morning and getting to the cafeteria early enough to make sure Don doesn't eat all the banana cream pie."

I chew on the inside of my cheek, trying not to laugh, but that's when Gil surprises me and throws his cards down.

"I've had enough out of you for today," he says to Stan, glowering. Then he pushes back from the table and slowly stands. "Rusty, thank you for the Coke. I'll see you next week." He pulls the box of soda from the pile next to me and walks gingerly away from us.

Stan sighs.

"This Peggy thing sounds like a sore subject," I offer, trying not to make any judgments.

"Oh, he's just mad because he didn't have the cojones to ask Peggy out in high school and Fred did," Stan says, waving a hand dismissively in the direction that Gil just went. "You have to go after the things you want in life, even if it's scary, and Gil was just never willing to take risks."

"And it would have been a risk to ask Peggy out?"

Art chuckles. "You should have seen her brother. You think I'm a big guy? Marty Orsen was the *biggest* guy."

"Nobody would ask her out because we were all afraid of Marty, which is why the fact that she ended up with Fred was such a shock." Stan reaches out and begins collecting the cards Gil threw down. "He was a nerd, you know? Small guy. But he was smitten with Peggy, and he didn't let Marty intimidate him."

"Treated her like a queen, too. And *that's* what impressed Marty the most."

They continue to tell stories about Fred and Peggy for a few minutes before we begin playing a quiet game of rummy, our typical backup when there are fewer than four of us.

My mind flits over what Stan said about Gil, him not going after Peggy when he had the chance. Part of me thinks I should be taking mental notes for myself, but it's hard to compare my situation with Bellamy to what happened with Gil and Peggy, or even Fred and Peggy. It sounds like Gil was too afraid to give her more than a look, and Fred was an upstanding guy Marty approved of.

Boyd wouldn't ever approve of me dating his sister. We've been through too much. He's seen me at my worst lows and knows most of my most embarrassing moments, so even though I don't doubt that he loves me, there's no way I'd ever be seen as worthy in his eyes.

Not a chance in hell.

chapter fifteen
bellamy

I'm lazily perusing a handful of recently posted jobs for un-licensed accountants online when my phone rings, Stace's name flashing on the screen. I debate whether or not to answer.

She seems like a really nice person, but she's also engaged to Connor, who is rapidly falling from his long-standing perch on the shiny throne of my admiration. I can only imagine she's calling to schedule another coffee date, and to be honest, I'm on the fence.

Ultimately, my inability to let people down forces me to accept the call.

"Hey."

"Hi, Bellamy. How's your morning going?"

I snort. "Dreamy. Just staring at my computer screen, bored as hell and wishing I were doing just about anything else. How about you?"

"My day is going a little better than yours, I think. Connor took some time off for the three-day weekend, and we're heading out on Mr. Pruitt's boat today."

"That definitely sounds like a lot more fun than this."

"I love that you say that, because I wanted to invite you and Rusty to come along."

Internally I groan. *Shit.* An afternoon on a boat with Connor? I can't imagine something I want less.

"You know, I think Rusty's busy today, but I can call him and check," I offer, hoping for a way out.

"Yeah, give him a call to see, but you should come either way. Sounds like you could use a break from whatever you're working on."

I instantly realize my mistake. I've basically painted myself into a corner. By saying I was bored, I've implied that I have free time. By saying going out on a boat sounds fun, I've already made it clear that I'd enjoy going along.

Shit.

"Alright, well…I'll check with Rusty and let you know."

"Awesome! I think we're leaving in like an hour or so. Just text me."

We say our goodbyes and I rest my forehead against my desk, thumping it gently against the wood a few times for good measure. Me and Stace and Connor on a boat together…god, that sounds terrible.

After giving myself a few seconds, I call Rusty, hoping like hell he answers his phone.

"What's up?"

"Please tell me you're free today."

There's a pause, and I can imagine his serious face thinking it over before responding.

"Why?"

I sigh. "Can you tell me if you're free first?"

"No."

Groaning, I push back from my desk and walk over to my bed, dramatically flopping down on my mess of blankets, my bed still unmade from this morning.

"Just tell me what's going on."

"Stace invited us to go out with Connor on his dad's boat for the day, and I can't imagine something more horrible, so I'm hoping you're free to come with."

"If you can't imagine something more horrible, just say you can't go."

"I already basically said I can."

Rusty is silent again for a long moment.

"I mean, this is why we're fake dating right? This is the kind of thing you agreed to do."

I don't mean for it to sound the way it comes out, but I'm also not expecting the curt way Rusty responds.

"I know what I agreed to, Bellamy." He sighs, and I can almost feel him bristling through the phone. "When are they leaving?"

"In an hour."

"Send me the details."

Before I can even say anything—*Thank you, you're the best, you're saving my life*—he hangs up.

I'm pretty sure the Pruitts keep their boat in the south marina near the resort, but when I flick a text off to Stace to let her know we can come, I also ask her to tell me where they're docked. Then I push myself out of bed and begin digging through my dresser, looking for a bathing suit.

It only occurs to me right then that Rusty will be seeing me in a bikini, and I'll most likely be seeing him in swim trunks. I mean, we live near a lake and I've known him long enough that we've certainly seen each other in bathing suits before, but things feel different now than they were when I was younger.

Rusty's not just my brother's friend anymore. He's a man I've kissed, a very attractive man I've kissed more than once.

And one I'd like to kiss again if I wasn't so sure he'd push me away.

It wouldn't make sense for Rusty to come get me since my house is in the opposite direction, so we agree to meet at South Bank Marina. When I finally find a parking spot amidst the holiday weekend surge, I spot Stace and Connor almost immediately at the end of Dock 2, loading a cooler and a few bags of stuff onto Mr. Pruitt's boat. I slowly unload, hoping to delay long enough so Rusty will get here quickly, but he texts to say he needs to swing by One Stop and will be a few minutes late. So, I head off toward their boat on my own.

"Hey, girl!" Stace says, waving with an outstretched arm and a wide smile.

I drop my heavy beach bag at my feet. "Thanks for the invite."

"I'm so glad you could come. I thought Rusty was coming, too?"

I nod. "He is. He just had to swing by the store. He'll be here in a few minutes."

Stace grins. "Awesome. I'm glad he's coming along." She bumps me with an elbow, her voice lowering just slightly. "Maybe Rusty can rub off a little on Connor, huh?"

She laughs at her own words just as Connor hoists himself up off the boat.

"Hey, Bells," he says, smiling.

I really wish he'd stop calling me that.

"We're almost ready to go. I'm just gonna run back up to the car for a sec. Forgot my sunglasses."

He jogs away down the dock, leaving Stace and me behind.

"Come on, let's get comfortable." She steps down into the boat, and I hop in after her, putting my bag on one of the seats.

I'm not a huge boat person. I know just enough from living at a lake and being around people who enjoy boating and lake life, and even *I* know Connor's dad's boat is really nice. It's long and sleek and has a canopy thing for shade and seats that are warm from sitting in the sun. Everything shines like it's brand new, and there are two big engines on the back and a big metal beam I'm pretty sure is for wakeboarding.

"I grew up near the water, but we weren't really water people," Stace says, interrupting my thoughts as she plops down in one of the captain's chairs. "I think I've been out on the water like…maybe three times in my whole life, so I have been *begging* Connor to do this ever since we got here."

I grin. "Holiday weekends can be a little wild, but lake days are always fun. Nothing feels quite like soaking in that vitamin D, and there's just something about swimming in the middle of a massive lake like this that's freeing."

She rubs her hands together. "I'm not sure I'll be brave enough to get in the water."

"What?" I laugh. "Come on, you have to!"

"We'll see." But she's shaking her head no even as she says it. "Maybe if Connor gets in with me."

I open my mouth to mention that the boat probably has life jackets, but I get distracted when I spot Rusty halfway down the dock and heading our way. He's wearing a pair of tan board shorts, a loose tank, flip flops, and sunglasses, and he's carrying a cooler up on one shoulder, a towel flung over the other.

"Damn, the way you look at him is just as awestruck as how he looks at you."

I glance over to Stace, finding her watching me with a smile. I want to tell her there's no way he looks at me like this—like I'm a piece of meat he wants to devour—but I keep my mouth shut. I can barely admit to *myself* that I'm looking at Rusty this way.

His muscles flex as he drops it down to the ground next to the boat, and he glances at me with a smile. "Hey, babe."

"Hi." I say it almost shyly, and I want to kick myself.

Rusty chuckles and takes a step into the boat, lifting the cooler with him. Once it's securely on the ground, he leans down to me, slipping his hand behind my neck and kissing me on the lips. It doesn't surprise me as much as the first time, but it packs just as much punch.

"Missed you this morning," I tell him, the words slipping out of my mouth naturally, as if I really did miss him when I woke up.

Did I?

"Sorry, just had a few things to get done. But I'll make it up to you." He says the last part with a grin then turns to look at Stace. "Good to see you again."

She nods. "You, too."

"We were just talking about how Stace is nervous to get in the water."

"Oh, no, really?" Rusty shakes his head. "It's so worth it. You're gonna have a blast."

Stace just shrugs. "We'll see."

The three of us each start talking about what we have in our coolers—Rusty obviously brought the beers, and Stace and Connor packed snacks—and the general weather for the day until Connor gets back a few minutes later. He thumps down into the boat, his sunglasses firmly in place, and steps right up to Rusty.

"Fuller," he says.

As if it's possible, Rusty seems to stand a little taller as he extends his hand.

"Pruitt."

They shake, and for whatever reason, it feels like I just witnessed two rival football captains sizing each other up before a game. Thankfully, the vibe between them eases as they step away from each other. Connor heads to the helm, and Rusty sits down next to me and drapes his arm around my shoulders while Stace walks over and slips into one of the seats at the bow.

"Alright, time for a day on the lake," Connor says, switching the engine on and backing the boat out of its slip. "North Bay?"

"Sounds good," Rusty answers.

We're mostly quiet as we travel through the low wake zone surrounding the marina, just enjoying the sun and the light breeze from being out on the water. When we pick up speed, Rusty's embrace grows more secure around my shoulders, tucking me in tighter to his side, and I don't complain, enjoying the feeling of being next to him.

After about fifteen minutes, Connor drops the speed of the boat, and we cruise slowly into North Bay, an area of the lake that is reserved just for town residents. It's not a policed area or anything, but you have to have a Cedar Point address on your driver's license to be eligible for a pass, and non-residents will get a fine if they're found in the vicinity.

I've never been a fan of exclusivity—I am definitely a 'the more the merrier' kind of girl—but there is something really nice about being able to enjoy a quieter area on the lake during busier months, and *especially* on a holiday weekend when the lake feels overly full. We passed a few party boats on our way here, and I have no interest in dropping anchor near one of those.

"This a good spot?" Connor asks once we've gotten to a little cove that's fairly empty about 10 yards or so from one of the community beaches. We all nod, and a few seconds later I hear the release of the anchor as it begins its descent to the lake floor.

"God, this whole town is so gorgeous," Stace says, coming back to where we're sitting, her hair wild and untamed from the wind that whipped it around as she sat in the front. "The trees and the lake and the rocks…I mean, look at that house."

I glance over, spotting my favorite house on the lake, an older home with a kind of Nantucket, east coast vibe and a large grassy yard that extends before it hits shoreline.

"That's one of the only houses on the lake that's built on a beach," I tell her. "It's my favorite."

She shakes her head and tugs open the cooler she and Connor brought. "Absolutely gorgeous. It has such a warm vibe about it. I would *love* to live in a house like that."

"Nah, you don't want that," Connor says, shaking his head and looking like he smelled something bad. "I can only imagine the maintenance problems you get with a house that old."

Stace rolls her eyes. "But that's just one of those things you deal with because you love the house."

He shrugs. "I'd want something much newer. I don't want to deal with any problems, or anything super old."

"It's all about how you look at it," Rusty interjects. "Newer construction might *seem* to have less problems, but really it's all just masked with money and flash, and a lot of times, that covers up poor construction or shabby materials. Older builds have proven they pass the test of time and are more reliable."

Connor crosses his arms. "Or they're just old and broken down and useless."

Rusty grins. "You can usually look at something older and tell if it's broken down by the way it's been maintained. That house looks to be in incredible shape." He pauses. "And you should see the size of the kitchen. It's massive."

I glance between the two guys, trying to understand what's happening, because I'm getting the feeling they're talking about something else entirely.

"Connor, stop being weird," Stace says, her eye roll heavily implied by the tone of her voice.

That seems to snap them out of it. Rusty tugs a few beers out of the cooler and pops off the tops before passing them around to everyone. Connor messes with the stereo, turning on some classic rock, and Stace lays out a towel on the front bow and strips down to her bikini, a tiny neon thing that shows off a lot of ass. She declares that she's gonna get a little tan before stretching out on her back.

"Well, I'm ready to get in the water," I say, turning to Rusty. "Wanna join me?"

He grins and takes off his sunglasses, his bright, beautiful eyes sparkling as he looks at me. "Absolutely."

Suddenly, I feel a bit self-conscious about getting down to just my bathing suit, and I go to the back end of the boat and look out to the water as I pull off my top and chuck it on the seat then kick off my shorts. I flick my head over and bunch my hair into a knot then loop a rubber band from my wrist around it so the long, thick strands stay out of my face.

"Alright, which end are we jumping off of?" I ask, turning around.

But when I look at Rusty, he looks angry. It's only brief, barely there and gone in a flash, before he takes my hand in his and leads me up to the front of the boat, past Connor who is lighting a cigar where he sits in the captain's chair, edging by Stace where she's tanning.

"Ready?"

I grin, unable to hold back my smile. "Yeah."

"One, two, three, jump!" he says, and I squeal as we go feet first into the water, plunging into the cool lake, my body chilling instantly.

When I break through the surface, I'm laughing, and so is Rusty. God, laughter looks good on him.

Kicking my feet to stay afloat, I begin swimming toward the rear of the boat, wanting quick access to a ladder out of the water. My teeth are already chattering even though I've only been in for two seconds.

"I always forget how cold it is, no matter how long I live here," I say as I brace my hands on the step at the back, near the motor.

"If you're cold, I can warm you up," Rusty tells me, a mischievous grin on his face as he drifts in my direction, having followed me around from the other end of the boat.

I assume he's joking, so I laugh, but then he tugs me toward him, his arms wrapping around me as we float together, the warmth of his body soothing compared to the not-quite-frigid temps of the lake.

"How are you already an ice cube?" he asks me, rubbing up and down on my skin under the water in a way that feels both caring and sensual in the same movement.

"I just get cold very easily," I answer, my teeth continuing to chatter. "It's genetic—my mom and Briar are the same way—but I love being in the lake, so I usually just suck it up."

Rusty chuckles and shakes his head. "I'm always a furnace," he says. "I wear nothing to bed, even during the winter, because I'm constantly a million degrees."

I'm sure he's just saying it conversationally—I mean, what other reason could there possibly be to tell me he sleeps naked?—but my mind still tries to conjure up a vision of Rusty, nude and reclined on his bed, his long, strong frame and contoured muscles laid out in repose.

"Abby's like you, though," he continues. "Always cold, so we were constantly fighting over the thermostat. I'd wake up sweating because she'd snuck down the hall and changed it to 75 in the middle of the night."

I make a face. "Okay, that I can't get behind. I am a firm 68 degrees at night kind of girl. I just pile up blankets and wear a good pair of fuzzy socks."

His lips tilt up. "You seem like a fuzzy sock kind of girl."

"And what does a fuzzy sock kind of girl seem like?" I ask as Rusty continues to rub my arms and shoulders to warm me up.

He shrugs under the water. "Like you."

I snort. "Well, thanks. That's a lot of help."

"I just mean, you seem like someone who likes to…I don't know, snuggle up with a good book, you know? And those people tend to like fuzzy socks and comfy blankets and little reading nooks. And tea, they always like tea."

I giggle. "Okay, well show me the type of person who *doesn't* like those things, because all of that sounds absolutely divine."

At that, his head falls back, and he laughs, the sound echoing across the water.

"Told you," he eventually says. "Fuzzy sock kind of girl."

We float there for a few more minutes, and it's hard not to feel lulled into a state of comatose bliss in Rusty's hands. At this point, it feels less like he's trying to warm me so I can stay in the water and more like he's just touching me anywhere he can reach.

His hands run up and down my biceps before gently doing the same on my thighs, lightly brushing my stomach as they move. I feel that gentle graze like I've been struck by lightning, my entire body erupting in goose bumps, and I know Rusty can feel them, because he's continuing to rub my skin.

My breathing picks up, and I catch him staring at my lips. It feels like we're suddenly so much closer to each other than we were just a few minutes ago. The thought of kissing him crosses my mind, but I instantly tamp it down.

I promised him I wouldn't do something like that again, and even though we're here with Connor and Stace, even though I'm sure I could explain it away just like Rusty's mild kiss when he first got on the boat, I can't break my promise to him.

I can't let him down, no matter how desperately I want to kiss him in this moment.

"I should probably get out of the water," I say, my voice calm and quiet, even though I feel a riot of want and need rushing through my veins.

He watches me for a long moment, and for just a second, I see the thought reflected on his face almost like words as it runs through his mind, the thought of kissing me.

Then he lets it pass and backs away, giving me the space to climb onto the step and hoist myself back onto the boat. I grab my towel and wrap myself up, enjoying the way the warmth of the air and the heat from the sun-baked fabric feels on my skin.

When I glance back at Rusty, I find him still floating in the water, looking up at me.

"I'm gonna swim over to the shore." He turns and swims off, his body strong and fast as he cuts through the water, heading to the beach a little ways away.

Clearly, he needs some space, too.

chapter sixteen
rusty

I stretch out on the sand, catching my breath and enjoying the feel of the sun as it heats my body.

I swim several times a week, so the short distance from the boat to the shore wasn't anything that tired me. The reason I'm trying to slow my breathing is because of how it feels to be around Bellamy, and the fact that she has this undeniable way of leaving me breathless.

God, I can't believe I'm even admitting that to myself, but I almost kissed her again. I need to stop doing that. I need to remember what's at stake here: my closest friendship.

There isn't a bone in my body that could imagine a world where I'd betray the one man who stood beside me when my universe fell apart. When my parents died, it was just me against the world. Sure, I had Abby, but I had to be *her* support.

Boyd was mine, and through it all, he was there for me, listening to me cry or bitch or just sitting in silence with me as I fumed about how unfair it all was. Not only was he my greatest support emotionally, he was also one financially by investing in Cedar Cider when I was scrambling for a way to make our lives in Cedar Point stick.

I didn't have many options. I know almost nothing about cars, so keeping dad's shop was out, and I sold that off to liquidate so Abby and I could keep the house, which—by the time we got it all figured out—was months behind in mortgage payments. There were death taxes and my college debt, and I knew I'd need to come up with something if Abby wanted to go to college.

When I began fucking around with making my own beer and it tasted damn good, it felt like a possible saving grace, but it *never* would have gotten off the ground without Boyd. I approached both banks in Cedar Point, and neither would give me a loan. I even drove down the mountain to see if I could find some other way to make it work but ended up scrapping that for fear of ending up with a loan shark who would take our house or something. It was a mess.

Then Boyd said he wanted to buy in, said he believed in the product—believed in *me*.

I nearly cried when he said it.

So when I say Cedar Cider wouldn't exist without him, I mean exactly that, and that's why I can't forget about my friendship with him, no matter how intoxicating each new moment is that I spend with Bellamy.

Damn if I don't feel lit up by her on the inside in a way I can't remember ever feeling before.

And I mean ever.

I'm not saying this is the best I've felt since Hailey. I'm saying this is the best I've felt, period. Hard stop.

She makes me feel light inside, like the world isn't this heavy dark place that's hard to manage and hard to face on my own. Bellamy's smile—the way it sits just slightly crooked on her face with that little dimple I always want to kiss—and that damn fucking giggle when she thinks something's really funny…it just hits a rough spot inside of me that I didn't even realize was there.

It's pretty clear to me now that turning off these feelings for her isn't something I'm going to be able to do overnight. It'll just need to happen on its own.

But that doesn't mean I can give in to how it feels, which is why I swam off once she climbed back into the boat. It felt like I needed to put physical distance between us, like I needed an actual lake separating us to make sure I didn't drag her toward me and press my lips to hers.

I was barely able to look away when she took off her clothes and stood standing in her bathing suit, a little blue number I'd like to peel off with my teeth. It sits low on her hips and the small triangles fit snug on her perfect tits. Then I got hard just by warming her skin and feeling my hands pressed against her body, a real feat considering how cold the water is.

Like I said—intoxicating.

I'm thankful, though, that she had the ability to pull away from me when I couldn't manage the strength to do the same. That's Bellamy, though. She promised me she wouldn't try to make something happen between us again, and she's the type of woman to be believed when she makes a promise. It just makes me admire her even more.

I spend quite a while on the shore, lost in my thoughts and the quiet of North Bay before I decide to head back out to the boat. As much as I'm enjoying the solitude of being here on the beach, I also know each minute I'm here is a minute Bellamy has to be with Stace and Connor without me. If I can't be *with* her,

I can at least be next to her so she doesn't have to face that little shit on her own.

I stride into the cold water—a much more difficult task than just plunging in now that I've been warmed by the sun—and begin swimming back out to the boat.

God, I can't stand Connor. He's such a little prick. He reminds me of all the frat bros Jackson was friends with during college. It was one of the few things that has really tested our friendship, and it ultimately proved to me that I can't judge a person until I get to know their character. Jackson is definitely a man with character.

Connor, however…there's just something about him. He's got this cocky arrogance that needs to be smacked out of him. That whole 'old house' conversation was as infuriating as it was laughable, at least to me, just another example of his entitled attitude.

Apart from the fact that we were very clearly arguing about our own ages, the value of youth versus longevity, there's also an obvious insinuation there about the importance of money. Of which Connor has plenty, and I have…not as plenty.

I might be running a successful business, but finances are always tight. My primary profits go to Boyd and Jackson and back into the business. I only take enough to keep me afloat—pay the mortgage and the utilities, food, gas, etc. Connor's dad owns the resort, the most profitable business in Cedar Point. We're very much in different tax brackets.

I mean, even this boat demonstrates that. I examine it as I approach, my long strokes slowing as I near the step at the back. They own a Cobalt, which is *not* a cheap power boat by any means, and it looks to be brand new.

Abby and I share my father's old fishing boat, David Buoy,

and it does the trick of getting us out on the water, but it is an older vessel through and through that I have had to put a lot of work into maintaining.

As I pull myself out of the water, I glance at Bellamy. She seems to be enjoying Connor's boat, laying out on the extendable mesh that hangs almost like a hammock over the water. It makes me wonder briefly if she'd enjoy *my* boat.

Her head tilts when she spots me, and she smiles. "Enjoy your swim?"

I nod. "I did."

"Good. Glad you got in some alone time."

My hands pause as I'm drying myself with a towel, her words hitting me. The idea that she'd notice that I like alone time, that I need it, crave it…it's surprising to me, because I can't remember ever having someone vocalize it out loud like that, as if it's not a big deal.

Abby is an extrovert, and she always seemed upset when I'd tell her I wanted to go hiking alone or swimming alone or any other thing, because she assumed it was to get away from her.

I mean, technically, it was, but not because I needed to be away from her *specifically*. It was because being alone is how I recharge, how I think through the things that matter, how I keep myself level and focused and moving forward. Somehow, Bellamy gets that, almost immediately.

Instead of stretching out along the back bench, I climb out onto the hammock next to her, suddenly realizing that, after my time away from her, it's almost like I'm even more interested in drawing her near.

She giggles as my still damp skin rubs up against hers, and then we just lie there, baking in the sun. We're both wearing sunglasses, so I can't see her eyes, and she can't see mine.

But something tells me we're both looking at each other for quite a while.

It's late in the afternoon by the time we pull back up to the dock at South Bank, and I feel exactly like you should after a day on the water: slightly sticky, overly warm, and incredibly tired. So when I get to my Blazer and see the flat tire, I groan, not wanting to deal with it today—or any day, for that matter, but definitely not today.

"Leave it and come back tomorrow," Bellamy tells me, giving it a gentle kick. "I'll give you a ride."

After our goodbyes with Stace and Connor and promises to do it again soon that are a bald-faced lie on my part, I squeeze into the passenger seat of Bellamy's little Honda CRV and we head toward my house.

"Thanks," I tell her as we unload the cooler and carry it inside together. I don't tell her I could have brought it in alone, especially now that it's far more empty, and that's partly because I'm not ready for her to leave.

"No problem," she says as we set it down in the kitchen. She unclips the lid and opens it, tugging out the remaining beers and putting them in the fridge.

My eyes rove across her as she bends and rises over and over again, taking in the faint pink on her skin and the wavy, untamed wildness of her hair from being out on the water.

"What are you up to for the rest of the day?"

She closes the fridge and leans back against it then turns and presses her face against the stainless steel, closing her eyes.

"Honestly, I'd like to just stand here and enjoy the coolness of this against my skin," she jokes, a tired smile coming across her face. "I'm exhausted."

"You have any water today?"

She shakes her head.

"You're probably dehydrated."

I step up to the counter and grab a glass from an upper cabinet, filling it with tap water and handing it over. She downs it greedily, like she hasn't had anything to drink all day even though I know she had a few beers and several sodas.

"Thanks. I needed that. Now I just need to go home and figure out a way to bathe in lotion." Bellamy holds her arms out. "I think I might have gotten a little burnt."

I shrug. "Don't we always get burnt on the first lake day of the year?" I ask, knowing it's happened to me pretty consistently over the years.

"Yeah, I guess so, but I think I might be worse on my back." She rotates her arms and winces. "I can already feel it."

Making a twirling motion with my finger, I say, "Let me see."

Bellamy eyes me for a second before turning around and lifting her shirt, revealing her mostly bare back, only the string of her bikini top wrapping around it. I touch it lightly with my fingertips and she shivers, goose bumps erupting across her flesh.

"Yeah, it looks a little red. Do you want me to put some lotion on it? I have this stuff Abby swears by that's supposed to help keep the skin hydrated so it doesn't peel."

She drops her shirt back down.

"Um…sure. That would be great, actually."

I cross the kitchen to a cabinet in the corner where I keep medicine and bug spray and sunscreen, reaching to the back in search of the white bottle of Maui Babe, reading the information and confirming that it's to help nourish skin that's been in the sun.

"Alright, here it is. Do you wanna, um…" I pause, realizing what I was just about to ask her: if she wants to take her top off.

"How about I sit on one of the chairs?" she suggests, taking the lead and heading over to the small kitchen table with four chairs. Bellamy pulls one out and sits sideways, so the back is to her left and I'm given unfettered access to her shoulders and back. Then she quickly takes her shirt off.

I swallow thickly, my eyes roving across her exposed skin again. My intentions were mostly honorable, offering to rub in some lotion for Bellamy so her burn doesn't get that much worse by peeling, but a part of me knew I'd also be touching her skin, massaging the lotion into her body.

I clear my throat and step forward, opening the bottle and squeezing some into my hands. I rub them together briefly before reaching out and touching Bellamy. Her muscles shift when I first touch her, reacting to the feeling of the coolness of the lotion against the sun-kissed warmth of her skin.

"This okay?" I ask as I begin massaging it in along her upper back.

She nods. "Yeah."

I know I should make quick work of it—a get in and get out kind of situation—but I can't seem to force myself to do so. Instead, I brush long, slow streaks between her shoulders, making certain the lotion has settled into her skin before moving lower, avoiding where the string is tight across the center.

"Do you want to…" She pauses. "…to untie my top?"

I freeze, my hands halting their movements, but I find myself nodding.

"Sure."

My hands pull gently, and the knot releases, both strings falling.

I squeeze more lotion into my palm and begin massaging again, getting all the exposed skin down to her hips before coming back up to the top to get her shoulders. As I work my hands, her head dips forward slightly, and I press my thumbs in more firmly, focusing more on massaging her muscles, the lotion sinking into her skin a happy byproduct.

When I hit a particularly tight spot, Bellamy moans, and we both freeze. God, I'm getting hard just from touching her like this. After the same happening in the water, I'm starting to realize that's apparently just what touching Bellamy does to me. My hands stroke gently along the line where her neck and shoulder connect, and I can see her visibly shiver, the tiny hairs on her body rising at that soft touch.

"Okay, I think I'm done," I tell her, my voice quiet as my hands reach out and retie the strings around her back.

"Thank you," she replies, standing and turning around.

My eyes glance briefly at her chest before coming back to her eyes.

"You're welcome."

We stand there for a long moment until Bellamy's eyes fall from mine.

"I guess I'll see you later?"

I nod. "Yeah. That sounds…"

But my words trail off. I don't want to see her later. I want to see her now. Suddenly, I realize I can't resist her anymore, can't resist the way she pulls me in and lights me up.

Without allowing myself to think about it too much, acting almost entirely on instinct, I step forward so we're just inches apart. Her eyes widen and she looks up at me, her lips parted in surprise as I dip my head and press my mouth to hers.

She tastes like heaven, like sun and beer and everything bright and colorful—things that are the exact opposite of me. Bellamy moans into my mouth, wrapping her arms around my shoulders and deepening our kiss, flicking her tongue against mine. We both drink from each other as if we've been parched for so long and have finally found an unlimited supply of water. With my mouth against hers, I feel nourished in a way I haven't in years…maybe ever.

"You made me promise," she says, pulling away, her eyes closed and her forehead against mine. Her breathing is heavy. "And I don't break promises."

I shake my head. "You're not. This is all me." I dip down and kiss her again, not wanting to give myself the chance to think better about what I'm doing.

Then we're moving slowly out of the kitchen and into the living room, where I pull Bellamy down onto the couch on top of me. The weight of her feels amazing, and when she spreads her legs and shifts her hips so her core presses against my dick, I groan as pleasure shoots through my veins.

Bellamy sits up and reaches back, untying her top again, though this time, she pulls the entire thing off, and my mouth waters at the sight of her gorgeous breasts, white and creamy in contrast to the slightly tan skin surrounding them.

My hands come up immediately, taking them both into my palms and squeezing. She moans quietly and moves her hips again, her hands resting on my chest and pressing her tits together where I'm holding them. I sit up just slightly and suck one nipple into my mouth, letting my tongue flick against the little nub until it grows hard and Bellamy whimpers.

"Rusty," she whispers, her eyes closed and her head falling back.

"Let me hear you," I growl, my hands dropping to her hips and pressing her more firmly astride me. "I want to hear what I do to you."

Her eyes connect with mine. "I don't…know what to say."

"Say exactly how you feel."

But I can tell when I look at her face that she doesn't feel comfortable with it, or maybe just that the effort of thinking of something to say would distract her from what we're doing. So I tug her down for another kiss, my hand slipping back to her shorts and sliding under the hem, gripping her ass.

Eventually she pulls back and climbs off of me, unbuttoning her shorts and letting them fall to the ground. I match her movements, undoing my own and shoving them down to my ankles before flinging them off the edge of the couch.

My eyes scan up and down as she climbs back onto the couch between my legs, and when I take my dick in my hand, her eyes follow my movements. She licks her lips, and I groan.

"I want your mouth on me," I tell her. "So fucking bad."

Her eyes move to my dick again, then she leans forward and kisses the head, giving tiny licks and gentle teases. It sends a scorching heat rushing through my body.

"Fuck, Bellamy." I can barely keep myself together, especially when she takes me into her mouth, the warm wetness enveloping me. I groan, feeling desperate.

She wraps her hand around the base and begins to jack in tandem with her sucks, and fuck, it has clearly been a while for me, because I'm already ready to blow.

I tap her shoulder. "I'm gonna come."

Her eyes glow, and she sucks harder, her other hand coming up to play with my balls, giving them little tugs that have me shooting hard into her mouth as my orgasm rushes through my body, the tingling sensation traveling up to my scalp and down to my toes.

When I finish and the last tremors rumble through my body, I sag back into the couch, physically depleted and entirely exhausted. Bellamy grins at me then crawls over my body and presses her lips to mine. I tuck my hand into her hair and give her a deep kiss, tasting myself on her tongue.

"That was amazing," I murmur, my hands roaming across her naked body pressed to mine.

I shift us so we're both on our sides and she's tucked between me and the back of the couch. She grins, almost like she's embarrassed, and moves so her leg is flung over mine. I rest my hand on her thigh, gently stroking, light touches in broad sweeps as we just lie there together. I feel more tired and ready to fall asleep right now than I have in a long while, but I also want desperately to continue touching and teasing this woman at my side.

Tugging her leg up further, I stroke my hand toward the apex of her thighs. Bellamy whimpers and tucks her face into my neck as I reach her lower lips and run a single finger through the wetness that has gathered there.

"You're soaked," I groan, feeling my dick begin to harden at the thought. "God, you must be aching."

She keeps her face tucked against me, but I feel her nod. I rub at her slowly, stroking between her lips before circling her clit then dipping back down to press a single finger into her. Bellamy's breath huffs out through her nose, and I can feel her hips begin to move against my hand.

"You're so sexy," I whisper, adding a second finger and pumping in and out.

She shifts back, her eyes meeting mine for just a second before her tongue is licking at my lips and we're kissing again. There is nothing like this moment with Bellamy, the feeling of her body pressed against mine, my fingers inside her, stroking along her inner walls. There is nothing like being able to give her the same pleasure she just gave me.

"Rusty," she whispers again, her face returning to that crook in my neck as her hips move faster, and I know she's getting close.

I pull my fingers out and she whimpers, this time with frustration, but it's quickly replaced by a moan of pleasure as I adjust my position, crawling down and pressing my mouth between her legs. My fingers slip back in, and then my tongue is stroking against her, circling her clit and rubbing at that soft spot deep within her that has her tossing back her head in pleasure and crying out loudly. Her inner walls clamp down on me repeatedly, and Bellamy shakes as her orgasm rocks her body. I grin, enjoying the look of absolute bliss on her exhausted face.

But my smile falls when I hear the front door open, and I scramble to the edge of the couch, grabbing a blanket and covering us both with it just as Jackson walks into the room.

chapter seventeen
bellamy

Heat sears my cheeks as Jackson freezes at the end of the entry hallway then turns around, giving us his back. I still cover my face with my hands, feeling absolutely mortified.

"Uh, sorry," he says, chuckling awkwardly. "I just came by to grab some of my stuff."

"I thought you guys were in San Francisco this weekend," Rusty says, his voice easier than I would be able to manage. Then again, this probably isn't an uncommon occurrence for Rusty considering how often he used to hook up with women before we started fake dating.

Another wave of humiliation sweeps through me at the thought. I know I'm not just another notch on his bedpost, but it's hard not to wonder how many other women have had an orgasm on this couch. Here I was, lost in my feels, wondering if maybe I'd gotten this thing with Rusty all wrong, and this right here is a reminder of why that would be a foolish direction to allow my mind to go.

For Rusty, sex is casual. I can't let myself forget that. Whatever little…weird thoughts I had during our sexcapade today need to go firmly in the 'do not revisit' pile along with my brief interest in yoga and that horrible red dress my mother bought me when I was in high school.

"We were supposed to, but Ruthie's daughter is home sick, so Abby needed to go in to work to open the store." He clears his throat. "We rescheduled for next weekend."

"Alright, well…if you could head to another room of the house and give us a few minutes, that would be great," Rusty says, again sounding nothing but calm and collected.

"No prob. I'll just…" Jackson points to the stairs and heads up, taking them two at a time before disappearing entirely.

Rusty turns onto his side and gives me a sheepish smile. "Sorry about that, but we were fully covered, so…no harm, no foul, right?"

He must see in my face that I'm upset, because his smile falls.

"Hey, it's okay."

"No, it is *not* okay." I push him away and climb off the couch incredibly ungracefully, searching frantically for the clothing I chucked away without a care. "Being walked in on when I'm naked is *not* okay."

I find my bikini bottoms and shorts and yank them up in one quick movement then grab my shirt off the edge of the couch, tugging it over my head without even trying to find my bikini top.

"I've only had sex with one guy—Connor—and I've done almost nothing else, so this was…and to have Jackson walk in, to know he's probably going to tell other people…" I shake my head, feeling a fresh wave of embarrassment. My throat tightens and I can feel tears pricking my eyes.

"Bellamy." Rusty has hopped up and is pulling his shorts on faster than I realize, and then he's in front of me, his hands on my shoulders, holding me in place and trying to meet my eyes.

I can't look at him, so I just keep my eyes on my feet.

"Jackson's not going to share like it's high school or something, okay? And I can talk to him as well. I swear, he won't say anything." His arms rub up and down my biceps, similarly to how he did in the water to keep me warm. "Besides, we're both adults, right? If we want to fool around in the living room, that's up to us."

Even as he says the last bit, I can see he looks a little less comfortable than he did a few minutes ago, a bit more overwhelmed by the thought of it now that it's been spoken out loud.

"I'm gonna go, okay? I just need to go home."

Rusty immediately lets go of my arms.

"Yeah, okay. If that's what you want." He scratches the back of his neck. "But I want to make sure you're alright. I don't want to send you off feeling..." He trails off. "I don't know what you're feeling."

I take in a deep breath and let it all out. "I'm just overwhelmed. There was a lot of emotion when I slept with Connor, and he was someone I thought I was in love with. There are going to be some feelings about hooking up with a guy who sees it as just another way to pass the time."

Rusty's face flinches when I say it, but I don't take it back.

"I mean, I knew that going in, you know? It's not new information. I just need some time to process."

He nods, but he looks more sullen and withdrawn. Ultimately, I don't focus on that, though. Right now, I need to focus on my own mind and my own thoughts and feelings. What just happened was a big deal to me, and I highly doubt it matters at all to Rusty.

I grab my keys off the kitchen counter and give him a small wave then walk out the door, heading home where I can crawl into my bed and cover my face with a pillow.

I have some serious thinking to do.

Later that evening, I'm lying sprawled out on the dock behind our house, staring up at the sky, when I feel the vibration of footsteps moving toward me.

I glance over my shoulder, spotting a familiar figure coming my way, and I let out a sigh, feeling equal parts embarrassed and grateful: embarrassed because I shouldn't have run out of Rusty's like that earlier, grateful because he's clearly not a man who lets things go unaddressed for long.

"Your mom said you were out here," he says, his feet a few inches from my head as he looks down at me. "I don't know what I was imagining when you said you lie on the dock to think, but I didn't realize you meant you actually lie on the dock to think."

My lips tilt up. "I typically mean exactly what I say."

"I'm realizing that."

Rusty dips down and sits then lies flat, our bodies in opposite directions but our heads side by side.

"You get your tire fixed?" I ask.

He nods. "Jackson helped me."

I sigh. "I can't believe he walked in on us."

"I'm sorry that happened."

"It's not your fault," I reply. "You couldn't have known he would come home. I mean, doesn't he practically live at Abby and Briar's?"

He snorts. "I like to pretend I don't know where he sleeps at night, but yeah, I'm pretty sure he stays most nights with Abby."

"See? Not your fault."

"No, not the Jackson part, but I shouldn't have instigated things in the first place."

I hum. "Well, we were equal instigators, so you can't take all the blame for that, either."

Rusty sighs, and we lapse into an easy silence, both of us just lying there, thinking. I'm not sure what's on his mind, but mine returns to what I was considering before he arrived. The intimate moments I shared with Rusty earlier were incredible. I mean, I've not had a lot of sexual experience, but I can definitely say my time on the couch with him was lightyears away from my awkward fumbling with Connor last summer.

Maybe the real issue is just that I've always placed so much importance on sex, putting too much pressure on it to be this perfect thing when it's seeming more and more like that might rarely be the case. Instead of shielding myself from men and sexuality, maybe I just need to experience more of it. Maybe that would…dilute what happened with Connor, and a guy like Rusty who has all the experience and skill and isn't at risk for developing feelings might be the perfect guy to help me expand my sexual horizons, so to speak.

I don't even know how to pose that kind of question, so I decide to start with something less daunting.

"Can I ask you something?"

189

Rusty turns his head and looks at me briefly before returning his eyes to the sky. "Sure."

"You've had sex with a lot of women, right? I mean, we've established it's not thousands, but it's a lot."

He chuckles. "Yeah, sure. Why?"

"Well, is it better that way? Having sex with a lot of people versus just a few?"

"I'm not sure it's better. I think it's just about how you view sex and what the function of it is."

"What do you mean?"

"Well, some people think sex is only for marriage, and others think it's simply to express love. Some consider it a form of exercise or stress relief. I tend to be in the latter camp. It's primarily because of the enjoyment I get out of it."

"So it's never been about love for you?"

Rusty pauses, seeming to consider my question before he eventually replies.

"It was once. With one person."

"What happened?"

Again, there's a beat that passes, and I get the feeling Rusty either doesn't want to tell me this story or is trying to figure out what parts to share.

"I had a girlfriend in college. Hailey Melbrook."

I'm glad he isn't looking at my face because my surprise at that bit of information is surely evident in the way my mouth opens.

"We met during orientation as freshmen, and we were together for almost three years. With her, the sex was about love… or at least what I thought was love."

I turn my head and look at him, but he continues staring straight up.

"What changed?" I ask.

His jaw flexes.

"My parents died. I made the decision to drop out of college and move home to take care of Abby. Hailey told me she didn't want to be a 21-year-old mother of a teenager and wife to a college dropout. 'That isn't the life I signed up for,' she told me."

Something twists in my chest. I can tell Rusty's trying to not be emotional about it, but the pain I hear in his voice is still there.

"I was...well, it really fucked me up. To lose my parents and drop out of college and have to move home with no job to take care of my sister was bad enough, but to add my girlfriend dropkicking me like a piece of trash was just...the fucking icing on the cake. I decided from then on out that sex was going to be the one thing that was for me. It would be the one thing I really gave to myself, and it would just be for fun and to feel good."

I want to hug him. I want to snuggle up next to him and hug all that pain away, because damn. I can't imagine.

"Did they really die on your birthday?"

I whisper the question, because I can't believe I'm asking it, but part of me has to know. Rusty nods, and when he speaks, it's with the kind of clinical distance you can only achieve after a decade of dealing with your grief.

"They came to visit me at campus. We'd originally planned to celebrate me turning 21 when I got home for the summer, but they surprised me. Took me and Hailey out to a fancy steak dinner before I went out to get wasted with all my friends. When I woke up with a hangover, it was because a university admin-istrator was at my apartment door. They'd died while I was out partying."

I've always felt like I know Rusty. I mean, he's Boyd's best friend. The two of them and Andy spent their entire childhood running around together, and I always felt like I got a good picture of who he was when I was a kid looking up to them.

But I guess it really is true: you never actually know someone until you hear the deepest, darkest parts of their lives. There's something about hearing the quiet shame in his voice when he talks about his college girlfriend and his parents dying that gives so much more weight to his fears of letting everyone down. It feels so much more understandable.

I shift closer to Rusty, pressing the side of my face to the side of his and closing my eyes, hoping he can feel my sorrow on his behalf. The life he has faced has been so incredibly unfair and has left him facing so much alone. No wonder he's considered such a grump by most of the town; I'd be fucking grumpy too if I were him.

"Why did you ask?" Rusty says, his voice still calm and quiet. "About the sex, I mean. That was the original question, right?"

"Oh, yeah," I reply, having completely forgotten about the initial purpose of what we were talking about. "Yeah, I, um…I was just thinking about my own sex life, I guess. In comparison."

"You mean sex with Connor."

There's something kind of terse about his voice when he says it, but I figure the guy has had to travel a depressing path down memory lane to answer my questions, so I try not to take it too personally.

"Yeah, I mean sex with Connor. And I think…that's my point—that I've pretty much never had a sex life, and I'm just wondering if that might have been a mistake."

This time, I can feel Rusty turning his head to look at me, and I keep my eyes trained up at the sky, not wanting to see his expression. Part of me thinks maybe I've already said too much, but then I consider how Rusty basically just shared the most depressing, shitty things that have ever happened to him, and I decide if he can be vulnerable, I can too.

"Like…maybe I should have had more sex and then sex with Connor wouldn't have mattered as much as it did. But since I can't go back in time to change that, the only thing that would make sense would be to have a bunch of sex moving forward to reduce his impact…right?"

When Rusty doesn't say anything, I finally turn my head to the side and find him watching me, his eyebrows furrowed.

"You're saying you want to have a lot of sex so when you think about sex, you don't only associate it with Connor?"

I nod. "Yeah. And I was thinking, since you're, you know, a guy who enjoys sex and sees it as fun, and clearly we have some sort of chemistry…maybe you could be the one who helps me feel more comfortable about it."

His eyes scan my face for a long moment before he looks back up at the sky, and I see him swallow, almost like he's uncomfortable.

"I mean, you don't have to," I say, trying to backtrack. "It was just an idea. And I figured since you weren't having sex with other people for a while because you're doing me the favor of being my fake boyfriend, maybe I could…"

"What?" he interrupts. "Do me the favor of having sex with me?" Rusty sighs and sits up, looking far more upset than I thought he would.

I mean, he's clearly at least somewhat attracted to me, and I'm offering him sexy times, so I'm kind of confused about why he looks like I said something outlandish. I sit up as well, thinking maybe this is a far more serious conversation than I was anticipating.

"Sex is not a bartering chip, Bellamy," he finally says, looking across the lake, twinkling lights showing where other homes are hidden within the trees. "I don't want you to have sex with me as a favor."

"Well…I didn't mean that, exactly. I meant more like, clearly we would both enjoy it, you know? And we'd both get more than just the enjoyment out of it. You'd get your stress relief, and I'd get more experience."

He's silent for a while, his arms resting on his knees, his hands clasped together. Eventually he turns around and looks at me.

"You're serious. You want to just have sex for fun."

I nod. "And with you, it *was* fun. With Connor it was… there was so much pressure built up in my mind because it was this guy I'd been in love with forever and now it was finally happening…" I shake my head. "It was *not* a good time, and I don't want to feel that way with the next guy."

Something inside of me feels icky when I say that out loud, and I want to take the words back. I shouldn't be referencing some other, hypothetical guy in the future when I'm talking to Rusty. It feels wrong, somehow.

"So, basically, you're asking me for sex lessons."

At that, I giggle, my cheeks flushing and slight nervousness running through me at the thought.

"Well, kind of. I guess."

He shakes his head, but there's a hint of a smile there, too.

"Bellamy Mitchell, what are you getting me involved in? First a fake boyfriend, and now sex lessons?"

It's a relief that the serious tone he had just a moment ago is gone, something lighter and more teasing having taken its place.

"I guess I'm a lot more interesting than either of us ever gave me credit for, huh?"

Rusty watches me for a long moment, his eyes searching my face.

"We'll talk more about this, okay?" he eventually says, pushing up to standing and reaching out a hand to help me up as well.

I nod. "Yeah."

We walk down the dock together in silence, the nighttime quiet of the lake surrounding us. When he takes off in his Chevy and sticks an arm out the window to wave, I can't help the thrill of excitement that rushes through me.

I'm not sure what the next few weeks with Rusty Fuller will look like, but I'm sure excited to find out.

chapter eighteen
rusty

I started noticing it almost immediately after that night when Bellamy and I kissed at The Mitch. I'd be doing a delivery or picking something up at a store around town, and people who hadn't really ever had much to say to me before would start asking me random questions or striking up a conversation.

The first time, it was Roy Pulasky, the owner of the hardware store.

"Hey, how's Bellamy doing?" he asked me.

I was so surprised I didn't really know how to answer, so I just said, "She's great."

He nodded. "That's good to hear. You know she used to come in here with her daddy when she was young, asked all kinds of questions. Curious little thing."

"She's pretty smart," I responded, struggling to know what to say.

Roy finished ringing me up with a smile. "Well, tell her I said hi, would ya? Haven't seen her in a while."

Of course I agreed, because what else was I going to say? No? I can count on one hand the number of times Roy has had anything to say to me outside of my order total and asking whether I'm paying with cash or card, so it felt particularly unusual.

As it turns out, Roy isn't the only one who suddenly has things to say to me. Maryanne Charles, one of the cashiers at One Stop, tells me they're doing a free shopping bag day with a big smile on her face when she almost never smiles at me.

"You and Bellamy should both come and do your shopping together. They're really nice bags, and you could get more than one."

Even Nick has started tossing out a "Give Bellamy my best" when I leave the construction site. Suddenly, it feels like I'm getting more smiles and hellos than I've gotten in a long time.

"It's because you're dating Bellamy. Duh."

I pin Jackson with a look as I pull into a parking spot outside The Mitch on Friday night.

He shrugs. "It's the only explanation that makes sense. I mean, I've only lived here for what, six months? And even *I* can hear the difference in how people are talking to you. It's because of Bellamy."

I ruminate on what he's said for the rest of the evening as we sit at The Mitch and Bellamy flits up and down the length of the bar grabbing beers and chatting with patrons. I don't think I've ever noticed how friendly she is with everyone, asking each customer—some of whom I don't even recognize, let alone know their name—how their family is doing or about their kid's graduation or some other very personal thing that shows she's regularly asking questions and paying attention to the people around town.

My parents used to have that quality, that interest, knowing everyone in Cedar Point and investing in their lives. I, personally, haven't bought into it—not because there's no merit for someone else, but because I just haven't had the bandwidth. The mental strain of raising my sister and starting a business consumed all my energy for years, and by the time I might have gotten around to caring, I was on pretty much everyone's shit list because I'd been uninterested for so long. Now, though, people seem to be associating me with Bellamy, linking us together and connecting her friendliness and welcoming attitude with us as a pair instead of paying any mind to my naturally bristly demeanor.

Part of me doesn't know how to handle it. I've never gotten so many unnecessary questions in my life, and I've kind of just been dealing with it as it comes. But there's something small in my chest that stands a bit taller when people want to talk to me, even when it's about Bellamy and not *me*. Bellamy is amazing, and there's something I can't deny about how it feels to be associated with her, with her and her kindness and willingness to open her heart and soul to just about everyone.

I chat with Jackson for quite a while and Andy when he shows up later on. All the while, my eyes never leave the woman who has very nearly taken over my every waking thought. I can't get our conversation from Saturday night out of my head.

Sex lessons.

The idea is hot as hell, even though it shouldn't be. I *should* feel like a creep, enjoying the thought of teaching Bellamy more about her body, about the things she likes, what gives her pleasure.

But I don't.

Instead, I feel like a fucking lion, the king of the pride. It's almost animalistic, the kind of primal need that zips through me when I think about taking her back to my place after she's done working tonight, when I think about getting her naked and laying her back on my bed, spreading her legs and stroking my tongue through her folds until she's shaking.

Her eye catches mine, and she must see something in my expression, because she bites her lip and looks away, almost shyly. It's been almost a week since our conversation on her dock. We texted a few times on Sunday, and I told her we should take a few days to think about it, to figure out our boundaries and the rules of engagement.

I'm pretty sure my rules are going to piss her off, but I also don't doubt she'll get over it. Or at least, I'm hoping she will, because I've been jacking off to the image of her straddling me, tits squished together and head tossed back, every night since she said she wanted me to be her sex tutor.

Our undeniable chemistry is growing harder and harder to resist, and now, I feel like a live wire, my entire body strung tight, like just a simple touch might send me careening over the edge.

Bellamy was the first on tonight, which means she's the first one cut, thankfully, but it's still pretty late when we walk through the front door of my house.

"Want something to eat? Or drink?" I ask, heading to the kitchen.

"No, I'm alright."

I nod, grabbing a glass of water for myself and drinking the entire thing down.

"Well then," I say once I'm done, turning to look at Bellamy where she hovers at the edge of the living room near the stairs. "Should we head up?"

She gives me a nervous smile then turns and starts upstairs, and I follow in her wake. Once we're both in my bedroom, I tell her to take a seat on the edge of my bed, and I lean back on my dresser, crossing my arms.

"So, tonight probably isn't going to look like what you think it will."

Her head tilts to the side. "What do you mean?"

"We're not going to have sex."

One eyebrow rises high.

"Tonight is going to be about learning to have fun with your body in a sexual way. I don't want you to be stressed in the back of your mind about when the sex is coming. Tonight is just about fun."

"I thought sex is supposed to be fun," she counters, and I have to say, it's hard not to laugh when I see how irritated she is.

"Yes, but you can do other things that are fun too, and sex tends to be *more* fun when you're comfortable with yourself first." I can tell she doesn't entirely believe me, but at least she isn't protesting. "Alright, so tonight…" I turn to power up my little Bluetooth speaker and scroll through my phone, pulling up the playlist I preselected. "We're going to strip for each other."

Bellamy freezes, then bursts into laughter.

It cuts off when I press play and a slow R&B song comes through the speaker with a deep bass.

"Neither of us needs to be an expert," I tell her as I move to a spot in front of her, about two feet away. "We don't have to be good at dance moves or know how to shake our hips a certain way."

I step toward her and take her hands into mine then slide them under my shirt, slowly guiding them over my pelvic muscles and then up along my abs. My dick begins to throb in my jeans.

"We just have to feel confident in our bodies and the fact that the other person is turned on by us."

Her eyes are wide, her pupils dilated as I bring her hands up to my pecs.

"Do I turn you on, Bellamy?"

She nods, though I can barely see it, and I grin when she drags her fingernails gently along my skin when I bring her hands back down.

"Do you like touching my body? Looking at it?"

She nods again, her hands beginning to move on their own as I pull my shirt over my head.

"I feel the same about you. And your body."

Her eyes connect with mine, and I bite my lip before leaning in and pressing my lips to hers, loving how quickly she opens for me and tangles her tongue with mine. I pull back, take a few steps away, and finish my horrible striptease. I've never been great at this, and it's not like I'm trying to be Magic Mike. Even so, there's something erotic about stripping for her, and I'm already fully hard as I unbutton my jeans and slide them off, leaving me in just my boxers.

"Now, your turn," I tell her.

Bellamy looks at me with wide eyes again, and I take her hand and gently pull her up, standing her where I just was then taking her place at the edge of the bed.

"Remember," I tell her, "you enjoyed touching my body, you enjoyed looking at me as I took my clothes off. I feel the same."

I rub my hand over my boxers, squeezing my cock through the material. "Trust me. I am *very* turned on."

Bellamy licks her lips then begins to sway her hips to the music with her eyes closed. She runs her hand over her body— her stomach, her thighs, her breasts—then up into her hair before moving it back down again.

When she opens her eyes and looks at me again, I can tell she found that little bit of confidence she needed. She moves slowly, taking off her shirt then slowly unhooking her bra and letting her gorgeous tits bounce free. I grip the edge of the mattress to keep from reaching out for them.

She begins unbuttoning her shorts, shimmying slowly as she pulls them down and turns to show me the apples of her cheeks as she reveals her light blue thong and the gorgeous ass cheeks I want to sink my teeth into. Eventually, she drops them to the floor then turns to look at me, continuing to sway and move, before ditching the script and approaching me, wrapping her hands around my shoulders and straddling my hips. She presses her warm center against my aching dick where it's still trapped beneath my boxers.

"Fuck, Bellamy," I whisper, tugging her down for a kiss that slowly shifts from measured to filthy.

Our tongues tangle and she drops her mouth, kissing along my jaw before stroking her tongue down my neck, but she doesn't stop there. She continues to kiss and lick a path down my chest, kneeling before me and gripping my hard shaft through the fabric with both hands.

I groan. She slips my cock through the fly and then shocks me when she pulls it snug between her tits and begins to jack me off. I grit my teeth, fighting to control myself because *holy shit*.

I don't care what she has to say about her past experience—

this girl doesn't need sex lessons. I tug her up and bring her back to me so we're kissing before I turn her and lay her out on the bed, returning her teasing by licking and kissing all over her body.

"Rusty," she moans.

"Tell me," I say. "Tell me what you want."

"I want you to lick me."

"Where?"

She pauses before she speaks, and I know she's building up the courage.

"Lick my pussy."

I grin. "Gladly."

Kissing down her body, I get to her panties, tugging them to the side and licking through her lower lips in one firm stroke. She moans, and I continue, fluttering my tongue against her clit as I slip one finger inside of her, then another, flicking them deep. Her back arches off the bed, but I don't let up until I feel her clamp down on me, until I feel her splintering apart at my touch.

I only stop once she has collapsed on the bed, her breathing heavy, looking like her world has been thoroughly rocked. Once I've kissed my way back up her body, I kiss her mouth, loving how she moans into mine.

"I love watching you fly apart like that," I tell her.

She gives me a mischievous grin and pushes me back then begins to slowly remove my boxers. When her warm mouth surrounds my dick, my head falls back, the pleasure almost too much for me to keep watching. It doesn't take long for me to tip over the edge as well, and then Bellamy is crawling back up and snuggling against my side.

"See?" I tell her. "It's fun to just play with each other."

She nods. "I get it."

We lie like that for a long while until I eventually hear a soft snore that tells me Bellamy has fallen asleep. I know I should wake her, should send her home or to Abby's room, or *I* should go to Abby's room or the couch downstairs.

But I can't make myself do it.

Instead, I tuck her in more snugly and cover us with a blanket, enjoying the closeness of having her here against me, allowing my mind to consider what it might be like if things were different and this could be real.

As much as I'm telling Bellamy we aren't having sex because she needs to learn to play, we're also not having sex because I'm not sure I can handle it. After all the women I've been with, after every hollow one-night stand and quicky fling I've had, I finally found someone I want sex to mean something with, and all she wants is something meaningless.

How ironic is that?

chapter nineteen
bellamy

Stace invites me out for coffee again on Sunday morning, and this time, I enthusiastically say yes. We had fun last time, and I really enjoyed talking to her when we went out on the boat last weekend.

When I get there, though, it's Stace *and* Connor I spot standing in line. I flick off a quick text to Rusty, letting him know and asking if he might be nearby. Then I tuck my phone away and join them.

"Hey, sorry," she says, giving me a hug and looking a little irritated even through the smile on her face. "I mentioned getting coffee and he really wanted to come."

I wave a hand, telling her it's not a big deal. Would I rather not be around Connor at all? Sure, but it's becoming less and less important for me to avoid him now that I'm caring less and less about his opinion on…well, anything. I might have called my fake boyfriend to join us, but it's less about making sure Connor knows I'm into someone else and more about just having an additional buffer.

"No worries," I say, smiling at them both. "Let's order. My brain is still a little fatigued."

"Late night?" Stace asks, giving me a look filled with meaning before bumping me with her elbow.

I smirk. "A lady doesn't kiss and tell."

Stace laughs. "Well I must not be much of a lady then, huh?"

We both start giggling and step into line, Connor looking indifferent about being here even though it seems to have been his idea.

Ultimately, it doesn't matter, though. We order and take a seat outside once we've gotten our drinks, and Stace and I have a great time chatting. She asks all about how studying for my final exam is going and what the job prospects look like. Then I redirect back to her.

"So you have one year left, right?" I ask, referencing what we talked about last time we had coffee.

She nods. "Yep. One more long-ass year."

"And then what?"

Stace opens her mouth, but Connor speaks before she can say anything.

"She'll be moving here so we can start our family."

There's a stilted silence, and I glance between the two of them.

"We haven't ironed out all the details yet," Stace eventually says. "But yes, Connor would love for me to move back here so I can be a nurse in town."

I want to point out that Cedar Point doesn't have a free clinic, which is what she said she really wants to do, but I keep my mouth shut. Those are conversations the two of them need to have, preferably when I'm not around.

"Hey, guys."

I turn, spotting Rusty and Jackson approaching, probably having walked over from the new Cedar Cider site.

"Hi." I can't help the way I beam at him, and something shivers through me when he leans down and presses his lips to mine in a kiss that feels much less friendly than the way he used to kiss me in public. Now, there's some extra lip action, and it lights me up inside.

"Stace, good to see you," Rusty says, smiling. Then he glances at Connor. "Pruitt."

Connor grunts but doesn't say anything else, and I'm beginning to wonder how I *ever* was attracted to him. He's so incredibly self-absorbed and, frankly, boring. Definitely something to run over in my mind later when I'm on the dock.

"Wanna sit?"

"I'll join you for a few minutes if that's cool with you, Jackson?"

Jackson nods. "Sure. I'll grab you once I'm done." He heads off down the street.

"So anyway, what were we talking about?"

"Oh!" Stace exclaims. "I was going to ask you guys—what else is going on this summer? I heard there's some kind of festival in August, right?" She rolls her coffee mug between her hands. "I don't want to miss out on anything fun."

"Summerpalooza is in August," Rusty confirms.

"And there's a bonfire night every Sunday," I add. "Though I'm pretty sure you knew that."

Stace nods.

"There's also the TBA Swim in a few weeks." Connor puffs his chest out. "I'll be competing."

I barely refrain from rolling my eyes.

"What's the TBA Swim?"

I look at Stace. "There and Back Again is a swimming competition that benefits the local library. Technically, the library was torn down a while back, so now all the proceeds go toward the rebuild. We're really close to meeting the goal, and they're hoping to break ground next spring."

"Oh, that sounds so fun! Rusty, are you competing, too?"

Rusty opens his mouth, but Connor chuckles under his breath before taking a sip of his coffee.

"Care to share what's so funny with the rest of the class?" Rusty asks, his tone sour.

Connor grins. "Just the idea of you trying to swim from South Bank to Miller's Landing and back." He shakes his head. "Sorry, old man. Leave the athleticism to those of us who haven't passed our prime yet."

I narrow my eyes, prepared to give Connor a piece of my mind, but Stace interjects with her own thoughts.

"Why do you have to be such an asshole sometimes?" she says, giving him a look that resonates with how I feel inside as well.

Connor laughs. "Oh come on, I was just teasing."

"Bullshit." I glare at him. "You expect us to believe that?"

His smile grows forced, and his eyes narrow in my direction. "Some people will believe anything you tell them."

A ripple of pain slithers through my body, and I can't hide it on my face. I stand up, pushing my chair back with my knees and moving to shove it back into the table.

"Sorry, Stace. I'm going to need to cut this coffee short."

Her face reflects her distress at my leaving, but I don't change my mind.

"I hope you two have a nice day. Feel free to give me a call next time you want to do a girls' morning."

I walk away, feeling emotionally beaten down by just a few words, but then suddenly, I feel a warm hand in mine, and when I turn, I see Rusty at my side. He gives me a gentle squeeze, and we walk down the street together.

We're sitting on the back deck of my parents' house, sucking on popsicles, when Rusty finally asks, "Do you wanna tell me what that was about?"

I shake my head, letting my hair fall like a curtain separating us. "Not really."

Rusty scoops up my hair and pushes it behind my shoulder, tucking some of it behind my ear. Then he uses one finger against my chin to raise my head back up and meet his eyes.

"Will you tell me anyway?"

I sigh, nodding and taking a bite out of my popsicle to stall.

"You probably remember me mentioning that last summer, I tutored Connor in math. He'd failed a class and needed to take it over summer so he didn't fall behind and not graduate on time. It was the first time we ever spent any real, solid time together. Before that, it had always just been a kind of crush from afar. He used to flirt with me a lot when he'd come home from school during the summers, and I guess I just always thought we were building toward…something."

I bite into my popsicle, the sweet strawberry flavor in such contrast to how sour I feel inside.

"He told me he thought I was beautiful and he wished he'd paid more attention to me when we were younger, started saying these things about..." I pause, feeling even more embarrassed. "...about what it would be like when he came home from college. All these bullshit things about us, together, like he saw some kind of future. And I was stupid enough to believe him."

Rusty wraps his arm around my shoulder. "You weren't stupid," he says, his tone warm and kind.

"It feels stupid, especially because I slept with him before he left to go back to school, as if it was some kind of grand thing for us to share, something special. It was awkward and uncomfortable and he was only focused on himself, which I thought was maybe a thing that I didn't know about sex. I thought maybe *I* was bad at it."

He snorts. "You're not. Trust me."

My cheeks flush at his proclamation. "Well it felt that way, and when I tried to talk to him about dating, he kind of brushed it off, like he was going back to school and needed to focus on his classes and graduating. It sure seems like he found the time to date, though, so his comment earlier was a dig at me being stupid and naïve, giving him my virginity because of a bunch of bullshit I thought meant something." I shake my head. "I can't believe I was *ever* attracted to him."

We sit in silence for a few minutes, finishing off the last of our popsicles. It feels good to tell someone about Connor and the emotional struggle I've been facing since last summer, but there's also this sense of failure I'm dealing with. It's embarrassing, because as reassuring as Rusty is trying to be, it's hard not to feel like I was incredibly dumb to believe anything Connor said to me.

"I feel like I just had this idea of what it could be like, this perfect kind of love story, you know? We're both from small-town families, and I was thinking maybe we could work together a bit. My parents love his parents, and how cute would it be to have had this crush on him for forever and to have him finally notice me."

I glance at Rusty, finding him watching me with an unreadable expression.

"You don't have to tell me how stupid it sounds," I continue, shaking my head. "I can hear it now. I thought I was in love with him, but it turns out I never even really knew him."

"I don't think you're stupid," he says again. "I think you just focus too much on things being perfect."

At that, I chuckle just a little bit. "Doesn't everyone want something perfect?"

"No, actually. They don't," he says, surprising me. "Besides, life rarely gives us anything perfect anyway. I mean, look at my life."

I wince inside, realizing how insensitive it was to say that. "I'm sorry."

"Don't be sorry. It's just a simple truth, you know?" He lets out a sigh. "I had a perfect vision for my life once, and it did not include moving back to Cedar Point."

I turn my body toward him, feeling shocked by this revelation. "What?"

He nods. "I always wanted to go to graduate school, like Jackson did. That was our plan. We were going to apply to grad schools, probably move out of state, start a business together. I was considering marrying Hailey and taking her with me." Rusty shrugs. "And sometimes, I wonder what my life would have been like if those things had worked out, or even if I had continued with my plans even though my parents died."

"Wow."

"Even though I'd rather my parents be alive, I'm thankful my idea of perfect didn't happen. That I'm back in Cedar Point and things didn't work out with Hailey, glad she showed her true colors. Otherwise I might have married her, and who knows how long it would have been before I really knew her. That's the problem with perfect—it doesn't leave room for something real."

What he's saying makes sense, but it's still a hard lesson to learn.

"The same goes for you and Connor," he continues. "It's better that he showed what a selfish little shit he is now so you can be thankful you're not together."

I smile at his 'little shit' comment. I've heard him refer to Connor that way once or twice now, and it always makes me laugh.

"Well, I'm definitely thankful we're not together," I tell Rusty. "I can't imagine a world where I'd want anything to do with the real Connor Pruitt, and that's not just bitterness talking."

He wraps his arm around me again and gives me a squeeze. "Good, because you deserve so much better than that little shit."

"...little shit," I say, finishing his sentence at the same time.

Rusty raises an eyebrow, and I start giggling.

"You just love calling him that."

"Well...it's accurate."

I giggle again then let out a long sigh. "Thanks for listening to me." I pause. "Thanks for *asking*—for caring to hear why I'm upset. It means a lot."

He rubs my bicep affectionately then tugs me in and places a kiss on my temple.

"I know I give you shit, but I'm here if you want to talk. About anything."

I nod, enjoying how it feels to be snuggled up next to him… maybe a little too much. Even though Rusty is saying he's there for me, I doubt it's as anything other than a friend. We might be more intimate with each other now that we've seen each other naked and explored each other's bodies, but the point of it all is to be casual. Friendly. Just have some fun.

At least, that's what I need to convince myself of.

Eventually we head inside, and I walk Rusty to the door, thanking him again for spending the time talking to me. I watch him as he walks out to his Blazer, waving as he turns his car around and heads down the drive. It's starting to occur to me that maybe I don't need Rusty to be my fake boyfriend anymore considering the fact that I've finally come to the realization that Connor is an asshole.

A little shit, if you will.

I grin as I take the stairs up to my room, but it fades when I think about telling Rusty we can probably call it off. Something about that idea pinches the inside of my chest.

I take a seat at my desk, staring unseeing at the textbooks spread out and waiting for me to dive in. It wouldn't make sense for Rusty and me to break up right now, I tell myself. It's only been a few weeks, and even though I might not care about Connor anymore, it still can't hurt to have Rusty as a buffer. Besides, we still have more sex lessons to attend to.

My cheeks flush at that thought, and I close my eyes, remembering what it was like to mess around on Rusty's bed, to touch him, to have him touch me…

A shiver races through me, and it feels divine. If I were to ever classify *anything* as perfect, it would be the way it feels when Rusty and I are pressed together, naked and open to each other in a way I never could have imagined before him.

I clear my throat and open my eyes.

Casual. Friendly. Just for fun.

I repeat the words to myself a few times, hoping they'll stick, hoping I'll believe them.

chapter twenty

rusty

The next few days go by fairly quickly.

Things with the brewery site continue to progress, and Nick's crew wraps up the final electrical and plumbing components in record time, which means it's time to install the brewing equipment ahead of schedule. To say I'm thrilled is an understatement. The sooner we transition to this new gear, the better, especially if we want to have good batches ready for the opening in September.

Jackson and I are at the construction site much more than I anticipated, so I have to work longer hours to keep on top of local deliveries and normal Cedar Cider business functions. That also means I don't have extra time to go into The Mitch or get together with Bellamy like I've been doing since we started this thing up.

Part of me thinks it might be better this way, though. After some of our more revelatory conversations recently, we might both need some time to cool down a bit and remind ourselves that this thing is supposed to be fake.

It's fake for her, at least. For me, it's been borderline real since the night she yanked me across the bar and planted a kiss on my lips that I felt in my toes. I try not to think about that when we're together, though, because I can't risk falling for her any harder than I already am.

I'm completing my delivery at South Bank Resort when I hear my name in a sweet feminine voice, and I turn, grinning when I see Stace approaching. I might loathe Connor, but Stace is great. If anything, I like her so much it makes me dislike Connor even more, because I don't think he deserves her.

"What are you up to?" I ask, giving her a quick hug.

Stace shrugs. "Just bumming around the resort. Apparently it's *one of the perks* of dating the owner's son." She says this with an eye roll, and I laugh.

"Hey, don't shit on enjoying that pool. It's one of only three in all of Cedar Point, and the other two are privately owned."

"Ah, so it really *is* a luxury," she replies, her tone playful. "Good to know." Her eyes scan over the dolly of beer I'm standing next to. "I'm actually really glad I bumped into you. I'm wondering…I mean, I know you're working, but once you're done delivering that, would you have a few minutes?"

I blink, a little surprised. "Um…sure. I could probably give you ten minutes."

She smiles. "Awesome. Go ahead and do your"—she waves her hand at the beer—"stuff, and I'll just be out by the pool, okay?"

I nod, and she heads off toward the pool that overlooks the marina.

It only takes me about fifteen minutes to sort out my delivery to the bar, and the entire time, I'm wondering what Stace could possibly want to talk to me about. The easy answer is Connor and Bellamy, and something uncomfortable slides through my stomach at the idea of Stace sharing something about the two of them that I don't know.

I'm fairly certain Bellamy's interest in Connor is long gone, but I've learned the hard way that you never really know someone until they prove to you exactly who they are. As much as I'm getting to know Bellamy and feeling more connected with the heart of who she is, there's always the possibility that someday she'll reveal something I'm not expecting.

Once I've completed the delivery and returned my dolly to the trunk of my Blazer, I head out to the pool. It's not a hugely popular place on a gorgeous Thursday afternoon since most people are probably out at the lake, but there are still plenty of families scattered about sunbathing and playing in the water. Stace is seated at a table under an umbrella, her legs up on another chair and sunglasses on, reading a book. When she senses my approach, she looks up and smiles.

"Oh, that was quick! I thought I'd get in a full chapter."

I take a seat in the chair across from her. "What are you reading?"

She dog-ears the page and closes the book, showing me the yellow cover. "It's just a book about believing in yourself and learning to trust your instincts."

"I like it."

"I do too. I'm trying to do that more, you know?" Stace sets the book on the table then leans back in her chair in a casual pose, her feet still up. "Doubt myself less. Trust myself more. Kick a little ass."

I chuckle. "Sounds great."

"It's actually one of the reasons I wanted to talk to you."

She's wearing sunglasses, so I can't see her eyes, but I can still tell when her expression becomes more serious.

"I really admire your relationship with Bellamy. It seems like you guys talk about stuff and treat each other really well. I just like it. I like both of you." She pauses. "I'm wondering if you have any advice for how Connor and I can build something like what you guys have. We have a very active sex life and I thought that was enough, but…I don't know, watching you and Bellamy makes me want that kind of deep connection. Especially if we're getting married, you know? I just assumed relationships looked like this, and now I'm starting to realize there might be something more."

She shrugs and lifts her sunglasses up on top of her head.

"I mean, you know Connor pretty well, right? You guys are friends? I just thought it would be great to get a guy's perspective—a *good* guy's perspective."

I scratch at my beard, feeling a little out of my depth at her request, not only because I can't remember the last time someone lumped me in with the 'good guys,' but also because I'm *not* dating Bellamy, not really. The admiration she feels about our relationship is based on something other than reality.

I'm also *not* friends with Connor, nor do I know him well. I might feel like I understand exactly what kind of guy he is— one who is definitely not the type of person I would want to be friends with, hard stop—but I don't have some great insight to reveal. I'm not exactly sure how to answer her without sharing all of that.

"Well, first, I think it's important to say I don't know Connor well. He's more of a friend of Bellamy's from high school, so I can't really speak about him from that perspective because I wouldn't consider us to be friends."

I'm just trying to be honest, but she looks kind of dejected, her shoulders sinking slightly.

"Oh, okay."

"But here's what I *can* tell you," I say, thinking maybe I can give her some advice, even if it's not much. "I think people are pretty honest about who they are and what they want. They speak their interests and desires out loud, for the most part. You can see it in how they treat the people around them, who they spend their time with, where they direct their attention." I shrug. "Is there something about Connor that makes you think he'd give you a deeper connection or closer relationship if you asked for it?"

Stace licks her lips. "I'm not sure. I really haven't given something like that much thought before."

"Knee-jerk reaction—you and Connor having long chats about your dreams."

Her eyes fall from mine, and I can tell she doesn't like her own thoughts.

It makes sense to me that she'd eventually realize she and Connor might not have the connection she originally thought. Stace is clearly an intelligent, thoughtful person, and the fact that she got caught up in Connor is just another example of how manipulative the guy really is.

When Bellamy said she thought she loved him until she realized she never really knew him, she couldn't have been more right. Even his own fiancée feels adrift when it comes to their relationship.

"I think the fact that you're reading a book that's all about trusting yourself and asking for what you want out of life and relationships is a great indicator of you wanting more." I pause, trying to decide how best to phrase this. "Maybe Connor has already shown you who he is and what he's capable of."

Stace looks away, over to a group of children playing in the pool, lost in her thoughts. She tucks a loose piece of hair behind her ear then looks back at me.

"Yeah," she finally says, her voice soft and a little bit sad. "I was kind of thinking the same thing."

We sit together for a few beats before she gives me a smile that doesn't reach her eyes and stands.

"I think I'm gonna head out on a walk," she says. "Thanks for being willing to chat for a bit. I really appreciate it."

I nod. "Any time, Stace."

She heads back inside, and I stay out by the pool, thinking over our conversation. As brief as it was, it was pretty heavy, much more so than I anticipated based on her original request.

The truth is that she wanted me to tell her how to make Connor a person who cares more about others, and you can't force that into someone. You just can't.

I might have had my fair share of no-strings hookups, but the reason I'm great with Bellamy is not because we're faking our relationship.

It's because I care, and not just about her—about everyone: my friends, my family, the people in this town. There's an element of selflessness that goes into loving others and caring about them, and selflessness is something that translates into very specific behaviors.

Listening when they have something to say.

Helping when things are hard.

Communicating even when it isn't easy.

Learning how to be more intentional.

And most importantly, changing when you realize you can be better.

Bellamy: When's our next lesson?

The sight of a text from Bellamy on Thursday afternoon has plenty of thoughts running through my head about when we might meet up next and what it could look like. I've been imagining our next *lesson* ever since our first one, and only this morning as I stood in the shower with my dick in my hand and Bellamy on my mind did I settle on what it would be.

Me: When are you free?

I've barely sent it through before the text bubbles pop onto the screen letting me know she's responding.

Bellamy: Tonight. I swapped on the off chance you'd be free.

I smirk.

Me: Someone's eager.

Bellamy: I'm an excellent student, especially when I have a great teacher.

Biting my lip, I set my phone down. Something has shifted in the way Bellamy talks to me. We've been texting more often, and it always feels like there's a somewhat sexual undertone to everything.

I mean, in this context, we're actually talking about sex, but it's not just this. A few days ago, I asked if she wanted a tour of the construction site because she'd asked me about that. Her response? *I always want you to show me around.*

Now, maybe it's just me. Maybe I just have a filthy mind. But I don't think so.

Me: Come over tonight. 7-ish? Wear a skirt.

*Bellamy: *salute emoji**

I laugh and send off one more text.

Me: And no panties.

She doesn't reply, and for a minute, I wonder if that's asking too much or if I've crossed a line somehow. Eventually, I let it go and get back to work, prepping the paperwork to update our insurance to reflect our upcoming business expansion.

Before I know it, it's six-thirty, and I wrap things up and head upstairs to shower quickly and change. I'm just coming down the stairs when I hear a knock at the door. I pull it open, a smile on my face, but it morphs immediately into shock when I see Boyd standing at my doorstep.

"Hey, man," he says, giving me a hug that I awkwardly return. "Good to see you."

"You, too."

He pulls back, his eyes narrowing. "You forgot I was coming."

"I forgot you were coming."

Boyd laughs and slaps my shoulder. "No worries. I figured you didn't put tomorrow on the calendar when I was talking with Jackson earlier and he was clueless, too."

I step to the side, waving him in, then close the door and follow him into the living room.

"What's tomorrow?"

"I told you two I wanted to do a bi-annual meeting, one in December and one in June."

My shoulders fall, my mind finally recalling the conversation we had in January. "You *did* say that."

"I did, but that's okay. I'm here until Sunday, so if you're busy tomorrow we can do it over the weekend."

Boyd steps into my kitchen and opens the fridge, pulling out a beer. We've been friends since we were in elementary school, so his comfort in my house and ability to just grab stuff is pretty natural. I feel the same when I'm in the Mitchells' house.

The only thing that's different is this whole thing with Bellamy.

Shit. Bellamy.

I grab my phone and flick off a text.

Me: Abort. Boyd is here.

But just as I send it, I hear another knock at my door.

"Someone's popular today," Boyd jokes as he drops down onto my couch.

I don't respond, instead returning to the front door and pulling it open, my mouth drying when I see Bellamy standing there in a short skirt and stockings. She lifts the hem of the skirt just a little bit so I can see that the stockings stop high on her thigh. When I don't say anything, she puts the hem back down, her teasing expression falling.

"Did I push it too far? I figured I had an idea of what you were getting at, but…"

"Your brother is here," I say, interrupting her so she doesn't say anything else.

Her head jerks back, but then she smiles. "Bishop's here?"

I shake my head. "Boyd."

Bellamy's eyes widen. "I'm not wearing any underwear," she whispers.

My eyes scan her up and down one more time, giving myself a last chance to appreciate the image of her panty-less in thigh-high stockings before I wipe it away.

"Bellamy?"

I turn, finding Boyd standing a few feet behind me, one eyebrow raised as he assesses the situation.

"What are you doing here?"

She beams at her brother. "I should be asking *you* that question," she says. "I didn't know you were coming to town."

He gives her a smile, but it looks less easy than the one he gave me when he first arrived, especially since his eyes keep flicking between the two of us.

"Yeah, we have a meeting."

Bellamy nods. "Cool. Well I guess I'll see you later at the house then." Her eyes connect with mine. "We can chat about the thing with Connor and Stace another time. See ya!"

She spins around and heads back out to her car, and I quickly close the door so Boyd can't see the bit of ass cheek that flashed me as she walked away. When I turn around, he's leaning against the wall with his arms crossed, a neutral expression on his face.

"Maybe it's good I surprised you," he says. "Now we can

have a little chat."

I take a deep breath and let it out then nod, and we head back into the living room. He takes a seat on the couch, and I go for the fridge, grabbing my own beer and popping off the top before joining him.

"We've been friends for a long time," he says, his voice deep and gravelly in a way that says he's taking this conversation seriously. "So I'm going to give you one chance to be honest with me about what's going on with you and Bellamy."

My mind flickers over it all—Connor and Stace, how things started, when they became physical, the fact that I'm crazy about her—and I consider trying to lie to him. There's a part of me that doesn't want to be honest because I am *terrified* of losing Boyd's friendship, but ultimately, I can't be that guy.

I just can't.

I try to be as honest as I can be without making him want to scrub his brain clean of the idea of me giving his sister sex lessons.

"Bellamy asked me to be her fake boyfriend because of Connor—that part has always been true," I start, wanting to reassure him that my intentions were always to help out his sister. "But we've been spending more time together, and it's starting to feel real in a way I wasn't expecting."

"But it's *not* real. You know that, right?"

I sigh, scrubbing my hands across my face.

"You're ten years older than her, Rusty. She's in a completely different place in her life than you are. She's just starting to figure out who she is, and to be frank, I don't want you to use her and then toss her away like you do every other woman you hook up with."

Wincing, I look down at the floor. *Use her* sounds a little

225

harsh.

"And if it's not a hookup?" I ask, forcing myself to look Boyd in the eyes. "If the things I feel about your sister *are* real, even if the relationship isn't?"

He grits his teeth and takes a swig of his beer.

"I love you, Rusty," he eventually says after sitting silent for a moment. "I really do, and I know you have a good heart, which is why I think it's important to point out that the question shouldn't be about whether or not your feelings are real. Feelings are *always* real, big or small, deep or shallow. They're always real."

Boyd pauses again, and I know I'm not going to like whatever he says next.

"I think, more importantly, what you need to ask yourself is if you're good for Bellamy."

My nostrils flare, his words cutting deep, but I don't look away. I want to tell him I *am* good for her, tell him I'm the kind of guy who could make her happy and all the other things you're supposed to say in a situation like this, but what I'm really realizing is that *she* is good for *me*.

Should she really be saddled with someone who is just going to weigh her down? Someone who falls short of everything her family ever hoped for her? What *she* hoped for herself? Because if my feelings for her *are* real, the best thing I can do for her is want what's best for her.

And what's best for her isn't me.

chapter twenty-one
bellamy

Rusty: Sorry about before. We'll talk later.

I look at his text from earlier again, a sense of foreboding coming over me even though nothing about his message necessarily says I should feel that way.

Knowing Boyd is in town just makes me nervous. I know it will be a reminder to Rusty that their relationship is more important than the one he has with me. He'll remember how young I am and that I'm not what he ultimately wants in his life—not that he was feeling any differently before.

I sigh and stare up at the ceiling of my bedroom, wishing I hadn't taken tonight off of work. I should have still gone in for my shift instead of switching with Danielle. She asked me to take her Monday lunch shift in exchange, and waitressing on Monday lunch is basically asking for five bucks in tips, total—not at all an even trade.

Glancing at my phone again, I try to come up with something else I can do with my time. I could…watch a movie. Or lay out on the dock. Maybe go on a drive and play some country music like I used to do when I was stressed about school.

But really, I just don't feel like being alone. On a whim, I scroll through my contacts and click on Emily's name. She's probably working, but Celine hired two new bartenders last week, so who knows? Maybe she's free.

"Hey, girl!"

I smile when she answers.

"Hi. What are you up to?"

"Oh, just watching *Chips* with Gam. A pretty wild Thursday night for us."

"Sounds like a blast," I say, laughing.

"Wanna join?"

I lick my lips, thinking it over. I was originally going to see if Emily wanted to go do something, but honestly, a night in my jammies, eating snacks with my friend and her grandmother sounds like exactly what tonight calls for.

"I can be there in thirty minutes?"

"We have 25 minutes left in this episode, so that sounds perfect."

I grin. "See you soon."

A little over half an hour later, I'm sitting on a very comfortable couch on one side of Emily, her Gam on the other, a bowl of popcorn in my lap.

"I've never seen this show," I say, tucking a blanket tighter around my feet.

It might be summer outside, but Gam's home is set distinctly in the tundra, and I am freezing. Nothing a cozy blanket can't solve.

"We just started. Gam's a big fan of Erik Estrada."

"I put the subtitles on to watch him in the telenovelas," Gam says, giving me a sassy smile. "*Dos Mujeres, Un Camino* is my favorite. Hearing that man speak in Spanish is so sexy."

I tuck my lips between my teeth, trying not to laugh, and Emily just rolls her eyes with a smile.

She's warned me before that her grandmother says some crazy things. Apparently the two of them did a binge-watch of *Sex and the City* over Christmas, and the things Emily texted, direct quotes from Gam that always included #gamandthecity, had me rolling.

We dive into *Chips*, a late-70s show about two motorcycle cops in LA, and snack on chocolate and popcorn for as long as Gam can keep her eyes open. Around nine, she begins to fade and ends up telling us good night before heading down the hall to her bedroom.

"Wanna go sit on the porch?" Emily asks, flicking off the TV and beginning to pick up the chocolate wrappers and soda cans from the coffee table. "Gam's hearing isn't great, but I try not to make too much noise after she goes to bed."

I wave my hand. "I can leave if you want."

"No, you should definitely stay. Sitting outside on summer nights is so much more fun when you're not alone."

That's when I realize...maybe Emily is going through the same thing I've been dealing with, the shadow of loneliness that comes with growing older and having your friends move away.

I might have been somewhat of a goody-two-shoes who everybody knew, but Emily was more popular in a traditional sense when we were in high school, so it's hard to imagine her being lonely or struggling for friends. That said, the reality of small-town life is that a lot of people leave, and the ones who come back don't do it until they're ready to settle down, so there's a big lack of 18-to-30-year-olds in Cedar Point who aren't here for just a week or two.

Emily and I each grab a soda and head out to the tiny porch that extends off their kitchen and looks back into the trees and mountains. It's not really a view as much as it is just a quiet space to sit and relax.

"How's Rusty?"

Even though that sense of foreboding is still there in the recesses of my mind, I smile. "He's good."

"What's he up to tonight?"

I snort. "Boyd is back in town, and I showed up at Rusty's wearing a short skirt and thigh-highs while he was there."

Emily covers her mouth, hiding her smile. "You didn't."

"I did." I shake my head and take a sip of my drink. "Thankfully, I was able to run back to the car before he realized I was dressed like a prostitute."

She giggles again. "Oh my god, I'd be mortified."

"I was. Trust me." I sigh, still laughing at myself.

"Has he been okay with you and Rusty dating?"

"Honestly? I'm not sure. I haven't really talked with him about it."

Mostly because I know Rusty already told him the truth about what's going on between us, or at least part of the truth— the part that doesn't include any sexy nonsense. I don't want to possibly contradict anything Rusty has said.

"Yeah, I get that. I wouldn't want my brother to know if I was sleeping with his best friend."

I hum in agreement but don't say anything about the fact that Rusty and I actually haven't had sex. Realistically, I know people probably assume because of Rusty's previous exploits, but that doesn't mean I should feel obligated to confirm or deny anything.

Besides, the last thing I want to do is even hint at the fact that we've been playing around with these sex lessons. Somehow, it feels a lot more dirty to say someone's teaching me to be sexual instead of just saying I'm having sex with my boyfriend.

"How have things for you been, recently?" I ask, eager to turn the conversation away from me and Rusty. "Everything work out okay with your car?"

She nods. "Yeah. That turned out fine."

Something in her tone gives away that there's more going on in her mind.

"Are *you* okay?"

Emily shrugs but doesn't say anything immediately.

"I'm just feeling a little...rejected, I guess."

"Why?"

"If I tell you, you can't tell anyone, okay?"

My eyes widen. "Sure. I am a literal vault."

She nods, sinking back into the little two-seater we're sharing. "You know Connor Pruitt?"

I blink. "Yeah?"

"Last summer, we had a thing."

My stomach twists and my jaw drops, shock ricocheting through my body.

"He was always at the resort, you know, because of his dad and everything, and he'd hang out at the bar and we'd talk for what felt like hours. We used to go up to Easy Street after my shifts and..." She trails off, her eyes closing, like she's remembering something fondly. "It was amazing—the best sex I've ever had. Then when he left for college, he told me he just needed to focus on school until he graduated."

I want to throw up. My hands are clenched and my jaw is

tight and I feel like hurling my half-empty soda out into the woods, except I don't want to litter.

"And then he came back engaged—like, what even is that? As if what happened meant nothing?"

I lean forward, elbows on knees, resting my face in my hands.

"Hey, are you alright?"

I look back at her, shaking my head. "I have something to tell you."

She looks confused at first as I tell her about tutoring Connor last summer, but when I begin to describe my own experiences with him—how he'd come into Dock 7 and sit in my section, flirting almost relentlessly, all the things he told me about how good we were together and how we slept together before he left—Emily looks enraged.

I thought she'd be sad, maybe cry, but she looks like she wants to light something on fire.

"That fucking jerk," she seethes, standing, her hands balled into fists. "He is such a...such a..."

"A little shit?" I offer.

"Yes." She points at me. "He is *such* a little shit. I can't believe he would pull something like that."

She turns and storms off the porch, down the handful of steps and across the driveway. She stomps angrily into the trees at the edge of the property and disappears into the darkness.

I sit up, my eyes scanning for her. Then I hear a thwacking noise, and I can picture Emily out there, stick in hand, hitting a tree over and over again in anger. I giggle to myself, not because I think Emily's reaction is funny, but because the entire situation is fucking ridiculous.

Absolutely fucking ridiculous.

I have never been so thankful to have had the rug pulled out from under me, to have had the wool removed from my eyes or whatever saying fits best. Honestly, I think all of them apply in some capacity. Connor really *is* a little shit, and nothing in this world feels better than knowing I learned the truth about who he actually is without having to absolutely ruin my life first.

Emily returns a few minutes later, looking far calmer, if not a bit sweatier, than when she first stormed into the woods. She plonks down on the couch next to me, puts her feet up on the railing, and downs the rest of her soda like it's a beer-chugging competition.

"I want something with lots of alcohol," she tells me. "You?"

I shake my head. "I'm mostly over my anger at Connor, but you go ahead. Get shit-faced. I'll be here to take care of you."

Her shoulders droop and she leans over, wrapping her arms around me.

"I wanted us to be better friends, but not the kind of friends who sleep with the same guy."

At that, I bark out a laugh.

She pulls back and gives me a soft but sad smile then heads inside to grab something harder to drink. I've been hoping to create a deeper friendship with Emily as well, so it feels good knowing she's on the same page.

We sit together for a long while as she gets progressively more tipsy and we both share stories about Connor and our lives in Cedar Point and everything in between. As strange as the night is, knowing we've both been treated so shitty by the same guy seems to really bring us together. It's wonderful in the most unexpected way.

And I guess, for that and that alone, we can be thankful to Connor Pruitt.

When I pull up to Rusty's at one in the morning, I'm thankful the rental car from earlier is no longer parked out front, meaning my brother is probably safely tucked away and asleep at mom and dad's. I can't believe I didn't even notice it earlier, parked on the street. I wouldn't have known who it belonged to, but maybe I would have thought twice about trying to pull up my skirt at Rusty's front door.

It occurred to me to text him first before just showing up tonight, but the truth is that I didn't want to give him the opportunity to tell me not to come by. My guess is confirmed when he answers the door, his eyes tired, and says almost exactly that.

"You don't think your brother will notice you didn't come home?" he asks as I step through his front door.

"Does it matter?"

"Considering that I told him we aren't really dating, yes."

I ignore the vibe he's giving—the one that says he wishes I wasn't here—and remind myself that I was invited here just a few hours ago. He must just have a lot on his mind.

"Well, I came over because I wanted to tell you about my conversation with Emily."

Rusty looks confused but waves for me to follow him, and we head into the living room and take a seat on his couch.

"Apparently, she had a thing with Connor last summer, too."

That bit of gossip wakes him right up.

"What?" he says, his tone both shocked and furious.

I nod. "He was visiting her at the bar inside the resort. She works there for extra tips during high tourist season, and apparently he was super flirtatious and they used to go have sex at Easy Street when her shifts were over."

Easy Street is the nickname we have for the overlook up in the mountains behind the resort, a popular hookup spot for high school students. While I haven't been there with a guy, I'm pretty sure most people I know have been there at least once, even into their twenties.

He rolls his eyes. "He *would* take someone there. The little shit seriously never grew beyond high school."

I feel kind of bowled over by that assessment, thinking it's probably the truest observation he's made about Connor.

"How are you doing with that bit of info?" he asks, his eyes flicking over my face.

"You know, I'm actually not that mad," I reply truthfully. "It almost feels easier to know he was even more of a jerk than I initially thought. At the same time, it's difficult to finally realize he probably just saw me as someone to keep in his pocket, someone who made him feel all puffed up because I had this stupid crush."

Rusty shakes his head, his hand coming out and resting on my knee. "You can't beat yourself up about it."

"I know. I know I can't…but it still feels bleh, you know?"

"Yeah," he says, his voice soft. "I know."

Even though I'm not actually that upset about tonight's revelation about Connor, I'm feeling a little…needy. I want him to ask me to stay the night. Not for lessons, but just to be in bed together, to sleep with his arms wrapped around me.

There's a safety in his embrace I never knew existed before, and tonight feels like the perfect night for it, to tuck myself into him. The last time I spent the night, I got better sleep than I can remember getting in a long time, but I can't buck up the nerve to ask, and when he doesn't bring it up, eventually I give up on the idea that he will.

"Tomorrow you're taking a practice exam, right?" he asks as he walks me to the door.

I'm surprised he remembered, the digital test something I mentioned in passing while we were out on the boat with Connor and Stace. "Yeah."

"Well good luck. I hope it goes smoothly."

"Me too."

I hover at his door for a minute, each of us just watching the other.

Ask me to stay.

I wish it in my head, one more time.

Ask me to stay.

But he doesn't.

Instead, he watches me leave, and I have an unsettling feeling that will never change.

The weekend comes and goes, and I don't hear from Rusty.

I tell myself it's because he's busy with work, because Boyd is in town and they have those investor meetings, but there's a niggling sensation I can't kick telling me he's gearing up to be done with this—with me. I feel like he, too, knows there's no reason for us to continue to pretend date, especially with this new revelation from Emily about the fact that Connor's an even bigger scumbag than I originally believed. Now, I can confidently stride around town not caring in the slightest what he thinks about me, but what I don't want is to stride around town without Rusty.

I don't know when this connection to him began or if it's always been there, but I'm starting to wish things were more than just pretend. I wish the way he looks at me and the way he holds my hand in public and the way we are together were real.

Part of me hopes maybe he might feel the same, hopes all those little things he does are actually just who he is, not some performative version of himself that he's affecting to help me prove a point to Connor. Thing is, I can't figure out how to determine that without revealing too much of myself to him, without making myself look like a fool who was just reading too much into things.

Clearly, I've done that before, and I'm not sure my heart can handle doing it again.

I take my practice exam. I work shifts at both Dock 7 and The Mitch. I get coffee with Stace again. We don't talk about Connor.

Then, on Monday, when I still haven't heard from Rusty, I decide to swing by the construction site to see him. He did promise me a tour, after all, and maybe the weird vibe I'm getting from him having not talked to me since Boyd arrived is all just in my own head.

When I pull in next to his Blazer and hop out, I don't see him immediately, so I walk over to the massive double doors at the entrance that are at least 10 feet tall, pulling one of them open just a little bit and slipping inside. The place looks incredible, and I can only imagine how cool it will be once they offically open. I love the vintage wooden walls and concrete floor, the large windows allowing bright light to spill in.

I'm so proud of all Rusty has accomplished. I know he attributes a lot of the success to Jackson and Boyd, but I know most of the sweat equity of this business is all Rusty. He has spent tireless hours building a dream out of disaster.

I can hear voices in the distance, and I follow them, rounding a corner to what is likely going to be the kitchen, smiling when I spot Rusty and Nick talking with a few other construction workers. When Rusty sees me, he gives me a tight smile, excusing himself and heading my way.

"Hey. What are you doing here?"

"You said to swing by any time I wanted a tour."

I can tell from his expression that today is not the right time.

"I'm a little busy," he says, his voice gruff.

"Oh, I just…" I pause, trying to shrug off the feeling of rejection that's trying to take over. "Okay. Another time, then. Are you going to come by The Mitch tonight?"

He shakes his head. "I don't think so. I have a lot on my plate right now."

I lick my lips. He always comes in on Monday nights. Even before we started fake dating, that was his routine.

"Alright, well…I talked to Celine about rescheduling me so I'm not working Tuesdays so I can do family dinners. Abby asked me about it the other day and—"

"What are you doing, Bellamy?"

I take a half-step backward. "What do you mean?"

He sighs, his hands on his hips, and looks over his shoulder, toward where the other men are coming out of the kitchen.

"I think it's time we have a talk," he finally says. "Can you come by after you're done at The Mitch?"

My heart sinks. My soul suddenly feels shrouded in dread.

"You're ending things."

Rusty palms his beard, scrubbing his face in that way men do when they're not sure what else to say.

"Just come over tonight. Okay?"

His eyes can barely meet mine before he turns and heads back to the group in the corner surrounding a folding table with paper spread out on it. I only allow myself to stand there staring after him for a few seconds before I accept that he's not going to turn around and look back at me.

When I leave, I don't look back either.

chapter twenty-two
rusty

I didn't come to the decision lightly, the idea of calling things off with Bellamy, but after my chat with Boyd on Thursday, I've been thinking about little else. It was the only thing on my mind all weekend. I thought about Bellamy in almost every moment, from the interactions I had at the grocery store with Maryanne, who made sure to remind me *again* that we should come in together so we can get more reusable tote bags, to my time alone on Saturday when I took the long hike up to Kilroy and camped overnight.

I ran it over and over in my mind, and the ultimate truth I decided on is that fake breaking up with Bellamy is the best thing I can do for her.

It occurred to me as I lay in a sleeping bag, staring up at the stars and wondering if Bellamy was on her dock doing the same, that the longer we're together, the longer she'll go without a real relationship, and that's what she deserves—someone to really love her.

Regardless of how I feel, I don't know if I'm even capable of something like that, not because I *can't* love, but because I'm not sure I want to.

You can only lose so much before you start to realize the smartest thing to do is protect yourself from losing anything else.

So this is where I'm at now, ready to push Bellamy away to save her.

And myself.

When she shows up at two in the morning, I'm still awake and sitting in the living room, trying to watch sports highlights but seeing none of it.

"You're ending things, aren't you?"

It's the same thing she said to me earlier today at the construction site, but when she said it before, her tone was light and airy, like she was surprised, like she couldn't believe what I was preparing to do.

Now, it's low and pained, like the truth of what's about to happen has finally hit her.

I can't say I don't feel the same.

"Yes."

"Why? Because of Boyd?"

I scratch at my beard, trying to seem as indifferent as I can manage.

"Because it's time."

She shakes her head. "But what if I don't want it to be time?"

"It's not your choice."

Bellamy watches me, her eyes growing glassy.

"As simple as that? I get no say?"

"I think I should break up with you in public," I tell her, ignoring her question. "That way, everyone knows, and it can be blamed on me."

"What?" Her voice is incredulous.

"I was thinking you could claim I cheated, you know?" It's the best plan I could come up with, the only one that would protect Bellamy entirely. "It'll be easy to believe I couldn't stay committed."

Bellamy shakes her head again. "No. We're not breaking up in *public*. That's ridiculous." Her tears spill over, and my stomach turns. "Can you just be honest with me? Please?"

I wait…wait for her to ask whatever she wants to know.

"Just tell me the real reason."

I could tell her.

I could tell her it's because her brother made me see I'm not what's best for her in the long run.

I could tell her it's because I'm falling for her, and I don't want to be.

I could even tell her it's because she deserves someone better.

All of those reasons are true, but what's also true is if I say any of those things to Bellamy, she won't let me let her go. So instead, I tell her the one thing I know will push her away.

"I'm just ready to be back out there again, you know? I miss being with someone more experienced, and I'm kind of done pretending to be something I'm not."

I can see the pain as it cuts down her face, even though she tries to mask it.

Bellamy's never been a poker player. It's how I know this is the only way to end things between us, because I can see in her eyes that she has fallen for me, too.

I brace for her to burst into tears and leave, knowing I won't be able to follow after her, but she raises her chin, and I watch as her eyes flicker over me, something in her expression shifting.

"You're lying."

I grit my teeth. "You can believe that if you want."

"How long are you going to do this to yourself?"

I narrow my eyes. "Do what?"

"Be the martyr."

My body freezes, surprise rolling through me like a wave. It's a tidal wave that slams me into the ground and doesn't want to let me back up to the surface.

"It's not your fault your parents died, you know."

My nostrils flare.

"You don't have to keep sacrificing everything good in your life for the people around you as some kind of penance for what happened to them."

"Stop."

"And deny it all you want, but we are good together. We're good for each other."

"Bellamy, stop."

"So are you going to sacrifice what you want again? Or are you going to decide it's worth it to finally take something for yourself?"

"I do take something for myself," I counter, glaring at her, my entire body strung tight.

This isn't how this conversation is supposed to go. She's supposed to accept my decision to end things and leave.

"Every night I've spent at a bar, searching for someone to lose myself in," I continue, "that was for me."

At first, I think it's enough, think maybe I've convinced her—but Bellamy just shakes her head.

"That isn't for you," she says. "Didn't you hear what you just said? You don't lose yourself in the things that bring you joy and happiness and fulfillment. You find yourself. You find the best version of yourself."

Bellamy stands, tears glossing her eyes again as she walks toward me.

"That's how I feel when I'm with you, like I'm found in a way I couldn't have understood before you, like I'm learning new ways to be the best version of me."

Her hands come to my cheeks, framing my face, and it takes everything inside of me not to close my eyes and lean into the feel of her skin on mine.

"And maybe the way we started was messy and strange and imperfect," she continues, "but aren't you the one who told me perfect is overrated? Because it doesn't leave room for anything real?" Bellamy presses her lips to my forehead, to my right temple and then my left before tilting my face up to look at her. "This is real," she whispers. "I know it is, and so do you."

She kisses me, and I'm lost in her.

No—I'm found in her.

That's what Bellamy makes me feel.

Like a lost boy who has found his home.

She pulls back after a moment, her eyes red, and she wipes at something on my face.

Only then do I realize...I'm crying, too.

"I'm not pretending anymore," she whispers. "And it's time you stop pretending, too."

Bellamy stands back up to her full height, dropping her hands and pulling her warmth away. She crosses the room to the kitchen island, collecting her purse and slinging it over her shoulder.

"I'm willing to fight for you, Rusty, because someone in your life needs to do it. But you have to fight for you, too."

She crosses the room and heads out the front door, leaving me behind to wonder what the hell to do next.

I spend the next few days trying to work when really I'm busy thinking about what Bellamy said to me: the claims she made about me being a martyr, her declaration that we're good for each other, how our relationship has stopped being pretend and turned into something genuine.

Not in a million years did I ever think Bellamy Mitchell would knock me on my ass like she has, and yet here I am, splayed out on the ground, wondering how I got here.

But I know how I got here, don't I?

She's been tripping me up since the very beginning, with her beautiful laugh that I hear in my dreams and the way she refuses to give up on the people she loves.

And I'm one of those people now, at least that's what I'm assuming. You don't make a grandstand like Bellamy did for someone you have a few feelings for. You do it for the person you have *all* the feelings for.

Even though she might not have said it, I felt it in every word as they poured from her lips: Bellamy is in love with me.

I might try to deny it, but I'm in love with her too, which still leaves me in the position I was in before, wanting her with everything inside of me but worried that by allowing myself to have her, I'm not only risking everything I've sacrificed but also robbing her of a chance at something better—some*one* better.

Because I'm sure there's someone better out there for her than me.

We finalize the installation of the brewing equipment and dive head-first into creating the first massive batch of Cedar Cider. I spent the past month reading through all the manuals to make sure I wouldn't be wasting any time once they were installed, so it's easy to jump right in.

The machines from BruWorks have ended up being not that different from Master Brewer, and by the end of the weekend, I've gotten my first batch fermenting and the countdown has begun to tasting our first beers on large-scale brewing equipment. It should be a celebratory day, and I'm grateful to have Jackson with me when I press the final button on the screen to get things going, but the desire to call Bellamy and share the news with her is overwhelming.

It's amazing how quickly I've become accustomed to talking to her about even the most mundane topics. We haven't spoken since Monday night, the longest stretch of time we've gone without seeing each other or talking on the phone since that first day at the bonfire when she cried in my car.

It almost makes me want to laugh, the idea of Bellamy crying over Connor. That feels like a lifetime ago, like another world, one where she was a toy to him instead of the fucking goddess I know she is.

Eventually, when I don't know what to do or who to talk to, I decide to call the one person who might be able to give me some advice, the person I think knows Bellamy the best.

"If you're calling *me*, something's seriously wrong," Bishop says, his voice carrying a warning through the phone that's impossible to miss. "If you've broken my sister's heart, I hope you remember that I am *excellent* with a baseball bat."

My lips tilt up. "I thought you knew we weren't really dating."

"I did, and I called bullshit on that the first night she told me about it."

I laugh. "How's that?"

"I've always thought you were a great guy, and I know my sister well enough to know it would be nearly impossible for her not to realize how much better you would be for her than that fucker Connor."

I groan. "He's such a little shit."

"Fucking thank you! I've been telling her that ever since she first told me about her crush back in high school. Like, the guy is the worst." He sighs. "But anyway, I'm not trying to say you guys are soul mates or anything, but I could see a mutual attraction happening from a mile away. That's my point."

"Well, that's why I called." I pause, closing my eyes and feeling a whole lot younger than my 32 years. "What if we *are* soul mates?"

Bishop's silent on the other end of the line, so I continue.

"Maybe I sound ridiculous, and maybe you're just waiting to laugh your ass off, but I'm crazy about your sister. I've never felt anything like this before. What if I think I can make her happy? What if I can love her best?"

I hear him sigh, and I brace for the worst.

"If what you're saying is true, I'm wondering why you're telling *me* and not her."

My eyebrows furrow. "What?"

"Go tell *her* you're crazy about her, not me. I'm her twin brother, sure, and I love her like she's part of me because she basically is, but her finding someone who makes her happy has nothing to do with me. It only has to do with her and what she wants."

"Boyd feels differently than you do," I tell him, just wanting to put that out there to see what he has to say about it.

"So?"

I chuckle. "What do you mean, so?"

"I mean, so what? Boyd's opinion is no different than mine. You and Bellamy are the only ones who can decide if the way you feel about each other is worth all the energy and effort a relationship requires. If my brother has a tough time with it, that's *his* problem, not yours."

I'm surprised by his answer, but also not. It wasn't that long ago when I had a similar talk with Jackson about *my* sister. I guess I just assumed I needed to let go of what I thought was best in order for Abby to be happy.

Maybe Boyd will do the same.

"I guess it would be stupid, then, for me to ask for your blessing?"

Bishop laughs. "My *blessing*? Come to me for that when you want to marry her, okay? Anything before that, make your own choices."

I shake my head, a smile on my face. "This conversation did not go the way I thought it would."

"Well, stop assuming you know how everything is going to work out," he says, his advice far beyond his years. "Maybe if you did that, you wouldn't feel the *need* to have this conversation with me."

"Alright well, thanks for the talk."

"Yeah, yeah. Send me a case of your summer IPA. It's my favorite and I won't get to have it again until I come home."

I laugh. "Consider it done. Later, Bishop."

"Peace."

He hangs up, and I stand for a minute in the middle of my living room just staring blankly in the direction of the windows looking out into the trees behind the house. I can't help but think, again, how differently that chat went than I assumed it would. I thought Bishop would rake me over the coals for going after his sister, not encourage me to keep going.

Eventually, I climb into bed and stare at the ceiling, replaying our talk. The thing that stood out to me the most was his comment that only Bellamy and I can decide if what we have is worth it. Really, that's the ultimate truth.

It isn't about Bishop. Or Boyd. Or even Connor.

It's about us.

It's about whether or not we think the connection we have is worth fighting for. It's basically exactly what Bellamy said to me, and I'm a little embarrassed that I needed it mansplained to me before I really saw the truth in it.

And the truth is that Bellamy has already declared she's ready to go to war. All that's left is for me to get on board, for me to decide how I feel about her is what I want, everything else be damned. It's bullshit for me to blame my reluctance on Boyd, as if his opinion carries more weight than mine.

It doesn't.

I can't help but think about what Stan said that morning a few weeks ago at The Pines, when we were talking about Peggy and how she ended up with Fred because he was the one who was willing to risk it all to go after the woman he loved, friends be damned, her brother be damned. Maybe our stories really do have more similarities than I assumed at first.

Truthfully, if I want to be with Bellamy, if I think what we have is something true and deep and real, there shouldn't be any question in my mind about whether or not it's worth it to put everything on the line. It's just hard not to allow myself to be firmly rooted in that same familiar fear, the fear that I'm finally going to take something I want, something I love, and I'll end up losing it in the end.

chapter twenty-three
bellamy

"Doesn't it look great?"

I wrap my arm snugly around my mom's shoulder, both of us sweaty and exhausted from a hard day of work in the yard.

"It looks fantastic," I tell her. "Gives the whole porch a great vibe."

We stare for a moment longer at the new plants we've just put in around the large deck that juts out from the back of our house. All winter long, mom was talking about digging up the hedge they planted right after they built the deck fifteen years ago to replace it with something "more inviting"—her words, not mine. I personally don't think it looks that much different than the bush that was there before, but hey, I promised my mom I'd help her in the garden. As long as she's happy about it, that's all that matters.

"Now, in the spring, beautiful flowers will bloom and give some gorgeous color when I look out the kitchen window," she says, clasping her gloved hands, beaming at the fruits of our labor.

While she rolls our wheelbarrow around to the garage, I collect the shovels and follow behind. Then we drop into the padded chairs on the back deck, each with a cliché glass of cool lemonade.

"Why do you always do lemonade?" I ask as I take a sip, referring to the fact that she always makes some to put in the fridge the night before we're going to do yardwork.

"Because when you were a little girl and we planted the trees around the guesthouse, you said you would only help if we gave you lemonade."

I snort. "I did not."

My mother grins and laughs, her eyes twinkling. "You most certainly did. You were adamant about it." She shrugs. "I just thought that was so precious, so I've always made lemonade whenever we're doing outside work."

Giggling, I take another sip then smack my lips. "Well, it sure is delicious. It's a little more sour this time, and I am definitely a fan."

"I'll make sure to note that for next week," she says, winking at me.

"I can help more, if you want," I offer.

She eyes me curiously. "Don't you need to be studying for your exam?"

I nod. "I have time for that, too."

"Bellamy." My mother pins me with a look that says she's not pleased with my answer. "You've been around the house a lot over the past week. Everything okay between you and Rusty?"

The woman is infuriatingly observant, always has been. It made life particularly difficult when I was in high school and wanted a little more freedom. Sneaking out was pretty much never an option. Thankfully, as an adult still living in her home, she hasn't been too much of a helicopter, but that doesn't mean she isn't still all-seeing at the most inopportune moments.

"Things are fine."

I'm a horrible liar, and I don't doubt my mom can hear it in my voice. Things are most definitely not fine. Rusty threatened to break up with me, we haven't talked in a week, and I'm feeling far more emotional about it than I ever expected. So no... not fine.

I've been hyper-focused on replaying our conversation and wondering if the things I said to him cut too deeply, if maybe I was overly worried about him giving up and lashed back too strong. But I know the things I said were true, even if they were hard to hear. In all our discussions about his work and his sister and his friendships, it's been so clear to me that he sees himself as the sacrificial lamb in every scenario. There isn't ever a reason for someone else to carry the burden, and if he keeps going that way, he's going to work himself into the ground and everything will suffer—his business, his relationships, his own sense of self-worth.

I can't imagine a world where feeling like your emotions and desires aren't worth tending to would ever allow someone to feel whole. So, even though what I said was tough and might have hit Rusty in a place he wasn't prepared for, it still needed to be said. My hope is that, with time, he'll know that, too.

I lean my head against the back of the seat, closing my eyes and hoping my silence is enough of a message to my mother that I'm not in the mood to talk about Rusty.

"I've always liked that boy," she says, either missing my cues or ignoring them completely. "Sometimes I feel like he was dealt the most unfair hand in the history of cards."

I nod, agreeing with her but keeping my eyes firmly shut. If she wants to talk, she can. That's fine, but I don't have to share.

"He always had a big heart. Even when he was younger, when so many kids don't know how to think about anyone but themselves, he was always the helper, always willing to take the back seat in any situation to give someone else what they wanted."

That sounds *exactly* like Rusty.

"When his parents died, he changed, though."

At that, I open my eyes, and I see she's staring out at the water, lost in memories of a time that was so painful for anyone who loved Everett and Gina Fuller.

"When he was younger, he was always happy to give to others, like it filled up something inside of him...like that was a part of him that gave him joy." She shakes her head. "But after they died, that light dimmed, as if he thought he wasn't allowed to be happy anymore, wasn't allowed to want anything. I always got the feeling Rusty thought he was expected to be the one to sacrifice but never feel good about it."

I think back to when Rusty told me his parents died on his birthday, coming home from visiting him. I've wondered since that conversation if he considers himself responsible for robbing his sister of a family, if he thinks he needs to serve some kind of sentence.

"I guess what I'm saying is...ever since you two started dating, I feel like I see some of that light back again." She looks at me, smiling. "And while I might not have initially understood the two of you together, I can see how happy he makes you, too. I can't remember the last time I saw you quite as bright and full as you've been the past few weeks, and I'm so glad you've both found someone who gives you such joy."

I don't have the heart to tell my mom the real story, that it began as a lie and has a good chance of fizzling out any day. There's also the fact that I don't really know where things with Rusty currently stand, so all I can do is hope he's taking this time to think things over.

I meant it when I said I would fight for him. I will—tooth and nail, to the death, ride or die—but he has to show me I'm what he wants.

That he'll fight for us, too.

We're finishing up our lemonade and about to head inside when I see a familiar brunette walking around the side of the house.

"Hey!" I call, smiling and waving, but when Stace's eyes connect with mine, my smile falls, and I push out of my chair. "Are you okay?"

She's been crying, that much is more than obvious. Her nose and eyes are red and puffy, and she looks miserable. Stace steps up onto the porch, and I wrap her in a hug.

"I just came to say goodbye."

My eyes widen and I pull back, my hands on her shoulders. "What?"

She nods. "My flight is tonight. I'm heading back to Seattle for the rest of the summer."

Shock rolls through me, not just at the fact that she's leaving, but also at the sudden realization I'm having that I don't want her to go.

"Why? What happened?"

"Connor and I called off the engagement." She wipes away the new tears that are beginning to fall with the back of her hand. "We broke up, and I just want to go be with my mom."

I motion for her to come sit, and my mom points to the sliding door, quietly heading inside to allow us some privacy.

"It makes sense that you'd want to go home, but…I mean, what happened?"

The last thing I want to do is see Stace marry Connor. She deserves so much better than him, so I don't doubt this is for the best, especially after finding out more about what a slimeball he was last summer. Even so, my new friend is hurting, and I wouldn't have wished this on her.

"I just realized we're too different, you know? We want completely different things, and I don't want to settle for less than what I really want."

I nod my head. "Well, good for you. It's hard to set those boundaries, especially when you love someone."

"I want what you and Rusty have," she continues, and my stomach twists, the guilt settling in hard and fast. "I don't want to be with someone who only kind of listens to me and doesn't really care what I think. A good sex life is not enough. I thought it was the most important thing, but after watching you and Rusty, I realized I want more than that."

Licking my lips, I have the sudden urge to tell her, about me and Rusty and how everything she saw between us was fake, but I can't bring myself to do it. It's partially because I don't want to ruin her hope of finding someone who treats her right, but also because if I admit it out loud like that, to Stace, I'm admitting it really was all just pretend, and I'm not entirely sure it was.

At the very least, I'm not willing to concede it just yet. My heart is too filled with how I feel about that man to ever claim what we've shared has been a total sham. No matter what happens with Rusty, I'm realizing for me, it will always have meant more, even if he can't admit it to himself.

Stace and I talk for a little while longer about her plans—she's heading back to Seattle for the rest of the summer to live with her parents and will return to college for her final year in the fall—before she says she has to go finish packing before her flight.

"I just wanted to come over and say goodbye to the one true friend I've made since I got here," she tells me, giving me a sad smile. "I really like you Bellamy—you *and* Rusty—and I hope our paths cross again in the future."

We embrace, then she walks down the steps and back around the side of the house, presumably to her car so she can head back to the Pruitts'. When I'm left with my thoughts, the first thing I want to do is call Rusty to tell him, but I don't. Even though I said I would fight for him, I still need to give him the space to figure out what he wants.

Even if it's the hardest thing I've ever done.

I can't help but notice the empty seat during my shift at The Mitch.

There was a part of me that hoped he'd come in and sit across from me like he always does, with that small familiar smile that has become more and more genuine over the past few weeks.

But hour after hour passes, and while many bodies occupy that stool, it's never the face I want to see.

"You've seemed…not yourself tonight," Emily says, hopping up on the counter on the opposite side from where I'm drying glasses and putting them away.

I give her a pinched smile. "Just have a lot on my mind."

She nods. "About Rusty?"

My hands pause, mid-motion, before I continue what I'm doing. "What do you mean?"

Emily shrugs. "I just mean it seems like he's always here, sitting across from you. I figured if he's not here and you're standing there looking like the sky is falling down around you, maybe something is going on?"

"You're as bad as my mother," I tease, shaking my head.

She just grins at me. "I'm very observant. It's my superpower."

I'm silent for a little bit, but Emily just sits there, waiting for me to speak. It occurs to me then how nice it would be to talk to someone about what's been going on with Rusty. As much as I love Bishop, he's my twin brother. Siblings don't want to hear about their siblings' sexual or romantic lives, and brothers *definitely* don't want to hear that about their sisters.

So, I decide to tell Emily the truth—well, an abbreviated version, at least.

"We aren't really dating, me and Rusty," I tell her.

Emily's eyebrows furrow, understandably.

"He agreed to be my fake boyfriend because I was upset about Connor. The *last* thing I wanted was for him to get a big ego because I sat around pining for him."

At that, her face morphs into something else. "Oh girl, if

anyone can understand, it's me." She snorts. "I wish *I'd* had the idea to drum up a fake boyfriend. I think you're a genius."

I give her a small smile. "Well, it was genius until I started to catch not-so-fake feelings for him."

Emily's face pinches. "Oh. Yeah, that's hard. Does he not feel the same?"

Sighing, I chuck my drying cloth onto the bar and lean back against the counter behind me, arms crossed. "That's what's making everything so difficult. I think he does, but there's a lot more at stake because he's best friends with Boyd and they run a business together, you know?"

She lets out a long breath, shaking her head. "I wish I had any kind of advice to give you," she says. "The best thing I can say is to just be true to yourself, you know? But I realize that might be a little too Disney."

I giggle. "I don't think anyone could really give me advice for this. I kind of just have to give Rusty the time he needs to think it over."

"Do you have any idea what he *might* be thinking about?"

Shaking my head, I pick up the empty gray rack and tuck it in the corner.

"I mean, I *hope* he's thinking about how incredible we are together, but there's no way to know for sure until we finally talk."

Emily's quiet for a little bit, but then she leans forward with mischief on her face. "Can I ask a question that might be insensitive?"

I narrow my eyes, but there's no heat behind it.

"Sure," I say, drawing the word out, feeling a bit nervous about what she might ask.

"Did you guys..." She trails off, then her eyebrows bounce

up and down a few times.

I burst into laughter and chuck the rag at her face. "Emily."

"What?" she asks, but she's smiling with a hint of embarrassment. "You hear things, you know?"

I sigh, my lips pursed, shaking my head. "Alright, I'll tell you one thing, but then my lips are sealed, okay?"

Emily beams at me and nods like I'm giving her the best gift in the world. Little weirdo.

"Okay." I pause and lean forward, lowering my voice. "The hype is real." Then I pull back and begin wiping down the counter.

"What?! That's all you're going to say?" she cries out, drawing the attention of the last few people in the bar over at a table in the corner. She shifts closer and lowers her voice. "You're giving me less than I already knew."

I shrug. "A lady doesn't kiss and tell."

Emily yanks the rag out of my hand and chucks it at *my* face, and then the two of us break into peals of laughter.

When I crawl into bed later that night, I replay our conversation, glad I decided to tell Emily the truth about me and Rusty. I've spent so much of my life carrying my own burdens, keeping my internal struggles to myself, always serving as the sounding board for everyone I know but never willing to seek that when I need it. There's something relieving about opening up, like by sharing, I've found a new kind of depth to some of my relationships that I didn't have before. Truthfully, I have Rusty to thank for that.

I think back to that night when we talked on the phone as I lay on the dock and I opened up to him, when I shared my conflicted feelings about Stace. It was like he cracked a hole in the dam inside of me, and throughout our time together, it grew and grew until it became a flood.

I curl onto my side and tuck a pillow against my chest. I'm afraid.

Afraid Rusty is going to push me away.

Afraid he won't be willing to fight for us.

Afraid all we will be to each other is a memory.

chapter twenty-four
rusty

When Jackson asks me if I want to BBQ together and watch the A's game on Monday evening, I instantly know something is up. I love my friend and there have been many days when we've watched sports and drank beer and eaten good food, but he's been a bit of a ghost ever since he started dating Abby. He's around for work stuff, and I see him at family dinners on Tuesdays. We supposedly live together—his bedroom door is right across from mine—but I can count on one hand the number of nights he has slept here, let alone was just at home for us to hang out.

At first I wonder if he's caught wind of what's going on with Bellamy and wants to chime in with his two cents. Then I think maybe there's something up with the business that he thinks we should talk about in a casual setting. All I know for sure is he's jittery when he shows up, and we've barely gotten the burgers onto the grill when he blurts it out.

"I want to ask Abby to marry me."

I stare at him, surprise likely coloring every single line on my face.

"I know it's soon—"

"It's very soon," I say sternly.

"—but I'm crazy about her. I love her more than life itself, and I know that's never going to change."

I don't doubt Jackson loves my sister. I see it constantly in how he talks to her, how he treats her, how he thinks of her in everything he does—but that doesn't mean he needs to ask her to marry him.

"What's the rush?"

He crosses his arms and leans back against the railing on the small deck off the living room.

"If you love her more than life and you know that's never going to change, what's the hurry?"

This look crosses his face, one I've never seen on my friend before, and as cliché as it sounds, I swear he's glowing, like he can't wait to tell me.

"Because loving someone so much you want to spend the rest of your life with them is a kind of love you don't just keep to yourself. It's meant to be shared, and I want to share that with her so she knows just how deep my love for her goes."

I swallow thickly, my eyes dropping to the burgers sizzling on the grill. I'm suddenly overwhelmed with an emotion I wasn't expecting.

"I know when I first started dating Abby, you told me you don't get to have an opinion on who she wants to be with. But I'm going to ask you anyway, because you're the most important man in her life." He pauses, and I see his eyes gloss over. "Rusty, I'd like your blessing to marry your sister."

My chest constricts and then explodes, the love I have for

Jackson growing in ways I didn't know was possible. I'm at a loss for words, and I feel bad, looking out to the trees in the distance, knowing I'm keeping him hanging. I want to make sure when I say whatever I say next, I say it right.

"You love my sister with a depth that makes me proud to know you," I tell him, placing my hand on his shoulder. "Of course you have my blessing."

Jackson tugs me in and we embrace, each of us overwhelmed by the moment. Something passes between us—a knowledge that we're going to be more than just friends. We're going to be brothers.

"And you're wrong," I say, patting him on the back. "I'm not the most important man in Abby's life. You are."

We hug for a moment longer before we pull back, Jackson turning to attend to the grill and me heading inside to grab us something a little more celebratory than beer. I think we each need a moment to ourselves.

Eventually, the burgers are done, and we settle in front of the TV, just shooting the shit and watching baseball. My mind struggles to focus on anything other than what Jackson and I just discussed, and I think we're both a bit distracted for the rest of the evening.

Later, as I lie in bed, staring at the fan oscillating above me, the full weight of our conversation hits me. My little sister is going to be getting engaged, and then married. She's found the man she wants to spend the rest of her life with, her forever kind of love.

It's one of those major moments parents always want for their children, and I know mom and dad would love Jackson and be so happy for the two of them. As the person who has helped to raise her and guide her ever since their passing, I can't help but feel something a bit like fatherly pride and satisfaction knowing she's made it to this big milestone in life. It almost feels like…a weight has been lifted off of my shoulders.

It's not that I consider my sister a burden in any way, but for the first time, I no longer feel the responsibility of being the only person she turns to for support. Sure, I've always known she had many others loving her and caring about her. Briar, for sure, and the entire Mitchell family. Definitely Jackson ever since they started dating, and plenty of people in this town have rallied around her—around both of us—since our parents passed.

But now, she's on a path to creating a new family, one that is uniquely her own. Somehow, knowing she'll have that highlights to me just how much I want it too, how much I've *been* wanting it but haven't allowed myself the chance to even consider it a possibility.

Bellamy was right when she said I need to take something for myself, need to fight for myself. For far too long I've been committed to sacrificing everything for the sake of the people I love. I can still do that, can still be someone who is willing to bend over backward to love and support the people in my life, but I don't have to do it at the expense of my own happiness.

In truth, giving myself permission to seek out the things that bring me joy, to find that happily ever after, will help restore me in a way I desperately need. In doing that—in giving myself permission to mend the fractured parts of my soul that have never truly healed—I'll probably be capable of being an even better friend, a better brother, a better lover.

My chest feels tight again as I lie in bed, thinking over all the things I want to do, all the ways I want to be different, all the love I want to give. It's like taking this weight off my shoulders didn't just make me feel lighter; it makes me feel like I can fly.

The following morning, I'm staring at the electrical panel with Nick and Jackson, discussing an issue we're having with the main circuit breaker, when I see an unfamiliar black Lexus pull up and park dead in the center of the gravel lot. To my surprise, Connor Pruitt emerges from the driver's side looking like he wants to strangle someone, and when he slams his door angrily and begins walking my way, I can only assume I'm the one he's looking for.

What I'm *not* expecting is for him to sucker-punch me as soon as he's close enough.

A chorus of shouts rise up around me, and Jackson presses a hand to my chest, holding me back while Nick and one of his guys grab Connor's arms, restraining him as he tries to shake them off.

"Fuck you, asshole," he shouts at me, his voice loud and furious. "Stace broke up with me and it's all your fucking fault."

I'm rubbing at the spot on my jaw that he hit—I don't care how big you are, getting punched smarts—feeling completely confused.

"What the hell are you talking about?"

"She fucking broke up with me," he repeats, finally shaking Nick and Jon free.

"And what the hell does that have to do with me?" I bark, pressing up against Jackson's hand, which is doing little to stop me.

"You're the one who told her to do it."

My head jerks back. "That's bullshit."

"It's not. She said she talked with you, and you made her see I'm not what she wants."

"Look, you little shit," I say, glad to finally tell him exactly how I see him, "as much as I'd like to claim credit, if Stace ended things, that was a choice she made entirely on her own." I lean in close, pointing a finger at the center of his chest. "And we both know she deserves far better than you."

He tries to come at me again, but Nick and Jon are right there, holding him back until he finally stops fighting them.

Then he laughs, the sound filled with something nasty and bitter. "You wanna talk about someone who deserves better? How about Bellamy? Huh? Because I can guaran-fucking-tee if anyone deserves better, it's her."

I clench my fists.

"You think there's any kind of world where someone like *you* could ever be enough for her? What do you have to offer, huh? Besides proof of an STD panel and a bottle of your shitty-ass beer."

My jaw feels like it's going to crack in half with how much I hate this guy, but I roll my shoulders, trying to let go of the rage. Even though he might be right, he's also very, very wrong.

"And that's where people like me and people like you differ," I toss back, smirking. "You had a good thing with Stace and you didn't deserve her, but you weren't willing to give her everything you have to prove to her she made the right choice." I tuck my hands into the pockets of my jeans, the truth in my words settling me even further. "*I*, on the other hand, know exactly how far out of my league Bellamy is, and I'm going to do every-fuck-ing-thing I can to make that woman so happy she doesn't doubt me for a single second."

Connor stands before me, his entire body vibrating, absolutely seething. I don't doubt at all that the way we feel about each other is mutual.

"Stay the fuck out of my life," he finally says before spinning around and storming back to his car.

I don't even watch him go, my mind already having moved on to Bellamy and the fact that I don't want to waste another second standing here in the middle of a construction site when I know I could be telling her how much I love her instead.

"I gotta go," I call out to Jackson and Nick, giving them a wave as I jog over to my car.

The last thing I hear before I slam my door shut is Jackson's laughter, and when I glance at him as I back out, I see him smiling, his hands in the air, clapping.

I chuckle and shake my head then pull away.

It's about a fifteen-minute drive from downtown to the Mitchell house, and part of me wonders if I should text Bellamy before I just show up. But I don't want to slow down long enough to pull over and message her safely, so I just keep going, breathing out a sigh of relief when I see her CRV parked alone in the driveway.

When I knock on the door, it takes a few minutes before she answers, and her eyes are wide when she sees me.

"It's real for me, too," I say before she can get any words out.

"It's the most real thing I've ever known, loving you."

Her mouth opens slightly, surprise crossing her face, and I lick my lips, suddenly worried what I have to say isn't enough. I spent the entire drive over here going over what I want to tell her, but now that I'm standing before her, I can't seem to remember half of it.

All I know for sure is how I feel.

"You are the most incredible person I've ever known, but it's hard for me to admit that, because I *am* afraid. My life has had some very dark moments, and I worry if I let myself love you, I'll lose it all again." I shake my head. "But I can't imagine living in a world where I had you and chose to let you go. Forgive me for not saying how I really feel sooner, for not fighting for you sooner. I promise, I won't ever let you down again."

Bellamy is silent for a beat before she wraps her arms around my neck, hugging me tightly. "You've never let me down."

She pulls back to look at my face then presses her mouth against mine, our lips parting and our tongues tangling like a familiar dance only we know.

The relief I feel is staggering, and I kiss her like I'll never be able to do it again, even though I know I'm going to spend every waking moment searching for my next chance.

After a moment, we step back, and she slips her hand into mine.

"Come upstairs."

I swallow, glancing around as I close the front door and then follow behind her.

"Nobody's home," she tells me, and a thrill skitters its way through my chest as we step into her bedroom and she closes the door.

It feels particularly devious, what we're doing, sneaking

up to her room to fool around while her parents aren't home. I waste no time, yanking her against me and putting my mouth back onto hers, reveling in her taste as my hands travel lower and grip her ass.

"I'm on the pill," she tells me as I kiss down her neck and lick back up.

"I haven't been with anyone in a while," I reply, our eyes watching each other. "Are you sure about this?"

She nods, tugging her top over her head. "As long as you don't mind that I don't really know what I'm doing."

I chuckle, toeing my shoes off and undoing my fly. "I think that's the first stupid thing I've ever heard you say."

She giggles, shimmying her jean shorts down her legs, hopping a little bit and making her tits bounce in a way that makes my mouth water.

"Everything about you turns me on," I tell her, ripping my own shirt off, shivers racing across my body when she places her hands on my abs and begins kissing my chest.

"Same," she replies, shifting to my navel before dropping to her knees.

Her hands dip into my boxers, and she tugs them down, my erection springing free, long and hard and desperate for her. She doesn't make me wait, her hand wrapping around my shaft and giving me a firm pump, then she licks me with the flat of her tongue from root to tip.

I tilt my head back for just a moment, lost to the bliss of it, but then I return my eyes to her, not wanting to miss a single second of anything she's doing. She puts her mouth around me and bobs her head, going so far that I bump the back of her throat and hiss with pleasure. I rest my hands on her head and thrust gently, but only a few times before I pull her up off the floor and kiss her.

"If you do that much longer, I'll come before I'm inside you."

She smirks. "I'm that good? I don't even have any practice."

I chuckle and urge her back onto her bed. "It's a testament to just how fucking turned on I am by you, but if you want to practice, please consider me a willing subject in the future."

Bellamy giggles, but it morphs into a moan as my fingers slide her panties to the side, slipping through the wetness gathered between her lips.

"Fuck, you're so wet," I tell her just before sinking a finger into her.

She cries out, her legs spreading and her hips beginning to gyrate against my hand. A second finger, and she moans deeper.

"I want you inside me," she whispers, her eyes on mine as she continues to rotate her hips. "Rusty."

I stay where I am, my fingers working her up, wanting her to be so far gone that all she can focus on is pleasure. Right before she tips over, I pull back. Her eyes open wide in surprise, and she makes a noise of distress, of disapproval.

But then I'm right there, hovering over her, my cock at her entrance, and I rub the tip over her clit and through the wetness at her core.

"God, Bellamy." I groan, lining myself up and looking her in the eyes. "I love you so much."

"I love you, too," she whispers.

I'm sliding into her in one long, slow movement, and she whimpers, her head falling back and her eyes closing. I stroke at her clit with my thumb as I pull back then push in again, just as slowly.

It's difficult to hold myself back, the heat around my hips

urging me to pump in fast and hard, but I know it's a lot for her, both my size and the newness of this moment, and I keep my movements leisurely.

Bellamy's hands grip my shoulders, her fingernails digging in, and when she opens her eyes to look at me again, I see the shift in her expression, which says everything in her is focused on the pleasure, not the pain.

I grin. "I love being inside of you."

"It feels so good," she whispers, her hips beginning to move against me.

Resting one hand on the pillow next to her head, I take the other and hold under her knee then begin to pump in and out, in and out, relishing the heat suctioning my dick and sending pleasure coursing through my veins.

"Fuck," I groan as the warmth in my lower back begins to spread. "I'm not going to be able to last much longer."

She nods. "Me neither."

"What do you need?"

Instead of answering, she moves one hand and begins stroking her own clit as I thrust. My eyes follow the movement, and I moan at how fucking hot it is that she's chasing her own release.

"You're so sexy," I tell her. "So beautiful. I love watching my dick pump in and out of your pussy."

She whimpers, and then I feel the muscles inside her clamp down like a vise.

"Oh my god."

I can barely hear her, and her hands wrap around me, her nails digging into my back as she comes. It only takes a few more thrusts before I'm falling after her, lost to the sensation.

I collapse on top of her, my arms holding me up just slightly as I kiss and suck at her neck before moving to her mouth.

Our tongues stroke each other in long, leisurely, erotic kisses, the kind you can only have with a partner you know intimately.

When I open my eyes to look at her, I'm struck again by just how much I love her, how desperately I want every part of her. I roll to the side, and we both tug her comforter over our naked bodies before snuggling up like we're in our own world.

"I'm so glad you came," she says softly, one arm under her head, her other hand lightly stroking the skin around my hips.

"I'm so glad I came, too," I joke.

She giggles and pokes me in the stomach. "You know what I mean."

I nod, smiling. "I do know. And I'm glad I'm here with you."

She licks her lips, her expression growing cautious. "What made you decide to come by? What made you realize…" Bellamy trails off.

"What made me realize I'm in love with you?"

She nods.

I bring one hand up and stroke a finger along the side of her face then gently comb my fingers through her hair.

"I realized I was in love with you that night on Abby's dock," I say honestly, "but I started falling way before that."

Her eyes widen. "Seriously?"

I nod. "I just wasn't ready to admit it. Thank you for not giving up on me when I tried to push you away."

Bellamy snuggles closer, her face in my chest. "Never."

My arms wrap around her, holding her as close as I can. I truly believe her when she says that, when she says she'll never give up on me.

Because Bellamy has proven time and time again that she means exactly what she says.

She tilts her head back and looks up at me, our eyes searching each other for a long moment before our lips meet again in the most passionate, beautiful kiss I've ever experienced. Even though I told her it doesn't exist, I have to admit...

It really is perfect.

chapter twenty-five
bellamy

We lie in my bed for a while, kissing, our hands exploring like we're mapping each other in a new way we haven't done before. It's wild to me that we've gotten to this point, and I can't help wanting to touch every inch of his body, my hands roving over each thick muscle and every tender spot. I feel him beginning to grow hard again, the length of him pressed against my thigh as our tongues stroke and lick, and an unfamiliar desperation begins to stir inside me.

After I was with Connor, there was a kind of relief that it was over. It was awkward and uncomfortable, and at no point did I feel a craving to crawl back into bed and do it again.

With Rusty, I don't ever want it to end. I can feel my need for him returning anew, and before I know it, I'm pushing him onto his back and crawling over his hips, straddling him. His eyes rove over my body, his hands moving to hold my breasts and pinch at my nipples. Both of us moan as I rest against his dick, as I slide my core, still wet, along his length.

"I wish it had only been you," I tell him, overcome with emotion.

But Rusty's hands come to my face, his palms on my cheeks, his thumb stroking gently as he shakes his head.

"It sounds romantic," he says as one hand tucks some of my hair behind my ear, "but we might never have found each other if we hadn't first been lost."

My lips tilt up, and I begin moving my hips again.

"You're getting awfully poetic," I tell him, my tone teasing, my moment of regret fading away.

His hands come back down, sliding leisurely along my skin before coming to a stop on my hips. "I can't help it…I've found quite an incredible muse."

I grin, rising up onto my knees and bending forward, pressing my lips against his. Shifting my hips, I notch him right at my core then slide down his length in one go, crying out at the way he stretches me, at how deeply inside of me he reaches.

I sit there for a moment, allowing myself to breathe and expand to accommodate him before rising up and sliding back down again. My jaw drops open, and I can't help the desperate sound that falls from my lips.

"There is nothing as incredible as being inside you," he tells me before pulling my mouth back to his.

He grips my hip tighter, his other hand moving to wrap around the back of my neck, and then he begins to thrust in earnest. I am overcome with pleasure, the feeling of his dick slamming into me over and over again unlike anything.

It takes longer this time, our bodies somewhat spent from our first orgasms, but Rusty is dedicated. He breaks out int a sweat as he continues to press up into me, until eventually he shifts our position, moving us so I'm bent over the bed and he's thrusting into me from behind.

My fingernails dig into my comforter, and I lift one knee up onto the mattress, opening myself to him further. When I turn my head to the side, I catch sight of us in the mirror hanging on my closet, and I'm enraptured by what we look like.

Rusty's tall, muscular body fucking me, his hands on my hips, his eyes on my ass. Me, my mouth open, a look of desperation on my face as I lie bent over my bed, my breasts swinging every time Rusty's hips meet mine. It's an erotic image, and I sear it into my mind as heat begins to build in my core.

"Fuck, Bellamy." Rusty groans, then slaps my ass.

I whimper at the feel of it, and it isn't much longer before I toss my head back, certain I'm going to tear my bedding apart with the forceful way my muscles seem to contract, the pleasure lancing through me. Rusty shouts out his release a moment later and stills before slumping over me, spent.

We lie there panting from the exertion for long moments, eventually crawling back into bed and entwining our bodies together, returning to our cocoon. We both fall asleep like that.

Safe, warm, sated.

And secure in each other's arms.

"You look disgusting."

My eyes widen at Bishop's declaration.

"Excuse me?"

"You're all in love and shit. It's gross."

I roll my eyes, leaning my phone against the paper towel holder in the center of the kitchen island.

"Call me disgusting again and maybe I won't answer your FaceTimes anymore," I threaten.

He narrows his eyes dramatically. "You wouldn't dare."

I give him a sassy smirk. "Try me."

Bishop shakes his head, but there's a smile there, and I know we're just teasing.

"Did you and the old man get things figured out?"

"Don't call him the old man."

"What? He's in his 30s."

"He's older, but that doesn't make him old."

"Sure."

I snort. "Anyway," I say, drawing out the word, making it clear that we're moving on from that thread of conversation. "Yes, we got things figured out, and we are dating for real now."

Bishop nods. "Good. He called me a while back, wanted my opinion."

"I know. He told me."

I was surprised at first, but it also made sense. Bishop might not live in Cedar Point anymore, but there is nobody in this world that I'm closer to. It's hard not to create a deep bond with someone when you share a womb and are then together 24/7 for 18 years. Ultimately, I consider him to be my best friend, so after hearing from Rusty about their conversation, I appreciate that the two of them talked.

"Thanks for saying what you did," I tell my brother, feeling truly grateful. "And Rusty wanted me to tell you a case of the summer IPA is already in the mail to you."

Bishop laughs, and we shift into conversation about how camp is going. It's being held at UCLA, and the main thing he complains about is being 'back in the dorms' after enjoying apartment living for the past two years.

Because he's in LA, he's been using his off days to enjoy the beach, watch Dodger games, and go out in Hollywood. It sounds like a blast, but I'm mostly jealous that he's also been able to see our baby sister, Busy, who decided to stay near her college in Glendale and work over the summer.

"You've got the draft thing and then you're coming home?" I clarify as we're preparing to get off the phone.

"It's called the Draft Combine," he says, chuckling. "But yeah, I'll be home when it's over."

I nod, knowing this is what he's been working toward for his entire baseball career. Bishop has often said he's totally okay with the idea of not going pro, but I know him too well to have ever believed that. He wants it more than anything.

He was also adamant that he wanted to finish his college degree first, so while a few of the guys from his team went to the combine last summer, Bishop decided to wait until this year. That's what this entire six-week program has been about—giving the players who received invitations a bit of extra prep before the week-long event hosted by the MLB.

"Well, I can't wait to see you," I tell him, meaning every word.

"Same, Bells. Same."

We say our goodbyes and hop off the phone after I make him promise to keep me updated during the combine, and I return my attention back to the prep book splayed open on my desk. I've scheduled my official final exam for mid-July, which gives me just a few more weeks to study.

I already feel prepared, but I'm the kind of girl who wants to take her time, so the timeline feels right. While I'm continuing to search for work and think about how to get my year of experience under my belt, I'm also not trying to rush it. For now, I'm happy to continue working at The Mitch and Dock 7, enjoy the summer, and spend time with my family—and Rusty, of course.

My eyes slide over to my bed, and a wave of heat rolls through me at the memory of yesterday. God, I'm so damn into that man.

Shaking my head, I force my mind back to my book and the far less interesting topic of variance analysis.

When Rusty texts on Thursday night to tell me we're going on a lunch date Friday, a thrill of excitement runs through me. The only date I've ever been on is our fake one at Dock 7, so I spend all of Friday morning tearing apart my closet, trying to decide what to wear.

A lunch date might be hiking or out on his dad's boat or even just grabbing coffee. It takes forever to settle on a pair of jean shorts and a loose green top I think is cute enough and flexible enough to do anything.

When we pull up in front of The Pines, I blink a few times, almost certain we're running an errand on our way to the date, but Rusty turns off the car and steps out. I hop out too, walking up to the front, and he takes my hand, a big smile on his face.

"I've been thinking about where to take you on our first real date," he tells me as we take the well-manicured path around the side of the building. "I figured…you've already been everywhere in town, you know? So, where could I take you for a meal you haven't already had?"

I smile as we come around a corner, spotting a table for two set up in the middle of the back courtyard with a tiny vase of flowers and two wine glasses. Rusty pulls out my chair and I take a seat, and once he's seated in his own, a pair of French doors open and several gentlemen walk out, all of them dressed in suits and carrying trays. I recognize one of them—Art used to be a librarian at the Cedar Point Public Library before it closed, and I love seeing his familiar smile.

"When I told my friends I wanted to take Bellamy Mitchell on a date at The Pines, they insisted on helping."

I can't help but laugh, my soul nearly bursting at how thoughtful and sweet this entire thing is. A tray is set in front of me, and I can tell immediately that this is all cafeteria food from The Pines. A bowl of salad. A small baguette with little pats of butter. A plate of spaghetti and meatballs.

"Your gentleman called ahead and was able to reserve you a coveted piece of banana cream pie," Art says, waving his hand at the tiny dessert in the corner.

I nod. "Thank you so much, Art. So good to see you."

He squeezes my shoulder. "You too, sweetheart."

"And this is Stan, and Gil," Rusty says, introducing me to the two other men, both of whom look familiar, though I'm not sure I've met before.

"Nice to meet you both."

Stan grins. "Nice to meet *you*. I heard through the grapevine that the two of you were dating, but I have to be honest, I didn't believe it."

Rusty winks at me. "Imagine that."

"You enjoy your lunch," Gil says, beginning to usher the

other men along. "We'll be back in a little bit to collect your trays."

"Thank you!" I call after them as they disappear back through the French doors, and that's when I realize there's a whole group of people inside watching us through the glass. I giggle, picking up my fork and digging straight into the banana cream pie. "You know, I've heard from my mom and Briar that this pie is so popular people try to hoard it and swap for extra meds."

He laughs. "That seems like it could be a problem."

"It's just Viagra," I say, shrugging as I put the pie into my mouth.

The flavors burst onto my tongue, and I moan.

"Okay, I get it," I add, shaking my head. "That shit is so good."

Rusty grins. "I'm glad you like it."

We dig into our lunches, and I find the entire tray of food to be far better than I was expecting.

"You know, when I share with people where I went on my very first date, I should make it a game and see if I can get them to bet money. There is no way anyone will ever guess you took me to eat at The Pines cafeteria."

We both laugh, but when it starts to trail off, I can tell Rusty has something on his mind.

"I'm sorry I didn't put more thought into our date the first time," he says softly, his eyes sincere. "It never occurred to me that it would be your first date, or how it would feel to have me take you to your work for dinner."

I shake my head. "You don't need to apologize." Reaching over, I place my hand on his. "Thank you for taking the time to set this up. It was fun and unexpected and special."

His lips tilt up at the sides. "Yeah?"

I nod. "Yeah."

We don't have a lot of time at The Pines. Rusty has to get back to work and I need to get home to study before my shift at Dock 7, but when we leave, he holds my hand the entire drive back to my house.

My smile never fades.

It takes me forever to find parking for the There and Back Again Swim Competition on Saturday morning, most of my go-to places already filled, and ultimately I end up in a spot in the gravel lot at the Cedar Cider construction site and walk the fifteen minutes to South Bank Marina.

In years past, parking was never an issue. Instead of milling about in the ticketed areas downtown, I used to sit on our dock with my dad, each of us having dragged down one of the chairs from our back deck. We'd watch the swimmers as they passed us by, heading up to Miller Landing, then again after they rounded the buoy and were on their return trip back to South Bank.

This year, Jackson accidentally let it slip that Rusty's competing. Apparently he didn't tell anyone, and the only reason Jackson knows is because Cedar Cider sponsors a swimmer and he happened to glance at the swimmer's name.

This year, it's Rusty.

I talked to Abby, and we bought a few of the remaining tickets in the seats set up at the finish line. It's going to cost me a few full shifts at The Mitch to pay for mine, but it's worth it, no matter what place he comes in.

"I still can't believe he's swimming in this race," Abby says as we stand in line to grab a drink before it begins. "And that he didn't tell us."

"I don't even remember him being a swimmer."

Abby nods. "He swam competitively in high school and even competed in some national events during college."

I think back to the day we went out on the boat with Connor and Stace, how he just sliced through the water like a warm knife through butter.

"Do you think he's expecting to win?" I ask.

She shrugs. "I'm not sure. I mean, I know he still goes swimming a lot, even when the lake is super cold, but I honestly can't remember the last time we actually talked about him swimming, so I don't know."

We chat a little bit more about how work is going for her at Ruthie's and the names she's been brainstorming for the social media account she wants to create before making it to the front of the line. We each order a hard slushy in a freezing cold collector's mug before meandering slowly through the crowd and over to our little platform of seats.

The thing I love about Cedar Point is that events like this are super successful because everybody comes out. There are fifteen sections of seats spread out on different docks throughout the marina, and I know there are many others along the shorelines at various parks stretching all the way up the lake to Miller's Landing.

People in this town are fans of supporting a cause, and since the desire for a new library to break ground next year is a big one, everyone is happy to pour their dollars in. Plus, the committee that plans the competition was able to get the competition on some kind of national swimming event website, so there were far more registrations than normal. With each person needing a sponsor and an expectation of raising funds for the cause, I'd guess the final amount raised will be staggeringly different than years past.

When we find our seats, I'm thankful to see we have a direct line of sight to the finish line. We can also see the group of swimmers at the edge of the water jumping in to get wet then climbing up a small hook ladder to line up. I've never watched the swimmers dive off the platform and into the water, and I'm suddenly overwhelmed with nerves not just for Rusty, but for all of them.

"I wonder what it's like to jump into the water in a big group like that," I say. "I feel like it would be really easy to get kicked in the head."

Abby laughs, and I join her, but it cuts off when I spot Rusty stepping up to the edge and glancing down at the water a few feet below the dock, shaking his arms and legs loose. My eyes scan him up and down, appreciating his trim, muscular physique in a speedo. I've never been a particular fan of the look, but Rusty has me reconsidering.

My admiration comes to a halt, however, when I spot another familiar face in the group of competitors standing just a few feet away from Rusty.

Connor.

The two of them stare each other down, and I can see them exchanging words, though I have no idea what's been said. After their brief interaction, Rusty walks away and Connor jumps into the water.

It's hard not to assume Rusty is competing because Connor is. The two of them have been in a bristly, low-simmer feud ever since I declared that Rusty and I were dating, and apparently, Connor blames Rusty for Stace breaking up with him and leaving Cedar Point. There's a small part of me that wants nothing more than a chance to tell Connor off, but ultimately, I'm over him entirely. The truth is, he just doesn't matter. Not anymore.

A loud voice comes over the speakers that are set up next to our seating area.

"All swimmers in heat one, please move to your assigned marker. We are at a one-minute countdown. All swimmers in heat one to your markers. We are one minute from the whistle."

My body begins to vibrate with equal parts nerves and excitement as I watch the first group line up along the edge of the center dock in two rows, Rusty among them.

"Swimmers, take your marks," the announcer says.

All of the men bend down, gripping the side of the platform, and when the whistle sounds, they dive in.

chapter twenty-six
rusty

The cool lake water envelops my body as I launch off the platform. I know there's a benefit to jumping in and getting wet before the race begins, but it always feels like just as much of a shock as if I were going in for the first time.

I break through the surface and begin swimming, one arm over the other, stroke after stroke, finding my rhythm fairly quickly. I've always been interested in participating in this competition, but I'm not going to lie...the prospect of going head-to-head with Connor was the ultimate reason why I finally filled out the paperwork a few weeks back.

It was after he called me an old man that morning outside Ugly Mug. I just knew in that exact moment that I wouldn't be able to let it go. I also—immaturely—envisioned shoving it in his face a little bit that an *old man* like me bested him.

Now though, it feels less about Connor and more about myself.

I used to love swimming. Even though I never imagined

myself doing anything with it long term, I was still good enough to be on the team during college. I got a tiny little scholarship, barely enough to cover my books each year, but a scholarship nonetheless, and yet when I returned to Cedar Point after my parents died, I didn't swim for almost two years.

Eventually, I got back into it, getting out into the water in the mornings a few times a week, but it never occurred to me to compete again. I just considered it a part of my past, one more thing I'd decided I needed to sacrifice.

After my confrontation with Connor at work when he suck-er-punched me and got in my face, I realized—I have nothing left to prove to him. It doesn't fucking matter if he thinks I'm an old man, or if he holds me responsible for his fiancée breaking up with him. It doesn't even matter if I come in last today.

What matters is that I start trying again, that I give myself permission to enjoy these things I love. So today, this race, is for me.

It's why I didn't tell anyone I was competing. I'm not look-ing for the praise. I'm not looking for anyone to cheer for me. I'm cheering for myself, for the first time in a decade.

It's an exhausting slog, and my arms start to feel like rubber as I circle around the buoy near Miller's Landing and head back to South Bank Marina. I've done a lot of swimming over the years, but this event is five miles roundtrip. I have more than a few moments where I wonder if I made a mistake by signing up without more practice. My primary swim route usually clocks in around three miles, and I'm always completely gassed by the end of it.

The muscles in my right calf begin to cramp during the last mile, so I slow and come to a pause in the water, trying to mas-sage it out. I glance around, thankful there's a bit of distance between me and the next competitor behind me so I don't feel like I'm losing ground by stopping momentarily.

After about a minute, I begin swimming again, my arms slicing in and out of the water. It would be nice to say I find a renewed energy after my brief stop, but the truth is it only feels more difficult. I feel weighted down, like I'm dragging something behind me, but still I push on.

Eventually, I can hear the cheers of the crowd in the distance, the indiscernible warble of the announcer's voice over the speakers as my face and ears dip in and out of the water. When I finally cross the finish line, I feel more exhausted than I ever have in my entire life, and I rotate onto my back, ripping off my goggles and cap and floating off to the side so as not to get in the way of others crossing behind me. I don't even care how I placed.

I finished.

I fucking finished, and I've never been so proud.

After a minute or two of floating there like a broken old man, I finally cross over to the hook ladder and begin to climb my way out, my muscles protesting the entire way. I'm barely up and over the edge before I feel a pair of arms wrapping around me.

Surprised, I look blearily at them as they pull back, smiling when I see Bellamy's beaming face.

"You are so incredible!" she shouts, jumping up and down with her hands in mine before embracing me again. Her words all come out in a jumble, her excitement a palpable thing.

I can barely understand her as she talks a mile a minute, my sluggish brain struggling to keep up. She yanks me down for a kiss then starts bouncing again, and that's when I spot my sister standing a few feet away, watching us with her own wide smile.

I'm surprised they're both here, but I'm even more surprised at how *glad* I am that they're here, the pride I feel that they've seen me complete something that was so draining, something that required me to push through with my heart and my body and my mind in equal parts.

Eventually, I shake off the post-race fog enough to really hear what Bellamy's saying. She leans into me, her arms around my waist and her eyes focused up at me.

"I'm so proud of you," she says.

It hits me square in the chest: it's been a long time since I've wanted to make somebody else proud, since it felt like it *mattered* how someone else felt about me. Having Bellamy here, hearing her say those words...

Well, it means more than I know how to express, even to myself.

"I love you," I tell her, leaning down and pressing my lips to hers.

I'm still drenched in lake water, but neither of us care. Her hands come to either side of my face, and she kisses me back like it's the only thing she ever wants to do.

"I love you, too."

I kiss her one more time, and then I turn to my sister.

"I'll pass on the wet hug," she says, laughing. "But I'm *also* proud of you."

It's the first time I've seen her since Jackson told me he wants to propose, and I'm not sure if it's the emotion of knowing she's going to be getting engaged soon or the exhaustion of the day, but I can feel myself getting choked up.

I ignore her comment and reach out, yanking her in for a hug. She shrieks, but it's mostly laughter, and she wraps her arms around me as well.

"It was great to see you competing again," Abby says. "You

know mom and dad would be here cheering their asses off if they could."

I nod but don't say anything. I don't doubt it in the slightest.

Abby, Bellamy, and I head to the swimmer station, and I grab a glass of water and a protein bar then collapse on a metal folding chair.

"Official swim times for heat one have been posted," one of the volunteers says, and I see a few guys get up and cross over to the piece of paper taped to a standing whiteboard in the corner.

When I don't rise to go check, Abby pokes me in the ribs. "Want me to look for you?"

I shake my head. "I actually don't want to know."

She rolls her eyes. "Don't be so dramatic."

"I'm not," I tell her, laughing. "I just don't need to know. My goal for today was to finish, and I did."

Abby narrows her eyes then darts over to the board to look, her eyes flicking over the paper. "Fourth!" she shouts, her hands rising into the air. "You came in fourth, oh my god!"

I smile. "In the first heat," I clarify. "There were two more after mine, and I'm pretty sure there will be a lot of people who beat my time."

"I don't even care," Abby says, pointing at my name on the paper again. "This says fourth and that's what I'm going to tell everyone."

I chuckle, amused by my sister's enthusiasm. After a few minutes, I slip into a pair of board shorts, a shirt, and a pair of tennis shoes, and we exit the swimmer tent. Abby gives me a big hug and congratulates me again on "finishing fourth" then jets off into the crowd.

As Bellamy and I walk slowly through the crowd, I get stopped a few times by various people in the community. People shake my hand and say I did a great job; a guy pats me on the back and thanks me for participating.

I spot Arthur, Gil, and Stan sitting in the stands in the seats I got for them, watching as other swimmers come across the finish, and when they see me, they all let out loud cheers and clamber out of their chairs.

"Rusty, my boy!" Art says, his arms wide as he walks my way. He's beaming as he pulls me into a hug. "Great job."

"You were incredible. Just incredible."

I nod at Stan. "Thanks. I appreciate it."

"I have to say, you really were something," Gil admits, almost reluctantly. "I'm proud of you."

I pull Gil towards me, refusing to let this moment go by without a hug. He's stiff at first but eventually pats me on the back. He only goes soft for a moment, ultimately pulling back and slapping me roughly on the shoulder.

"Alright, we'll see you for bridge next week?" he says.

"Wouldn't miss it."

They all wave then head back to their seats, settling in to watch the remaining heats as Bellamy and I slip back into the crowd.

"How did you guys know I was competing?" I ask her once we've made it out of the primary throng of people and are walking hand in hand through downtown, back to where she parked at Cedar Cider.

"Jackson let it slip when he and Abby came into The Mitch a few nights ago." She shrugs. "I couldn't *not* come once I found out. I mean, this competition is a big deal."

"Well, I'm glad you came."

"Why didn't you want us to know?"

I can hear the tiny tone of hurt in her voice, and I get it.

Bellamy is one of the most supportive people I know. It's in her nature to want to show up for people.

"I wasn't sure I would finish," I reply honestly. "And I just… didn't want to be thinking about anyone expecting me to cross the line and being disappointed when I didn't."

Bellamy brings me to a stop, right in the middle of the sidewalk, and she looks at me, her eyes earnest. "I could never be disappointed. What matters is that you tried."

I grin, remembering my own thoughts about the race earlier today, appreciating how similarly we see it. We turn and start walking again, but it's barely another minute before Bellamy says something I'm not expecting.

"I saw you talking to Connor before you got in the water."

I glance at her, finding a curious expression on her face.

"Yeah. He had a few choice words for me."

Bellamy rolls her eyes. "Of course he did. What did he say?"

I chuckle, remembering how intensely he glared at me.

"He said, 'Prepare to lose, old man.'"

She hums. "Sounds like Connor."

We round the corner to the gravel drive that leads to Cedar Cider, and once we come to a stop next to Bellamy's car, I gently push her up against it and cage her in with both arms.

"You didn't ask me what I said back," I whisper, kissing the delicate skin just below her ear.

Bellamy shivers. "Huh?"

I grin. "You didn't ask me what I said back, to Connor."

Pulling away a bit, I look at her, enjoying the way her eyes are closed and her lips are parted, like just that simple kiss was enough to distract her from anything else.

When I don't keep kissing her, she opens her eyes.

"What did you say back?"

I lick my lips, and my thumb lightly grazes her cheek.

"I told him…I'd already won."

She blinks a few times, then a soft, simple grin stretches across her face. Her arms slide around my neck, and Bellamy rests her forehead against mine.

"We both did."

I couldn't agree more.

epilogue
bellamy

...three months later...

The place is packed to the gills, and I'm not surprised to see what feels like half of Cedar Point here tonight. It's technically a soft opening for Cedar Cider, but with all these people here, you'd think it was their real opening.

There's a soft rock station playing lightly over the speakers, and the crowd is spread out across the tables and high tops in the main brewery space and out to the picnic tables on the patio.

I slip through the crowd, my eyes searching for Rusty in every corner before finally finding him in the doorway that leads to the kitchen, chatting with another couple, each of them holding a beer.

"I'm surprised he looks so calm."

Glancing to the side, I smile when I see Boyd and Ruby.

"Well, he wasn't calm this morning," I reply. "I can promise you that."

He got out of bed around five, far earlier than his seven o'clock alarm. When I managed to drag myself after him at around six, I found him in his office, looking over paperwork and going over everything he needed to get finalized today before this event.

"None of them were calm, I'm assuming," Ruby says with a smile. "Boyd was up before the sun, and the first time I saw him today was when I got here an hour ago."

I laugh. "Well, everything looks great," I say to Boyd. "You all should be really proud."

My brother's eyes scan the room, and a small, pleased smile curves his mouth. "Yeah, I think I am."

Boyd has been in town for the past few weeks, working with Jackson and Rusty to get the final components ready before opening.

Even though he's been mostly a silent partner in the past, Rusty told me Boyd has taken more of an interest in the day-to-day over the past few months. It wasn't a huge surprise when he came home for our yearly family reunion in August and just never left, claiming he wanted to stick around to pitch in however he could to help with the brewery launch.

I know Rusty was glad to have him around, though he was still a little bit concerned about how everything would play out considering it was their first time seeing each other since we officially started dating. Apart from an awkward reaction the first time he actually saw Rusty and me hand in hand, it's been smooth sailing.

I'm hopeful he reacts equally as calmly when he finds out I'm going to be moving into Rusty's in the next few weeks.

"Hey babe."

At the sound of his voice, I turn, unable to help the wide

smile that always crosses my face at the sight of him. Rusty wraps his arm around my shoulder and tugs me in, placing a kiss at the crown of my head.

"Everything looks amazing," I tell him, wrapping one arm around his back. "I'm so proud of you."

His chest puffs up like it always does when I say exactly how incredible he is.

"Thanks."

The evening passes in a flurry of conversations and beer, and by the time the night is coming to an end, I've come to the conclusion that it isn't half of Cedar Point here to celebrate, it's *all* of Cedar Point. And of course, that includes my entire family, with everyone, here to celebrate Boyd's success and help in any way possible.

My parents haven't stopped smiling since they arrived, and Busy—who drove all the way back to town just for this event— has been bustling around with trays of snacks and samples of beer along with Briar and a handful of other friends who offered to help.

Even Bishop, who has been sitting in a corner for most of the night with a frown on his face, managed to set his own emotions aside for a few minutes to give Boyd a hug and some kind words.

All in all, it's an incredibly successful night, and once we've closed everything down and returned to Rusty's, I collapse onto the couch, my feet killing me.

"You know, I used to spend most of my days on my feet," I say, slipping off my boot and massaging my foot. "How am I this tired after just a few hours?"

Rusty chuckles and drops down next to me then pulls my foot up onto his lap and begins rubbing at it with his big, strong hands. I moan, my head falling back at how delicious the pressure feels.

"Well, you sit on your butt a lot now," he answers. "Makes sense that your feet would hurt a little bit."

"Don't say I sit on my butt a lot," I reply. "That makes it sound like I'm lazy."

He laughs. "You sit at a desk for work. Is that better?"

I nod. "Much."

I really do miss working at The Mitch and Dock 7, but I'm so excited about how everything has worked out for my new job.

Taking Jackson's advice, I contacted George Sterling to see if he'd be interested in taking on an employee temporarily until he retires. He was actually thrilled by the idea, and we negotiated not just my employment, but my purchase of his business. Apparently, his clients were all very worried about him retiring, and he had been considering different ways to make sure they all found a good home with a new tax advisor.

Thankfully for both of us, the timing was absolutely perfect, and I started working for him as soon as I finished my last section of the CPA Exam in July. It's been a busy two months transitioning into full-time work, but it's everything I thought it would be and then some.

A little bit of guilt swims in my stomach, though, knowing that everything in my life is coming together so—dare I say it—perfectly, when my brother's life seems to have slowly fallen apart.

And unlike difficult times in the past when Bishop and I have turned to each other, for whatever reason, he seems to be retreating into himself and pushing me away. Things between us are strained, and I hope a day comes soon when he will let me back in.

I just have to be patient and keep trying.

Rusty puts my foot down then taps his lap, so I slip off my other boot and put my other foot in his very capable hands. I moan again, and he pauses.

"Make another sound like that, and I'll have to cart your ass upstairs," he says, a teasing look on his face.

Licking my lips, I shift just slightly, nudging at his lap with my foot, and I moan again.

He squeezes my foot, narrowing his eyes at me.

"Bellamy."

I squint at him playfully.

"Rusty."

He pushes up off the couch and crawls over me, scooting me so I'm lying flat on my back and he's hovering over me, his body gently resting against mine.

"You know what it does to me when you make those noises," he says, dipping his face into the crook of my neck and placing gentle kisses against my skin.

"I do."

He pauses and pulls back to eye me. "And yet you do it anyway."

I beam at him. "Obviously."

Rusty chuckles, then presses his lips to mine. We kiss lovingly, longingly, languidly, our tongues dipping and stroking and tasting each other in ways that have become so familiar over the past months.

I love the way it feels to be in his arms, to have his attention on me, to feel like I belong to him.

Because I do.

I do belong to him, and he belongs to me.

When we crawl into bed a while later, sated and snuggled

together, I feel incredibly thankful, not just that we love each other, but that we love each other in ways that feel so much deeper and so much more true than I ever thought love could be.

We might have started off as something fake, but each night I go to sleep in his arms, each night I feel his naked body against mine and hear his quiet breaths in my ear, I never have any doubts...

Everything about us is real.

For more stories from Cedar Point and the Mitchell family, visit my website:

www.jillianliota.com/cedar-point

jillian liota

acknowledgments
from the author

Creating Rusty and Bellamy's story was a labor of love. I began the first words in January 2021, only a few months after publishing *The Start of Someday*. And yet, it took me two and a half years to finish this story and finally put it out into the world.

But the final product could not have come to fruition without the additional eyes and ears of some incredible, supportive people, and I want to make sure to highlight them here.

Firstly - always firstly - to my husband, **Danny**. Life has been a wild ride recently, and I thank you for all you've done to give me the time I have needed to focus my attention on this project. I love you infinitely more with each day, and nothing I create would be what it is without you.

To **my family**, for continuing to cheer me on with each and every book and little achievement.

To **Marylou**, for relentless enthusiasm and encouragement, and the most incredible listening ear.

To **C. Marie** - I call you the best editor on the planet in every single book and I will continue to do so as long as you put up with me. Thanks for making me seem much more talented than I really am.

To **Jess**, for the many (many) writing sprints that led to this novel's completion. And to **Julie**, for the writing dates that helped me stay on track (and the critique that helped me create the new covers).

To **Grey's Promotions** for helping me launch this baby into the world, and to **Nina**, for some incredible feedback that helped me narrow my focus.

To **The Jillybeans**, for being my cheerleaders.

And to any reader who has picked up this book. Thank you for giving my books a chance, whether you bought, borrowed, or browsed this title...I appreciate you!

I love you all, and I look forward to seeing you back in Cedar Point again very soon.

<3 always,

Jillian

Continue to the next page to read the first two chapters of

The Echo of Regret

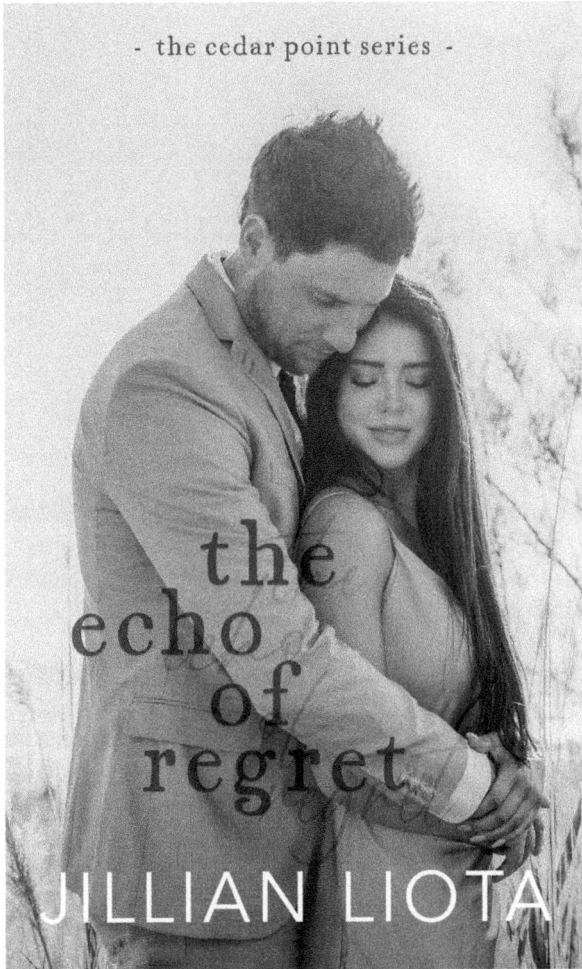

- the cedar point series -

the
echo
of
regret

JILLIAN LIOTA

chapter one
bishop

"I have a half-caff latte and an americano for Bam!"

Stepping forward to the drink counter to grab my order, I nod at the barista, who I recognize from high school. Doesn't matter where I go in this town—that nickname has stuck to me like glue for as long as I can remember. When you hold a record at your smalltown high school for most home runs in a single baseball season and your initials are B.A.M., it's easy for a moniker like that to take hold and never let go.

I eye the two drinks then glance down at my left arm resting tightly against my chest in a sling. One of the many inconveniences I'm facing with this stupid cast is shit like this. All I want to do is carry two cups of coffee outside. Instead, I have to ask for help.

"Hey, would you mind grabbing me a tray?" I motion to my arm.

"Oh, sure. Gimme just a sec." She dips down behind the

counter for a few seconds before her smiling face returns with a cardboard drink holder. "Sorry about that. Didn't even think about it."

I shrug, watching as she slips both drinks into the little slots. "No worries."

"How'd the surgery go? Is it true you won't be able to play anymore?"

I freeze for just a beat but manage to keep the easy smile. "Nah, everything went great. I'll be better than ever next season." I pick up the tray and raise it slightly in her direction. "Thanks again. See you around."

I turn, slipping quickly but carefully through the folks standing around the counter waiting for their own morning caffeine boost. I focus on the door, not wanting any more interactions like that one, before finally pushing out onto Main Street. The cool, early autumn morning is a balm on my soul, and I take a deep breath, inhaling the fresh, crisp air.

It doesn't surprise me that word has spread that I'm home… and home with an injury at that. Even so, I don't like knowing people are already speculating about whether I'll be able to play anymore. I've had surgery, and I have a rehabilitation plan I'll be following to the letter. What I need right now is relentless optimism, not people asking questions that lean toward the negative.

I drop into a seat at one of the open tables in front of Ugly Mug, set the tray down, then take a few seconds to adjust the straps of my sling that are starting to rub uncomfortably against my neck.

I'm no stranger to injuries. It's rare to be an athlete and never face a broken, pulled, or twisted *something*, but I've never had to have surgery before. Never had to wear a cast and try to keep my wrist as immobile as possible.

Yeah, can't say I'm a fan.

Slipping my cup from the tray, I raise it to my mouth and take a sip of the same caffeinated beverage I've ordered since I was barely a teenager. The piping hot liquid bursts onto my tongue, the warm melody of roasted beans and milk the perfect way to jumpstart the morning.

Sighing, I settle more into my chair and tilt my head back, closing my eyes and taking another deep breath. As much as being back in Cedar Point isn't ideal, the familiarity of a Monday morning on Main Street eases some of the anxiousness that's been a weight on my chest ever since I arrived home last week. I've been kind of tired and achy, holed up in my childhood home after my surgery, and it feels good to get outside.

"Hey, man. Sorry I'm late."

My head turns at the sound of Rush's voice, and I smile at the sight of him. I push to standing and we embrace briefly.

"No worries, man," I say, patting him on the back a few times with my good arm. "None at all. Just stoked to see you."

He pulls back, a grin on his face. Then his eyes fall to my sling-encased arm, and he shakes his head.

"Seriously, I can't believe your luck."

I scoff as we both take a seat. "It wasn't luck. Trust me." I push the tray his direction and motion to his americano.

"Thanks." Picking up his cup, he takes a sip, eyeing me over the lid as he does. "So, how've you been feeling?"

"Ah, you know. It hurts a bit still. But surgery went well, and that's all I can hope for."

Rush rolls his eyes. "Cut the shit, Bam. I'm not some reporter."

I pick up my own drink, chuckling. "Not shitting you, Rush. Things are fine. I'm gonna be better than ever once this thing has healed up. It's just inconvenient, that's all."

Fine and inconvenient: two words I've been using far too much. But what else am I supposed to say?

That I'm scared?

That I fucked up?

That there is a part of me—however small it might be—that worries I've done lasting damage to the body I've worked so relentlessly to hone?

Those are things I barely allow myself to think. I'm definitely not voicing anything like that out loud. Besides, those are the thoughts of someone who doesn't believe they'll be back, and I know I will be.

It's all that optimism that winds its way through my veins, keeps me looking on the bright side, trusting that everything will work itself out. It's been my greatest strength, my greatest ally, for as long as I can remember. It's gotten me through a few smaller injuries. It's gotten me through my hard days, my tough moments, my breakups. It will get me through this, too, and then I'll be back.

I know it.

"Well, if it's just *inconvenient*," he says, stressing the last word with a smirk, "maybe I can talk you into helping out with Fall Ball." Rush pauses, assessing me for a moment. "The team could use a batting coach. If you're up for it."

My eyebrows rise, both surprised by the offer and unsure if I should take it.

Rush and I have been friends for years—ever since Little League when we were both scraggly versions of who we are today—so my default desire is, of course, to help him whenever he needs it. He's the PE teacher at the high school and was just promoted to head coach of the baseball team last year. Last time we talked, he mentioned the workload was a bitch and he needed extra help, but I never imagined I'd be the guy he asked.

"You paying?" I joke with a grin.

He barks out a laugh. "A big ball player like you? Wringing your alma mater dry for giving some batting pointers?"

I laugh, too. "Now who's full of shit?" I ask, my chest shaking.

Rush shrugs, a huge, stupid smile on his face.

"You know as well as I do that Triple-A guys make nothing."

"No cushy signing bonus to sit on for a while?"

I snort. "I wish."

The reality of playing professionally—in any sport, at any level—is that it's rare for someone fresh out of college to get a massive signing deal. Most newbies get a pretty small bonus. The big money goes to the big players at the top level, and I have some work to put in before I begin truly making a name for myself.

The first step was signing with a team and playing at the minor league level, which I did about a month ago. I signed with the Portland Flame and went up to Salem to play for their Triple-A affiliate, the Kings.

And then I got injured. In my very first game. Broke my wrist and several fingers.

Thankfully, the season was practically over so I just followed the team doc's orders to get surgery and begin rehabbing, get myself better for next season. I could have stayed in Tacoma for the winter. I was planning to sus out some side jobs with a few of my new teammates, but it was mostly physical labor, and that's pretty much out for me at this point.

I thought it would be easier to manage at home with some extra help from my parents, so as soon as I had the surgery, I packed my shit and booked a flight home. I'm sure most 22-year-olds don't want to move back in with their mom and dad, but I have a pretty awesome family that I actually like to be around. My baby sister, Busy, is still in Los Angeles, going to college, but my older sister, Briar, still lives in town, and my brother, Boyd, is visiting for a while to help open up his brewery. My twin sister, Bellamy, still lives at home, too.,

While being back home isn't my dream scenario, it also isn't a hardship. Besides, maybe it'll do us Mitchell kids good to all be together for longer than a few days at a time for once.

Or maybe we'll annoy the hell out of each other. I guess only time will tell.

"I'm just teasing," Rush continues, rolling his cardboard coffee cup between his palms and drawing me back to our conversation. "I have a stipend for a part-time coach. I know the kids look up to you and would really benefit from your advice. I'd love to have you on board for the rest of Fall Ball if you have the time, maybe even the regular season if you're gonna be here in the spring."

I nod, my mind trying to digest the idea of coaching—even just for a little while—my old high school team.

"Let me think about it," I finally say, even though I know I'll probably say yes. "I can let you know in the next few days. But just to put it out there, I'm not sure how long I'll be in town."

Rush shrugs and gives me an easy smile. "Hey, if it works out, that's great. I'll take you for however long you're here."

We settle into other conversation points after that: family updates, childhood bullshit, the usual stuff we talk about when I come home. He doesn't ask any more about my arm, my recovery, or how long I'll be in town.

And I can't ignore the tiny thing inside me that breathes a sigh of relief.

Eventually, Rush heads off to work, and I leave Ugly Mug behind to begin a leisurely stroll down the length of Main Street, heading toward the lake stretched out in the distance.

Downtown Cedar Point is normally pretty calm this early on weekdays, even as we tip into the fall, our busiest tourist season. In an hour or so, there will be plenty of people littering the sidewalks, pushing their way into the shops that boast tchotchkes and "lake life" swag for people to lug home after they're done with their vacations.

But at 7:45am on a Monday morning, only a handful of stores are open, meaning it's mostly just locals dropping off dry cleaning or grabbing coffee before heading to work. It's not surprising that most of the people I see as I walk are faces I recognize: a few parents of old high school friends, one of our neighbors, a couple that hangs out with my mom and dad fairly regularly. I greet everyone with an easy smile, saying hello but continuing with my walk, not wanting to get stopped by anyone. I just want to enjoy the morning and the familiarity of being back in my hometown.

But then I see a face that is a surprise, so much so that I come to a halt in the middle of the sidewalk, old sensations rushing through me.

Gabriela Ventura.

She's standing in front of the hardware store, her arms crossed and an irritated expression on her face as she paces in front of the entrance.

A million memories rush through my mind, and a pang of…something hits me as I take her in. I've been on the receiving end of that look more times than I can count. I mean, I know Gabi's facial expressions better than I know baseball, and that's saying a lot.

Part of me wants to go to her and say hello, wrap her up in a hug and say how much I've missed her—a truth I've thought about more than a few times over the years. But I'm not sure how she'd respond, especially with the way things ended. Another part of me also knows seeing an ex for the first time in four years can be…awkward.

Before I get a chance to decide one way or another, her eyes connect with mine, and she stops moving. Her arms fall to her sides, her lips parting just slightly. She looks just as surprised to see me as I feel to see her, and for a long moment, we just stare at each other. A decade of memories races through me in an instant, the montage of our history playing like a silent movie in my mind.

Before I can move to say or do anything, the jingle of the bell on the hardware store's door rings as it opens behind her, startling us both out of whatever frozen moment we'd fallen into.

Gabi spins away, turning her glare on Roy Pulasky, the owner, as he steps outside.

"It's about time!" she barks, her voice bristling with the irritation that was evident on her body just a moment ago. "You were supposed to open at 7:30."

She blows past him and storms inside. She doesn't say a word to me, doesn't give me a wave or anything like that, just walks away, ignoring me entirely.

Part of me wants to laugh, because it's such a Gabi thing to do. She was always that way, quick to spin on her heel and dart away from…anything. Awkwardness. Conversations. Things she doesn't like.

She once told me she'd rather pretend a problem doesn't exist than face it head on because it means she doesn't have to deal with it as quickly. "It becomes a future Gabi problem," she told me, her eyes studiously focused on whatever she was working on in her sketchbook.

It felt funny back then. Maybe I'm reading way too much into our very brief non-interaction, but an uncomfortable feeling slices through me at the idea that *I'm* the future Gabi problem, one she'll deal with later. Or never.

Just as quickly as it arrived, that little part of me that wanted to laugh fades away completely, my heart feeling heavy in my chest. No matter what, Gabi was never that way with me. I was her safe place, the person she turned *to*, first as a friend, then as a boyfriend.

The realization that after all this time, after all our history, she'd rather flee than talk to me…

It hits me harder than I expect.

chapter two
gabi

The sound of the door slamming behind me announces my arrival before I do.

"I'm home!" I shout, marching through the house and into the kitchen then dumping my bags on the table.

My aunt glances over from where she sits on the couch in the living room, knitting next to the fireplace, and smiles. "Get what you need?"

"Yup."

The word comes out slightly more forcefully than I intend, and I can feel her eyes on me as I begin tugging my purchases out of the paper bags and placing them on the counter.

We don't have an art supply store in Cedar Point—a tragedy if you ask me and a missed opportunity, surely—but I'm able to get most of what I need online and a few items locally from the hardware store. My secret assumption is that Roy keeps some of the things I regularly need on hand just because he's hoping my

Aunt Leah will come shopping with me.

Roy's a nice guy and all, but he should know better than to think he has a chance with my aunt. *Nobody* has a chance. Leah is a confirmed bachelorette with no intention of changing things up. It's been that way for as long as I can remember. She mostly just keeps to herself, does her own thing, and enjoys being an old cat lady with no cats—a label she bestowed upon herself.

"Everything go okay?"

I sigh, trying to keep my mind focused on putting away a few grocery items I picked up at One Stop after the hardware store. I needed an extra few minutes of wandering around aimlessly to clear my mind after my run-in with Bishop, but when I look at what I grabbed—a half gallon of milk, some tomatoes, and a bottle of shampoo—I realize my mind must have been quite distracted, because I'm pretty sure none of this was even on our grocery list.

"It was fine."

It was not fine.

What is he doing here?

I mean, realistically I've always known that I wouldn't be able to dodge him forever. That we would eventually bump into each other. His family lives here. He grew up here. He visits a few times a year.

But after nearly four years of studiously avoiding town whenever I know he's home, I was far more surprised by Bishop's appearance this morning than I expected. It would have been different if it was still summer, or even the holidays, when he normally returns to Cedar Point to visit his family. At least then I would have been somewhat prepared.

Instead, it was a random Monday at the end of September.

I bristle. It's so like him to just…show up like that.

"Yeah, you're really selling me on the whole *fine* thing."

I look up, finding Leah watching me with concern. Narrowing my eyes, I shove the milk into the fridge.

She's doing the thing, the thing she always does where she tries to be both motherly and sisterly in the same breath. She hovers like a mom but wants to sass me like a sister, and normally, I'm fine with it.

Not today though. Not when I feel so…on edge.

"I'll be in the shed." It's all I say before I stride out of the room, cutting through the garage and out the side door, away from the additional questions I know are imminent.

I shiver slightly as I tromp my way across the space between our house and the shed that sits about 20 yards away, the cool breeze of the early fall morning raising the hairs on my arms and leaving goose bumps in its wake.

The last day of summer was just a few days ago, and I've been holding out hope that the warm weather will linger a bit longer. Clearly, Mother Nature didn't receive all my desperate requests. I'll need to pull out the space heater soon, one of the irritating 'quirks' of working in a poorly constructed shack that barely has any electricity, let alone something useful like insulation.

Better electricity, insulation, and central air and heat are at the top of the list when it comes to things I want to change once I've finished saving to build a new workspace. Just a few more months and I should be able to actually confirm construction dates for the spring or summer, an exciting reality that even a year and a half ago I wouldn't have ever believed possible.

Shoving the door open, I step into the shed and flip on the lights. The halogen brightness floods the room, and I wince just slightly before blinking a few times, letting my eyes adjust.

The dusty old shed has been my escape and home to all my creative inspirations for the past two years. It does serve partially as storage for my aunt's thrifting addiction. Leah's goodies are all tucked away in the back half, stacked precariously on top of each other.

The front half, though, is all mine. Three rows of shelves, an old drafting desk, a pottery wheel, and an electric kiln. A sink and cleaning area in the corner and hooks to hang my aprons and lay things out to dry.

There's nothing fancy about the place, nothing on the walls or hanging from the ceiling. No big, beautiful windows that look out to nature, just tiny ones along the roofline that barely let in any natural light. But it has served me well and provided me a place to do the work I love so much, especially when I'm irritated and need to be alone, which is more often than I like to admit.

There have been many occasions when I've come in here and chucked a mound of clay on the wheel in anger, allowing the methodical work of throwing a plate or bowl or vase to level me out. It calms me in a way nothing else seems to.

It's what I wish I could do right now. I am tempted, but I have more than a few projects that need my attention, ones that are due to clients in the coming weeks. So I turn my eyes away from my wheel and instead head to the kiln.

I never expected to end up doing ceramics as a way to make a living. Hell, I never truly believed I'd *ever* make a living off my art, but especially not when I was focusing on dark watercolors and edgy oils and smudgy charcoals. My fingers were always stained, and I just assumed I'd be doing the artist's hustle for the rest of my life: working on my passion when I could but filling my bank account with a paycheck from a "real job".

Then I went to art school, which was two incredible years of stripping me of everything I ever thought I knew about art and who I wanted to be and what I wanted to create. I took a ceramics class first semester as an elective, and it became my new passion. I still love to paint and draw and many other creative pursuits, but sitting at a wheel and literally forming something that didn't exist before? Then bringing it to life with underglaze and oxides and special design elements I come up with in my own mind?

It's magical. I love everything about it, especially how it focuses my mind when it feels so scattered and angry.

I grab a cup and plate set out of the kiln and carry it over to my workstation to sit and examine the etchings and indents. I'll need to do a bit of light cleanup work and apply glaze before I fire them again to finish everything off. I like to sit with each piece for a minute or two after each step of the process to make sure I've thought through the entire thing. It's my way of reminding myself not to move faster than I can think. That's how mistakes get made.

I sigh internally when I hear the door open, but I don't move or look in that direction. Instead, I continue examining the cup I'm rotating in my hands.

"You forgot your bag in the kitchen. Just wanted to make sure you didn't need anything from it before you dive too deep into work."

I hear the crinkle of the paper bag as she sets it down behind me. That's not why she's here. If I hadn't forgotten that bag, she would have found some other reason to poke her head in and check up on me.

"I didn't need it yet."

I'm lying and she knows it. There's no reason I would be up this early to pick up supplies from the hardware store if I didn't need them this morning. I actually need something from that bag to work on the cup currently in my hand, but this is how we do things.

She pretends to have a reason to hover.

I studiously avoid her.

Eventually we find some sort of middle ground after she's done poking and prodding.

The last thing I want to talk to her about, though, is the man I saw downtown this morning.

Bishop Mitchell.

God, even just his *name* makes my heart begin to beat erratically. It's been four years since I've seen him in person, and as much as I hate to admit it, he looks good. Like…really good. The grown-up kind of good that only comes after that last bit of youthful roundness fades away. Well, that and an almost religious dedication to fitness and exercise and athletics.

Bishop always had that, though. He was always moving, always running somewhere, always playing some sort of ball— football, soccer, baseball, you name it—until eventually baseball became his life. It became his life and led him away from me… from here…and the last thing I want now is to still be bitter about it.

But I am.

So, Leah can prod and poke all she wants this time. I have no intention of sharing.

I glance her way before returning my eyes to the mug I'm

still examining.

"Thanks for bringing me my stuff. I need to get to work."

It's a firm dismissal, and I watch her out of the corner of my eye as she crosses her arms and her hip pops out to the side.

"Fine, if you want to hide in here, that's your choice. Just know you're not fooling anyone. So why don't you just tell me what it is and save us from this back and forth."

I remain silent long enough that she sighs and finally leaves me in peace.

Leah's the best 'mom' a girl could ask for, especially considering the fact that she never actually intended to be one in the first place. Still, she has yet to accept the reality that I'm not a teenager anymore. I don't always want—or need—to talk everything out with her. Sometimes, I want to keep my thoughts to myself, and I wish, every once in a while, she'd let me.

Once I've finished adding in the gold leaf and glaze, I add my pieces back to the kiln and turn my attention to a different project. Technically, it's nothing I need to work on for at least a few more days, but I'm desperate to use my muscles and focus my energy on something creative. There's nothing that both consumes my energy and stokes it at the same time like throwing pottery.

I grab a block of clay and chuck it on the bat—a flat disc that sits in the center that allows me to swap out projects more quickly—then drop down into my seat and start the wheel. I add water and press my hands downward, putting the full weight of my body into centering the clay, until I've finally gotten it into a dome shape. Then I press two fingers into the center, pulling outward to open the mouth, before pulling up on the sides. It doesn't take long to get the shape right for the first of four bowls, each just slightly smaller than the last.

A version of this nested set is what first boomed my business online when one of the most popular food bloggers used my pottery to plate her food in a video that went viral. My website actually shut down because there was so much traffic, and I got close to 300 emails in just a few days asking if I had more of the bowls or other items for sale.

Needless to say, I jumped at the opportunity in front of me and took full advantage. I began posting 'in-progress' videos regularly on my socials, hired a friend in town to take professional photos of my work, leveled up my website with a shop, and updated my commission request form. I booked out for the rest of the year within just a few weeks, and I've never looked back.

I'm shocked at how lucrative it's been. I've been able to pay off my student loans, begin putting aside emergency savings every month, and actually start paying myself with the remaining profit. It's why I'm planning to build a new workspace, and I'm even thinking about hiring a part-time employee to handle some of the administrative stuff I'm not as good at. It's been a wild ride for the past two years as I've been figuring this business out, and I'm finally feeling truly settled into my life again, in my work as a creator, in my routine and my process.

Which is why it's so irritating that Bishop is here. I don't want him to disrupt the life I've finally gotten my footing in.

I might not be a big joiner, but I still hear town gossip. I knew he got injured during his first game, knew it was serious enough he needed surgery. I know far more than I should about his life, if I'm honest. Doesn't seem to matter if I'm studiously avoiding him when he's home or diligent about not snooping about his life online—which would be so easy to do and I've thought about more than once.

Smalltown rules are that you always hear about what your ex is up to, whether you want to or not. For most people, it might just be a snippet of news here and there.

I'm not so lucky. I'm the girl who fell in love with and dated a Mitchell, and this town *loves* to talk about the Mitchells, so I get regular updates. His batting percentage each year. The fact that he waited on the draft until after he graduated because he wanted to get his degree. His grades suffering sophomore year to the point that he needed a tutor. News about his girlfriend. How things went with the combine and then the draft.

There's no way I would have *not* heard about his injury— half the town was watching his first game for the Kings on a TV Melvin Kinny brought into The Mitch and got set up with a streamed feed. Leah boycotted the townie bar that night, even though I told her she should go. She was adamant, though.

"No boy who breaks my Gabi's heart is going to get even a lick of my time."

I love when she says that—my Gabi—but it hurts a little bit, too. I was always Gabriela until Bishop. He was the only one who called me Gabi for years, until Leah started using it occasionally as well. Nobody else has picked it up, and for that, I'm thankful, because Gabi *did* have her heart broken. She was a moody, lovelorn sap for far longer than she'd like to admit.

jillian liota

I don't want to be Gabi, Bishop's ex-girlfriend.

I want to be Gabriela, the artist. Gabriela, the creator. Gabriela, the *insert badass thing here.*

And I can't be her if I'm just the heartbroken girl Bishop left behind.

BISHOP AND GABI'S LOVE STORY CONTINUES IN

the echo of regret

AVAILABLE ON AMAZON AND KINDLE UNLIMITED

jillian liota

about the author
Jillian Liota

Jillian Liota is a Southern California native currently living in Suwanee, Georgia. She is married to her best friend, has a three-legged pup with endless energy, and acts as a servant to a very temperamental cat.

Jillian writes contemporary and new adult romance, and has had her writing praised for depth of character, strong female friendships, deliciously steamy scenes, and positive portrayal of mental health.

To connect with Jillian:

Join her **Reader Group**
Sign up for her **Newsletter**
Rate her on **Goodreads**
Visit her on **Facebook**

Check out her **Website**
Send her an **Email**
Stalk her on **Instagram**
Add her on **Amazon**

jillian liota

additional titles
from jillian

For an up-to-date list of titles, visit:
www.jillianliota.com/books

For bonus content, visit:
www.jillianliota.com/bonus

www.ingramcontent.com/pod-product-compliance
Ingram Content Group UK Ltd.
Pitfield, Milton Keynes, MK11 3LW, UK
UKHW040825011225
9280UKWH00024B/253

9 781952 549380